A CABOT CAIN THRILLER

ASSAULT ON AIMATA

CALIBER
BOOKS

Also from ALAN CAILLOU

CABOT CAIN Series
Assault on Kolchak
Assault on Ming
Assault on Loveless
Assault on Fellawi
Assault on Agathon
Assault on Aimata

TOBIN'S WAR Series
Dead Sea Submarine
Terror in Rio
Congo War Cry
Afghan Assault
Swamp War
Death Charge
The Garonsky Missile

Rogue's Gambit
Cairo Cabal
Bichu the Jaguar
The Walls of Jolo
The Hot Sun of Africa
The Cheetahs
Joshua's People
Mindanao Pearl
Khartoum
South from Khartoum
Rampage
The World is 6 Feet Square
The Prophetess
House on Curzon Street

MIKE BENASQUE Series
The Plotters
Marseilles
Who'll Buy My Evil
Diamonds Wild

IAN QUAYLE Series
A League of Hawks
The Swords of God

DEKKER'S DEMONS Series
Suicide Run
Blood Run

The Charge of the Light Brigade
A Journey to Orassia

ASSAULT ON AIMATA
Book Six

"All these people came crying 'tayo' which means friend, and gave a thousand signs of friendship..."

Louis Antoine Bougainville,
1729-1811

CHAPTER 1

The Champagne District of France, which extends over the whole of the Department of the Marne and the south of the Aisne, boasts some of the most gently relaxing scenery in the world.

The name itself means "a flat plain," and it's a misnomer. Certainly, there are no huge mountains, no deep rifts, no great gorges or towering hills; but it's not a plain, either. There's a rolling vista of softly undulating folds in the ground, all covered with the greens and russets of the patchwork vineyards, and with little stands of dense green trees where the river meanders lazily along as though quite careless of where it's going.

As far as you could see in all directions, the vines were strung cut on their horizontal trellises, neatly tied up by the highly skilled *vigneronnes*, the women who, at this moment, were standing around in hushed little groups and stating in dismay at the disaster that had struck their handiwork.

Half-hidden by the folds of the earth, the town of Epernay sat atop the vast labyrinth of its caves, cut deep in the huge and friendly layer of chalk where the good wines were stored, some three miles to the west of the little knoll that gave us our view of the cancer which had suddenly struck at these few acres—and these few acres alone, it seemed.

For here, draped like a dismal shroud all the way from the Chateau down to the tree-lined bank of the river, and more than three hundred yards across, was a dark-brown blanket of desolation, a horrifying patch of burnt-out stumps of what once had been the most productive vines in the region. It was a sore, a canker, a pestilence on the face of the lovely hillside.

It was as though, in the middle of all that ripe and satisfying greenery, a poison has been spilled by some giant hand, a poison that killed everything it touched, spilling over and down to the banks of the river itself, where the dreadful brown blotch came to an abrupt end. There was only one corner of this vineyard, up toward the old Chateau, where anything was growing at all; the rest was *leprous*.

Less than twenty-four hours had gone by since I'd received Gerard's letter, and he was still in shock, incapable of the coherent thought that this disaster needed—not that there was much anyone could do about it.

He had written to me in San Francisco, which is where I live, a sad and desperate note.

"For God's sake, Cain, come. They're all trying to tell us that it's the phylloxera again, but it isn't, it's something far, far worse, if only because we just cant's understand it. Your old friend Fenrek is here and seems to think your knowledge might be useful to all of us..."

Fenrek? The mention of his name came like a bolt out of the sky; it would only mean trouble—of a quite different kind from what Gerard seemed to have at the back of his mind.

Colonel Mat Fenrek is the head of Interpol's Department B7, with Headquarters on the edge of the Bois de Boulogne in Paris. The *phylloxera* is nothing but a vine louse with an infinite capacity for mischief. So what has Interpol got to do with lice? I had a feeling that Gerard, a man of subtle discretion, had thrown Fenrek's name in to make sure I'd obey his plea for help; it was a thought that warranted a certain amount of cogitation.

In case you don't know it, the vine louse—or *phylloxera vastatrix* as its properly called—came over from America back in the eighteen sixties. In was first found in Kew Gardens in England in the year 1863, and within ten years it had not only crossed over to France, the Mediterranean Islands, and North Africa, but it had destroyed, completely, all the vineyards of Bordeaux. In another ten years it had wiped out Burgundy and Cognac. In the space of those two decades every single vine in France had been utterly destroyed.

The louse was burrowing into the ground and attacking the roots of the plants. They tried flooding, without any success at all; how do you successfully flood a hillside? But at last relief came, also from America, where the French immigrant oenologists had developed a louse-resistant strain that was sent over and grafted on, and all was well again, after twenty-five years of absolute chaos and desperation in an industry that not only provides the country with a major part of its revenue but also gives those of us who have developed our palates a nectar which has, on occasion, changed the course of history.

And now, it seemed, some new disease had struck there. But what the hell did it have to do with Interpol?

I could only wait and find out for myself.

My name's Cabot Cain, and I have to admit, modestly, that I know more about most things than most people; I study a lot. And since a *mens sana* is not much good without a *corpore sano*, I also like to keep myself as fit as possible, simply because at six foot seven and two hundred and ten pounds, there's always someone who wants to show you how tough he is; so I know about *Hapkido*, and *Kendo*, and *Wu-Hei*, and *Kung-Fu*, and all that sort of stuff. But mostly, I use my brains, because there are very few of the world's miserable problems that can't be solved by the application of sound *knowledge*.

And it's surprising how much of that old-fashioned commodity a man can accumulate if he finds pleasure, as I do, in learning for its own sake. There's so much that's been recorded for study, right from the beginning of written history, if only you bother to read it—and remember it. I like to find out *all* there is to know about a subject, tuck it away for future polishing, and then move on to something else. After my first half-dozen doctorates I gave up counting, but one day, I'm going to list them—should make interesting reading.

The pleasure, of course, lies in applying what you know to the elucidation of what you don't, and I've always found immense satisfaction in fitting together the little bits and pieces that make up the jigsaw puzzles we all live with.

And therein lies my usefulness to Interpol. Mat Fenrek found out about my inquisitive mind a long time ago, and ever since then, by the sheer force of his personality and of his close friendship, he's sort of kept me at his beck and call. I don't really mind; he's a thoroughly nice guy, even if his thinking is bogged down in logic and reason.

These are two very misleading qualities.

I wondered for a while about Mat, thinking of his devious and secretive mind, imagining him lounging at his desk in Paris, with his feet up and his eyes glassily fastened on the ornate ceiling, saying to himself—almost in desperation—"Well, I'll have to get Cain in on this one, because he'll *know*..."

Know *what*, I was wondering.

I thought, too, how good it would be to see him again. And then I took the first Air France jet over, picked up the Jensen that I always keep in Europe (because the moment I settle down to relax at home, someone calls me out to work again), and drove fast down Route 3 to Meaux and Chateau-Thierry, on to Epernay without even stopping to sample the wine there, past the little hill on the right bank of the river Marne which is called Ay, and took the dirt road that crosses the old stone bridge (so much of history here!) and meanders on to a dead end at Gerard's place, the Chateau Bricard.

The grounds were swarming with police, both uniformed and plainclothes, and a red-painted van from the Institute was parked there, close by the small and charming cottage where the *maître de vendange*, the most important man on the vineyard, lived.

I gave my name to the officer at the gate, and he saluted politely and told me that Colonel Fenrek was expecting me. I eased the Jensen slowly along the driveway to the Chateau itself.

And there was Gerard Bricard, plump, worried, and fussy, looking more like an English country squire than a Frenchman in his heavy tweed jacket and his little green felt hat, a huge pipe, as big and bulbous as his nose, smoking horribly; he grows his own tobacco, quite illegally, and it's dreadful stuff.

And Fenrek was with him. Mat Fenrek, as smooth and urbane as ever, an old, old friend and one of the best men in the business. He's in his fifties and looks a lot younger: a lean, muscular man with a look of controlled and very efficient energy about him, tall, hawk-nosed, and far too elegant for his own good.

They came down to meet me as I drove up, and Gerard threw his arms around me and slapped me on the back, and Fenrek took my hand in a firm grip and put on that sly and gentle smile of his and said: "You made good time from Paris."

I am not a great believer in the misery of speed limits, and they are not as restrictive about them in Europe as they are in America, believing (quite rightly) that it's not how fast you drive that matters, it's how well. That, and the quality of your car, of course. The Jensen is probably the best car in the world, a monstrous American mill in a British chassis, the best of two worlds. I have an old FF, with four-wheel drive, and I had them cut the top off for me and make it into a convertible; there's nothing more discomforting than driving around with a lid over your head.

I looked over the vineyard and said, sympathetically: "It's a mess, isn't it?"

Gerard threw up his hands. "And they're trying to tell me its *phylloxera* again. Any fool can see that it's not."

"Then what is it?"

He said, shrugging expansively: "How should I know? That's what we're waiting for you to tell us, *mon Dieu*."

"Is it spreading?"

"Apparently not."

"Just this one patch? No traces anywhere else?"

"Isn't that enough? I'm ruined."

"Strange. I find that quite remarkable."

He looked at Fenrek and threw up his arms, "He finds it remarkable."

There were deep lines etched under his eyes; he looked as though he had not slept for some days. He said, anguished: "This was going to be one of the best years ever, and look at it. *Mon Dieu*, just look at it!" He was waving his arms around like a fat ballet dancer, gesticulating with that bulbous pipe. He raised his voice and said: "The whole of France, the whole world, is waiting for my *cuvée*, first quality growth..." He glared at me as though I were the personal cause of his misery. "What is it, Cain? What is it?"

I threw a look at Fenrek; he was impossibly bland and casual. And then a man in a green baize apron came out of the house with three very large snifters of cognac on a silver tray, and we took them and wandered down the slope to look at the huge, ghastly, brown patch that stretched right down to the edge of the river. I indicated the Institute van and asked: "And what have they come up with?"

Gerard shook his head. "Nothing."

I looked at Fenrek. "And you?"

"Me?" He raised an inquisitive eyebrow, as though there were no sense to the question at all; not his fault, really, it's more the result of his training.

I said: "Since when has Interpol interested itself in viniculture?"

"Oh, that," he said carelessly. "Not only this...this plague. There was a dead body. I happened to be down the road in Epernay, selecting some champagne. Gerard told the local police I was there, they invited me over."

A likely story. "A body?"

"More correctly, a skeleton. Fresh."

"What exactly is a *fresh* skeleton? I don't think I've ever seen one."

Fenrek tugged at his ear lobe and frowned. "A man who was alive and well, if you can call it that, at six o'clock in the evening, and was a skeleton at six o'clock the next morning."

It seemed a little offbeat, I said: "Sure it's the same man?"

Fenrek nodded. "No doubt about it. Identified from fingerprints, apart from anything else."

He waited for me to ask how come a skeleton had fingerprints, so I said nothing, and he sighed and went on. "A man called Villiers, a well-known petty thief from Rheims. A confirmed alcoholic. He was seen in Epernay at six in the evening, staggering over the fields this way. During the night, he broke into the *maître's* house, stole a bottle of cognac, and left his fingerprints all over the place. When we found the skeleton, the empty bottle was lying underneath it—same fingerprints."

"Unless there's more to tell, your deduction is faulty. It's more likely that Villiers was the murderer, even more probable that he had nothing to do with it at all."

He nodded glumly, "There's more, yes. And none of it makes the remotest iota of sense. Bridgework on his teeth, a dentist in Rheims. No, the dead man was Villiers, all right."

Like Gerard, he seemed to be blaming me for it all. He said furiously, losing his habitual calm for a moment: "We know that he was alive and well the previous evening, a dozen people have testified to that, in a dozen different places and circumstances."

I said: "Then, let's assume for the moment that we have a live man turned into a skeleton in twelve hours or so..."

He scowled. "Impossible."

"Tell me about his clothes."

He looked at me sharply. "More or less complete on his bones."

"Shoes too?"

"Shoes too."

"Socks?"

"Fully dressed. A fully dressed skeleton." He said wrathfully: "For God's sake, how do you get all the flesh off a dead body in a matter of hours?"

To my mind, there was a very simple explanation, but thought I'd lead him astray, just for the hell of it. I said: "You boil it."

"Oh, for God's sake."

A man in his position really ought to know his history better, so I reminded him. "The year twelve hundred and seven. They brought the body of the saintly King Louis back from the Crusades in Tunis, They stripped all the flesh off his bones by boiling, and they paraded the skeleton through the streets for the worshipping crowd to admire."

He wasn't impressed. He said sourly: "But they didn't have to get his goddam shoes and socks back on, did they? Without disturbing as much as a metatarsal."

I said politely: "Or even a hallux?" Gerard began waving his arms around again and shouted: "It can't be done, and yet someone did it! So tell us how, Cain!"

I said: "I'm more interested in the *why*. Tell me about Villiers. He was an old man, no doubt?"

Fenrek looked at me very suspiciously; they never deal in likelihoods at Interpol, only facts, and there's nothing more misleading in the world than indisputable fact; so it seemed that the obvious answer just hadn't occurred to him. He said, frowning: "Yes, he was in his late eighties. Why?"

11

"Who found him?"

I saw that the police were constantly taking little scoopfuls of soil over to the Institute's van; I wondered if they knew what they were looking for. Gerard said: "I did, and it was a shock, I can tell you. Of course, I didn't know who it was, so I called the police in." He sighed. "I still don't believe it was Villiers, fingerprints and bridgework or not. How the hell can it be *done*? You're suggesting someone killed him, put him in a copper cauldron of boiling water... And how long would that take?"

"In the case of King Louis, two days."

"And, for God's sake...why?"

We stood there on the little knoll and watched the police going along the rows of vines on their hands and knees, searching for...what? I sipped my cognac and asked Fenrek what the connection was supposed to be between the dead man and the damage that had been done to the vines. Or was there any?

He shook his head unhappily. "Who knows? Two, simultaneous events, both unlikely if not impossible. God alone knows if they're connected."

"And Interpol is here just by chance."

He said firmly: "By chance. I happened to be in Epernay at the time..."

"Yes, we know all about that."

Ag though on cue, the town's church clock started striking its doleful note. In this lovely old town, it's a modernish church that can only be described as hideous, though they try and palm it off as a tourist attraction. I suppose I have to admit that its sixteen windows, which are of *painted glass* from the sixteenth century, are curious enough to be interesting.

Fenrek grunted, knowing that I didn't believe him and not prepared to do anything about it at all; that's the way he is sometimes, secretive beyond any reasonable limit. We moved on down to where the Institute men were; they're very bright people, some of the best agronomists in Europe.

There was a young man in charge, a sallow-faced youth of twenty-five or so, dressed in a long white smock and wearing his lank hair in a rather disgusting ponytail, but I saw that he was doing the

12

right things. He had a bench set up nearby, on which was a stereoscopic, wide-field, binocular microscope, a very good Zeiss, and an impressive array of test tubes. He looked up as we approached, nodded pleasantly, and went on with his work, peering intently into the scope.

I said: "What's the pH count like?"

He rubbed a hand over his face and said: "It's four point nine, I can't understand it."

"That's a bit high for limestone soil, isn't it?"

He nodded. "Far too high. Probably residue from the winter's manure."

"Uh-huh."

"You don't think so?" He seemed gratifyingly unsure of himself, a young man searching for knowledge.

"Not if the horses they used were fed on clover."

"You've got a point there." He shot out a hand suddenly, and smiled; it brightened up his face considerably. "My name's Falleron, Mr.?"

"Cain. Cabot Cain."

"A pleasure, Mr. Cain. Yes, they do feed the horses on clover here, we should have more phosphate, shouldn't we?"

"What's the bacterial count, have you checked it?"

"Oh yes, of course. It's around forty-eight million per gram."

"Well, that effectively destroys any theories about a fungus, doesn't it?"

"Fungus? Well, that's what we thought of at first, of course, but...yes, I suppose it does, hadn't thought of that aspect, I must admit." He squinted up at me. "Are you a microbiologist, Mr. Cain?"

"Not practicing. I do have a degree tucked away somewhere, I seem to recall. The Sorbonne."

"Ah. I wonder if they've been using ammonium sulfate or nitrate?"

"It would account for a lot of things, but it's hardly likely, I'd say."

Falleron looked a question at Gerard, who seemed about to explode; understandably so. Falleron repeated the suggestion: "Potassium, surely, is your most important trace element, Monsieur

13

Bricard. What about nitrogen? Are you using chemical fertilizers?"

Gerard drew himself up to all of his five feet two height and said coldly: "I make champagne, M. Falleron. Not Coca-Cola."

Falleron had the grace to look embarrassed, and Gerard turned to me, picking up a point long dead, and said: "What was that about a fungus? I hadn't thought of it either, but now you mention it... it's quite possible, wouldn't you say?"

I said: "No. Not even a degenerate ascomycetes, a thought which occurred to me but got thrown away. The bacteria count wouldn't go past a mere fifty thousand." I was studying the labels on the test tubes and vials, and wondered a little about his choice. I said: "No silver salts?"

He was startled. "Silver salts? Yes, we must have some tucked away somewhere, but..." He broke off, worried, and squinted up at me again. "Silver salts? Yes, that's quite a recondite idea, isn't it?"

He began rummaging around in his box, and came up with a vial, unscrewed the top, and said happily: "I know what's on your mind, Mr. Cain, but if you're a betting man..."

"Taking candy from a baby."

He laughed. "No way. No way at all." He was dropping distilled water onto the filter paper, and using the tweezers with a delicate, professional touch. He slipped the slide in, glued his eye to the scope, and then looked up in acute astonishment and said: "My God. Did we bet?"

"No, we didn't. Metallic silver?"

"Yes. A definite trace of it. A very definite trace. That can't be!"

"And why not, Mr. Falleron?"

He looked around at the acres of dead, dead earth and said, extremely puzzled now: "Well, there's the proof, its formic acid, it can't be anything else. I'd never have believed it." He was staring out across the bare earth. "But can you visualize how much it would take to do this damage? A hundred, five hundred, maybe more than a thousand gallons to give us a concentration like this! It couldn't be done!"

I said sympathetically: "There's so much that can't be done unless you think in terms of likelihoods."

"Likelihoods?"

"The only way to go. The essential *fact*, if you must have facts to fool around with, is that it stopped at the water."

"Then we're back to the *phylloxera*."

"No, we are not. That's the one thing we can happily dismiss. The damage is too severs, and it was done too fast."

He stared. "Animal secretions, then?"

"Of course."

"You mean... You can't mean *ants?*"

"Something of that general nature."

"But...but...there'd have to be millions of them. *Billions*, even."

"I knew you'd catch on sooner or later."

Gerard threw up his hands in disgust. His fist caught the bowl of his pipe and sent it spinning across the brown earth, and he said *"Merde!"* and went to retrieve it. When he straightened up he said: "It's preposterous, Cain! Preposterous!"

"Tell me what else can deposit such huge quantities of formic acid in the soil overnight."

He lit his pipe again and puffed at it furiously. "Ants build huge colonies, so where are they? The only kind of ant that eats every living thing in its path is the African safari ant; and we don't have them here. They're tropical, and besides; they don't..."

He broke off. His ruddy face had turned white.

I said gently: "Your own words, Gerard. Every living thing in its path."

He said, very slowly, his voice a whisper now: *"Mon Dieu. Are you suggesting that...that that's what happened to that poor drunk? That he was eaten alive by insects?"

"Tell me what else can strip the meat off a man's bones in a few hours, without even disturbing the clothing?"

"Oh, *mon Dieu.*"

He was shaking, his jowls trembling. But Fenrek was standing there with his head tilted back a little, as though he were listening for the sound of a billion crawling insects. There was even a very faint smile on his handsome, aristocratic face. He said quietly: "What kind of ant, Cain? If it's ants, where did they come from? Where did they go? If they're flying ants, which are not carnivorous—or are they?—where are they now? How is it they haven't turned up somewhere else? We'd have heard."

I said: "Those are some of the questions I've been asking myself. I don't know the answers yet. It will help if you'll tell me why Interpol's here."

He shook his head stubbornly. "I told you, the purest chance."

"Balls."

Falleron had sat down heavily on his little stool, and was staring at his microscope almost accusingly. He said slowly: "It makes sense. It's the only thing that makes sense. Oh, my God."

One of the policemen was hurrying toward us, an envelope in his hand. He saluted and gave it to Fenrek, who took it from him, deeply preoccupied, read it, and said, frowning: "From the lab. They've finished the examination of the skeleton. Formic acid all over. The poor bastard."

Falleron had jumped to his feet and was dragging a shovel out of his van. He said angrily: "How deep can an ant burrow, Mr. Cain? Do you know that?"

"I know. But don't bother to dig, Mr. Falleron. You won't find any trace of them."

He wasn't convinced. He said: "It has to be a formicinae ant, it can't be anything else. They live in galleries in the soil. I should have gone deeper for samples."

"You'd have been wasting your time. A safari of warrior ants leaves a trail you can't mistake. No. Everything points to ants except for that one thing, so...look for something of the same genre, but with wings."

He was screwing his eyes up as though it might help him to think reasonably. "Locusts?"

"No. Again, too fast, and the damage too acute. Besides, if it were locusts, you'd certainly have found a few hundred dead ones. You'd be better employed examining the vines for teeth marks, under the microscope. And sifting through five acres of soil for even a single wing. It won't be easy and I doubt if you'll even find one. But you might. See if you can find a fragment of leaf somewhere, and look for slime on it. Then, if you've still the time, go through J.C. Faure's

Bulletin of Entomological Research, I think it was published around 1925. Try volume twenty-three or twenty-four. And, with luck, and patience, you might be able to identify this creature. Or at least get some idea of what it might look like."

He said, frowning: "A wing? From an *ant*?"

One of those old, old memories was at the back of my mind, fighting for recognition, an image of an old, old man with a thin white beard; it refused to identify itself, but I knew that it would, sooner or later. I said: "Some sort of flying ant is the best of the likelihoods, though there are a few others. See what you can find, sift over the surface soil, can you do that?"

He was slow in answering. I wondered if he were thinking of the stupendous amount of work involved. How do you sift over five acres of soil for so microscopic and elusive an object?

And then Fenrek said coolly: "He'll do it."

They pull strings in Department B7. Especially when they have cause to. And I knew that in the course of time, he'd have to tell me what that cause was. He looked at the delicate glass that was still in his hand, studying the amber of the cognac and carefully avoiding my look.

V.S.O.P. Fine champagne, it has to be sipped very slowly, every warm breath of it enjoyed to the utmost. But he gulped it all down at once with a shudder, even though he's a man of excellent taste and sensitivity.

He recovered his *sangfroid* very quickly, and said with a smile: "Well, with that pressing problem solved, I suppose I'd better get back to Paris. Plenty of work waiting for me on my desk."

I said: "I'll bet. So should I go home too, do you think?"

He wouldn't budge: "If that's what you really want to do, of course. Though I thought Gerard had invited you to stay for a week or two?"

"You bastard."

There was a strange look in his eyes that I can only call jubilant. Fenrek knows very well that when the likelihoods are all wrong. I have a driving compulsion—if only out of a sense of frustration—to worry at them until they begin to make sense, to plow under the obscuring murk and show them for what they really are. I could see all kinds of alarming possibilities ahead if I didn't find out *who* was up to *what*.

In other words, he knew he had me hooked.

Gerard clapped me on the back, reaching up a trifle, and said briskly: "Well, no good depressing ourselves any longer with the sight of my own perdition. Why don't we all go up to the house and be miserable in comfort?"

I thought that was a very good idea. Slowly, we walked up the hill to the Chateau. An old, wrinkled woman, one of the *vigneronnes*, was watching us, wiping at the tears in her eyes with the hem of her long gray dress.

CHAPTER 2

Ten days later, I was still a guest in Gerard's charming old chateau, sitting on my ass and waiting for all the research work to come in.

But not waiting *openly*. Nobody, it seemed, believed in the story of the ants, or whatever they were, at all. On the surface, it seemed that all my logical deductions had just not seeped into their intellects. And some very strange things were happening.

First of all, the newspapers, after the first frenetic outburst, were playing a very low-key note. Officially, the sudden plague was termed an outbreak of a new kind of *phylloxera*, and about the death of that poor bewildered drunk Villiers there was not even a mention—except a blatant lie to the effect that a skeleton found on the Bricard estate had turned out to be an ancient pile of bones stolen from the Epernay Museum and put there as a hoax.

As for the devastation of the vineyard, the Institute had sent out warnings to the vintners to be on the lockout for any sign of this new and inexplicable plague, which they thought might perhaps be some kind of recondite fungus; they could have been talking about a disease from outer space. But there was an obscure article in *Paris Match*—a widely read magazine that doesn't always bow to the dictates of hidden governmental authority—from a very learned entomologist who wrote at great length about insects gorging themselves on chlorophyll and then dying in great masses, which I thought was an intelligent observation; only he spoiled it by suggesting that they burrowed deep into the soil and perished there. He didn't explain the fact that no excessive amounts of calcium carbonate or phosphate had been found in the soil, a fact which effectively nullified his theory. To add to the confusion, a police spokesman—and on whose orders, I wondered?—even suggested that someone, to settle a grudge against Gerard Bricard, had sprayed his vines overnight with an oxidized combination of methyl alcohol and formaldehyde.

I thought what a lot of nonsense. That is the old-fashioned way of making formic acid synthetically; they would have used oxalic acid and glycerin, which of course is far more effective.

I was sure that I could detect the devious touch of Fenrek in there somewhere.

Interpol is not an investigative body at all; it merely coordinates the work of regular police forces and helps them out on occasion. It's not even a particularly secretive organization—except in patches. But Department B7 emphatically *is*, and it only takes its general authority from Interpol Main because it too is international in aspect, and it's a convenience to have a governing head office that is subscribed to by most of the civilized countries of the Western world. B7 is very hush-hush indeed, and its interests are diverse and spread over almost all the globe.

If the Moroccan ambassador in London is to, be assassinated, or the movements of the Seventh Fleet are being put up for sale in Korea, or someone is secretly manufacturing chemicals for biological warfare...then B7 moves in mysteriously and quietly. And from the hedonistic luxury of his Paris office, Colonel Mat Fenrek, as Head of B7, reaches out and pulls a few gently persuasive strings when he moves in for the kill it always turns out to be high-level mischief that he's been up against all the time, and of a highly *criminal* nature.

In other words, precious little to do with a blight on grapevines.

And there was one more incident of enormous interest.

Three wild-looking gentlemen appeared one morning, with a high-ranking and dignified French bureaucrat and a veritable posse of officers from the *Garde Nationale* in tow, to examine, very quickly, the disaster that had struck at the vineyard. They wouldn't speak to Gerard, or to his *maître de vendange*, or even to me; they virtually locked us up in the Chateau while they hurried along the rows of dead stumps. They had landed in two military helicopters three minutes after a flurry of local police turned up and herded us out of the way. They looked around for an hour, and then they were gone.

Gerard could only throw up his hands and say, in complete frustration: "But I know *nothing*, nothing at all."

He was furious, and I was mystified—a state of mind I do not entirely enjoy. I'd heard them talking among themselves, in hushed voices but with moments of voluble excitability. And they were talking Arabic; their accent was the accent of Libya.

I found it all very intriguing.

So I composed my soul in patience, enjoying Gerard's splendid hospitality and studying the reports that Falleron—on whose authority?—was sending me.

He'd come up with some interesting sketches of what he thought the new bug might look like, a sort of miniature locust no bigger than an ant, with a surprisingly large and efficient pair of wings (which meant it could fly great distances), a relatively large jaw with pronounced mandibles, and yet a tiny intestinal tract. I saw that he'd taken J. C. Faure's teaching very much to heart, and I was much impressed with the work he had done, even though it was mostly imaginative; but as Sam Johnson once said, with imagination a man could be as happy in the arms of a chambermaid as of a duchess, and with very little to go on he was obviously thinking along much the same lines as I was myself; clearly, a bright young man.

In the last of his reports he'd added a friendly, cheerful, personal note suggesting that I might like to talk with a young woman named Marie-Therese Vasco, who was studying soil microbiology with him at the Institute. And overplaying his hand (just as Gerard had done), he had added, quite incongruously and unnecessarily: "She's known to Colonel Fenrek, who thinks very highly of her."

Ha! There he was, pulling strings again. B7 has agents all over the place, each more secretive than the other.

I told Gerard, and we invited her over for a drink. It was she who told us about the Island of Faatua, which lies in French Polynesian waters between the Society Islands and the Tuamotus. In other words, in what is generally known as Tahiti.

I had been there some years before, when I was investigating—more as an intellectual exercise than anything else—the strange phenomenon of the occasional granite monoliths on the island, and their possible association with the people who built the temples, the *marae*, on the island of Huahine, some two hundred miles to the southwest. I remember it as possibly the most beautiful of all those lovely "Islands under the Wind," a splendidly luscious little hump of land rising out of a cobalt, green, and purple sea that changed its multicolors with every shift of cloud, wind, or underwater sand. There was a wide reef around a central mountain, entirely enclosing it except for one narrow passage where the coral had been cut through by the inexorable action of the river that cascaded down from its heights. This passage was the only way into the lagoon, and a dangerous one at that. I had spent a week there—the island was uninhabited—living off rock lobster and a hundred different kinds of fish, with yams, and taro, and bananas, and breadfruit, and coconuts, and the Tahitian chestnut they call *mape* growing in wild abundance everywhere. As on most of the islands, all you had to do for a meal was stretch out your hand; God took care of the rest.

It was a glorious, immensely satisfying corner of Paradise, and the memory I had of it, more than anything else, was of its flora.

This is perhaps the most startling aspect of all the Tahitian islands—the simple fact of color. There's a riotous blaze of it everywhere, and when you've returned to less fortunate parts of the globe, it's the memory of color that sets the slow, insidious sense of nostalgia working.

If you stopped to count the different individual shades of green alone, you'd be up in the hundreds, and confused, before you even skimmed the cream off the top. Their variety and brilliance is astonishing, and when you begin to think there can't possibly be any more greens, you turn a quiet corner on a deserted, rustic road, and there's another mass of them, deeper, lighter, denser, or more subtle than those you've seen before, the sunlight striking them through the high trees and changing their intensity all the time. Emeralds begin to look dull by comparison, and you haven't even started on the reds and yellows and purples.

It's a blinding, startling display that overwhelms the senses, under a brilliant sun that breaks through heavy clouds, leaden in both color and weight, and the air is so clear that you wonder what happened to the rest of the world that it should be so drab and uninspiring.

I know the islands well, and when I heard, and saw, what had happened to Faatua, the "Island of the Valley at Large," it was like a blow to the stomach, a shock that somehow held in it a premonition of even worse things to come.

The news that Marie-Therese brought with her was harrowing.

She was in her late twenties, and had graduated, she told me, from the Académie Ecologique in Nice. She was quite tall, and rather thin and scrawny, not unattractive, with a peculiar kind of articulation to her legs that seemed to waft her around like a zephyr. She had very long and untidy dark auburn hair that kept getting in the way of everything, and hazel eyes that were very bright and alert, as though they were always on the point of making some remarkable discovery. She wore the most inelegant clothes imaginable, a pair of faded blue jeans and a lightweight brown sweater that was far too small and was constantly being pulled down to hide at least part of her bare midriff, a section that was, however, very smooth and taut and satisfying to look at. She somehow gave the impression that she had worn that God-awful sweater for the last fifteen years, and that it had simply not grown with her.

She said, laconically: "It keeps shrinking, every time I wash it."

But she was very sharp and sensible, and a delight to talk to, Gerard loved her at once, puffing his pipe at her happily, and he was noticeably chagrined when the *maître* wanted to see him down in the vineyard and he had to leave us alone. She spoke very rapidly, as though there just weren't enough time for all she had to say. I showed her Falleron's sketches, and told her where he'd gone wrong (she'd seen them before, and she agreed with me, which I thought was very sensible), and she in turn gave me a set of photographs which made me sick to look at: Faatua, before and after.

There were 8x10 enlargements of Kodak transparencies, a whole batch of them. On one side of the island, the southern, every speck of green was gone, and there was nothing but the same cankered, dull brown earth, ten square miles or more of eroded, diseased, and horrible blight. Above it, on the mountain slope, all was well and just as it had always been. But all over the southern shore, that same dread sickness lay like a deathly pall.

I said, incredulously: "This is Faatua?"

She nodded. "Two days ago, one of our pilots flew over, went home again in shock, took off again with a camera, and sent us the pictures."

A likely story. The shots were very professional indeed; well, no. matter. She said: "On that side of the island, there's nothing left, no vegetation at all."

She tugged her sweater down over her navel, which had surfaced again, took a long drink of Gerard's cognac, and said: "Do you know what that is?"

That was the outline of a plane under twenty feet or so of very clear water, an alien object on one of the photographs, and I said: "Of course, it's a plane, what else could it be?"

"Oh. Well, yes, it's a plane."

"More specifically, it's a Piper, probably one of the new Warriors. Single engine, tapered wing."

She said admiringly: "Well, aren't you clever? That's exactly what it is. It was a private charter, on hire to an American tourist from Papeete for a general flight around the islands, over to the Tuamotus. He said he was going to Rangiroa."

"And what happened to him?"

She shrugged, and had a go at the sweater again. "They sent a schooner over, no dead bodies. There had been a rubber raft on board, and there was no sign of it."

"They sent a diver down?"

"Yes, of course they did, how else could they know the raft was gone? So the presumption is that he saved himself and is drifting around the ocean somewhere. But that part of the Pacific is *very* pacific, there have been no storms since then, no heavy winds. Provided he's got water aboard, or knows how to catch fish, he could survive quite comfortably for a very long time."

I remembered that a few years ago, a Japanese freighter had caught fire in those waters and had gone down, with only six survivors;

but those survivors had drifted around in an open boat for an incredible five months, living on water squeezed from the fish they caught and on an abundance of seafood. Rescued at last, they were found to be in excellent health.

I said: "What about the currents out there?" I knew the answer, of course, since oceanography has always been one of my hobbies; I did a paper once on the effects of terrigenous sediments on pelagic foraminiferal remains in deep waters. But I wanted to know the extent of her inquiries, and possibly who was behind her, pushing.

She said: "This time of the year, southwesterly."

"So he's heading for either Huahine or Tahaa, or possibly Motu Iti or Bora Bora."

She was agreeably surprised. "You know our Islands, Mr. Cain?"

"*Our* Islands?"

"Yes. I'm Tahitian."

"Ah, that's nice. Yes, I know them."

"And that's nice, too."

She kept looking at her watch all the time, when she wasn't pulling that absurd sweater down over her flat little belly; and the big ormolu clock in Gerard's comfortable salon seemed to intrigue her enormously. I kept catching her eyes on it, as though she were willing it to move faster.

I said: "Why don't you tell me what's on your mind, Marie-Therese?"

She contrived to look bland, and surprised, and guilty, all at the same time. "On my mind? Well, nothing, really. I was just wondering... They want me to go out there and take a look at Faatua. And I was wondering...*they* were wondering...if perhaps you'd care to come along too."

"Oh. Who, in this case, is *they*?"

"The Institute. They will, of course, pay your expenses. It might be rather interesting, don't you think?"

"Fenrek's idea, no doubt?"

"Oh." She looked at the clock again. "So you know about Colonel Fenrek?"

I said: "What do you mean, know about him? He's my best

friend."

"I mean...know that I know him."

"Falleron told me. Rather cryptically."

"Oh." She hesitated. "Well, Colonel Fenrek did speak to the Board, I believe. He may have said something about you, I don't know."

"Uh-huh."

Gerard came back then, looking thoroughly miserable. He said, gesticulating wildly: "Dig up all of our vines, that's what we have to do. Sterilize the soil, re-fertilize, wait two seasons before replanting, and even then we've no assurance that the vineyard will ever come back. My God, I make the best champagne in all of France, and now..."

He sat down heavily and started filling his pipe, and jumped up again when the phone rang. I saw that Marie-Therese was waiting for just that, and I said to Gerard: "It's Fenrek. Tell him I'm not here. Tell him I've gone back to San Francisco."

He grimaced, picked up the phone, listened, and grinned happily, and then said: "Yes, he's here. He was waiting for your call."

It was Fenrek all right. He was very smooth, and charming, and noncommittal (waiting for me to tell him, no doubt), and asked after my health, and had I met the charming young Marie-Therese? And what did I think of a few days in the South Sea Islands?

I said: "The suggestion was just this minute thrown at me, I'm surprised you know about it."

"Well, I do know about it, so what have you decided?"

"I've not really made up my mind yet. I was rather hoping that someone or other would tell me what all this is about."

He sort of grunted, and said peevishly: "I don't know why you have to be so difficult, so obstructive. A breath of Tahiti will do you a world of good. There's a plane leaving Paris at midnight, and all I want is confirmation that you'll be on it. Do you have your ticket already?"

"My ticket?"

I looked at Marie-Therese. She had been straining her ears to the utmost to get both sides of the conversation, and now she was pulling down her sweater with one hand and holding up two airline tickets with the other.

I said to Fenrek: "Yes, it seems I have."

"Splendid! Do keep me informed, won't you?"

He was being careful not to mention my name, and I knew what that meant. Whenever I get involved with Mat Fenrek, there's trouble ahead, and his Department hates it. I used to work for them; and they've never yet, after all those years, forgiven me all those upsets. So, in his office, they just pretend I don't exist, and it comforts them greatly.

I put down the phone, and Marie-Therese said cheerfully: "Can we go in your Jensen, Mr. Cain? I saw it outside, and it looks so much nicer than my Citroen. If we leave now, we should make Paris very nicely by midnight."

There was just time, it seemed, for me to pack a bag; hers was already in the Jensen.

During the long flight to Tahiti, I got to know her rather well.

And as soon as we landed at Papeete's Faaa airport, with the imposing silhouette of Moorea out there to the west of us under white puffs of cotton in the brilliant sky, she told me firmly that her name, now, was no longer what it had been in France; now, it was Maite, its Tahitian equivalent. She even found, right away, a highly scented *tiare* flower to tuck behind her ear, and I half expected her to change at once into a *pareu* instead of that God-awful sweater.

We chose to stay at the Royal Papeete, which is on the waterfront in the heart of the town, a pleasant and relaxing sort of place with an atmosphere of laissez faire which can only be described as pure Tahitian. We took two rooms next to each other on the upper floor, above the white-portico entrance, which overlooks the yachts at anchor and the broad leafy sweep of the Quai Gallieni. I took an unhurried shower, and came out with a towel around my waist to find Marie-Therese, or Maite now, sitting demurely on the edge of my bed, a red-and-white *pareu* tied around her tight little breasts and her long hair hanging loosely down over her amber shoulders; she looked absolutely delectable and it was astonishingly hard to reconcile the new aspect of this young woman with the image of the scrawny kid in France.

She fluttered her long eyelashes at me and said: "Better? You didn't like my European clothes, did you?"

I said: "Yes, and no, in that order. And now it's time for you to pass on to me the limited information Fenrek has told you to give me, and a great deal he told you *not* to tell me. First of all, I take it that you're a B7 agent?"

She looked me straight in the eye. "Yes. No one is supposed to know that, of course."

"Of course. Do go on."

I stood at the window and watched a young Tahitian girl on the wide street sweeping up the flowers of bright red bougainvillea, and thought idly about the great navigator after whom the plant was named; in the seventeen sixties, he'd stopped here in Tahiti for a while and had written about his journey with great humor and simplicity, an account which I had once translated into Urdu and Hindustani for the Navigators College in Bombay. Dressed in a *pareu* also, she swept all the flowers (they're not really flowers, of course, but bracts; the flowers are microscopic) into a large pile in one corner of the curb, and then sat down on a bench, the broom tucked between her wide-spread thighs, to watch the wind blow them all back again.

Maite said: "I don't suppose you heard about what happened in Libya the other day?"

I'm an avid reader, so I told her: "If it was published in the press almost anywhere in the world, I heard about it."

"This you would not have heard about from the press. Both B7 and the Libyans were absolutely insistent on hushing it all up, though God alone knows why..." She broke off and stared at me. "I wonder why secrecy should be so important in a case like this?"

"Unless you tell me what the case *is*, I can't really help you there, can I?"

"No, No, I suppose not. Well..."

She lay back on the bed and stretched her legs; I hadn't noticed before how good they were, long and smooth and very sensuous, and I wondered why she'd chosen to hide them in faded, grubby jeans. She said: "The same bug, two days after the trouble at Gerard's vineyard. Do you know about the operation that's been going on in the southern desert of Libya?"

"The wells? Yes, I know about them. A very interesting

project."

For nearly a year now, a joint American-Libyan team, the old enemies cooperating as they always can when they've a mind to, had been sinking wells of incredible depths down into the Sahara's sands, seeking out the water that had once made Libya a giant farm, back in the days of the Caesars and their Roman Legions. Using the most modern machinery and technology available, the alien experts had found underground rivers of enormous potential and were pumping up water so fast that Bedouin could only stare at it in disbelief. They'd planted millet and corn, and now that vast, empty waste of sand was well on the way to becoming a supermarket for North Africa's starving millions.

I said: "A thirty-two million dollar operation, but more—an answer to a very great problem, the problem of feeding a lot of people who've never had enough to eat. Or to drink, come to that."

"The millet crop was a foot high, and doing very nicely indeed."

"*Was?*"

"The same thing as the vineyard. Only here, two hundred thousand acres of badly needed crops were wiped out in just two nights. It's chaos, The Libyans have turned out the army, they've cut all communications except governmental to and from the area, and quarantined everyone there, American or Arab. No one's allowed in, no one's allowed out. They are the people who called in Interpol."

Ha! It was beginning to take form. I said: "Still an agricultural problem, and nothing at all to do with B7. So?"

It was almost painful for her to start talking; they train them well at Interpol. But, at last, she told me what I should have been told in the first place. She took a long, deep breath and said: "While you were pottering around Gerard's place, looking for traces of formic acid ..." She broke off suddenly and then said: "How did you know what to look for?"

"It was fairly apparent to anyone but an idiot. Go on."

"While you were there, the Libyan government had a phone call from Marseilles. The caller wanted to speak, if you please, to the irascible Colonel Ghaddafi himself. All he got was the Minister for Development, the number three man in the country after Ghaddafi and the War Minister. He was told to pay ten million francs, in cash and at once, or the new millet crop would be destroyed overnight."

"Now it's beginning to make sense. About time, too. How was the money to be paid?"

"Patience, patience... They were given a pinpoint on the beach near Benghazi where the caller said a launch would be standing offshore waiting to receive it. They thought at first it was a hoax, but you know the Libyans."

"I do indeed. They sent a patrol out just in case."

"Two army half-tracks with thirty men on board, backed up by a pair of fighter planes. By the time the planes got there, a little late, the half-tracks had been blown sky high, apparently by bazooka shells or missiles..."

"Which? It may be important."

"We don't know. Most of the patrol was killed, the launch got away, and the next evening the devastation started. *That's* why Interpol is interested. We couldn't pass the word on, because Libya, for reasons of its own, had demanded complete secrecy."

"They're a very secretive people. But it makes everything a lot easier, doesn't it? Do you mind if I get dressed?"

She nodded casually: "Go ahead. And why does it make it easier?"

"Well, I was thinking in terms of someone who wanted to make war on champagne growers and uninhabited islands, a rather otiose occupation. But instead, we have a simple blackmailer who has found a nice new weapon to play with. And that's the key word—weapon."

The light breeze coming through the open windows was cool, so clear and fresh that there was almost a flavor, a taste, to it; I suppose I'd forgotten what fresh air is really like—no dust, no oxides, no noxious chemicals. I found I was subconsciously filling my lungs with it.

I thought of the military aspect of a weapon like this, and said: "About ten years ago, defoliation became a household word. Of course, denying food to the enemy is a trick as old as civilization, and nowadays it's by defoliation rather than by simple burning... Our source material is there somewhere."

She turned those hazel eyes on me; I had not really noticed before how fascinating they were. She said: "Indochina?"

I nodded. "Later better known as Vietnam... The Americans were defoliating with chemicals, but long before then, in the days of the French, the army was experimenting with locusts. It didn't work, so they gave up."

The image was there again, the memory of an old white-bearded man, an entomologist. I said: "What did you do with Falleron's sketches?"

She was off the bed in a flash. "I'll get them."

I slipped into slacks, a shirt, and sandals while she was gone, and when she came back I said: "Let's go down to the Vaima for a beer, I'm thirsty."

"All right."

"We'll need a map too."

"I have one."

We strolled down the Quai Gallieni and the Quai de Commerce and on to Bir Hakeim (named for a battle in the same Libya where our new battle was beginning), and found an empty sidewalk table at the Café Vaima. An elderly lady with no teeth, brown-skinned and cheerful, placed *leis* of *tare* flowers around our necks and passed on casually about her business. I took out Falleron's sketches and studied them; in his minute, scholarly handwriting, he had written on one of them: "*Doccio Mel? poss. Cress*," which had not, up to that moment, meant very much except that he was thinking in terms of the *Docciostaurus Melanoplus*, which is more or less a miniature version of the ordinary Moroccan locust.

But now that we were thinking of a *weapon*, the annotation *poss. Cress* took on a certain importance.

Maite was ordering beer, the Hinano which is made locally but put into bottles brought all the way from France, a matter of some thirteen thousand miles, and when it had come I said to Maite: "What do you know, if anything at all, about entomology?"

She sniffed; I don't think she liked the "anything at all." She said: "Not my field, but allied with it. I know enough to argue with Falleron about it." She tapped one of the sketches with a long, slim finger. "He hasn't got the teeth right, if he's thinking of locusts. And that's what the *Doccio* means, presumably."

"He's got the teeth *exactly* right."

"Ah yes, you told him to look for teeth marks, didn't you?"

"But the jaws are probably wrong, and so, I'd say, is the pronotum. Did you ever hear of a man named Jules Cresson?"

She frowned. "Who's he?"

"An elderly entomologist in a long white coat, with a long white beard to match. He dropped out of sight about ten years ago, a French-Canadian scientist of extraordinary ability. He was working in Indochina on the defoliation problem. I wish I knew more about him..."

The bells were ringing at the back of my mind, and they sounded a jarring, nasty note. I was lecturing a body of anthropologists once, in Iceland, on the Theory of Mandibular Growth in the Oligochaets (a group of the twenty-two hundred known species of earthworm), and there was an elderly Frenchman there who had the impertinence not only to dispute some of my reasoning but also to prove that he was right; I never forgot the experience. I'd even followed his career to a certain extent, but insects don't really interest me very much, except academically, so I'd let him sort of get away from me. Now the memories were all dropping into place.

I said: "Jules Cresson was experimenting with a minute locust, no bigger than an ant, which he wanted to call the *Cressonus*, but it wouldn't mate, if I remember correctly, and so it never came to anything. Or did it, I wonder?"

Her face was bright, her eyes wide. "When Falleron first used the term *Docciostaurus Cressonus*, his superiors told him, rather crossly, that there was no such insect. And since he has an eye to his own future in the Institute, he chose not to argue with them. But he spent a lot of time and energy analyzing the excreta he found in the soil..."

"What an occupation."

"And he said to me once, excitedly: 'Everything points to a *Cressonus*.' Since I'd never heard of Cresson, I didn't pursue the question, because I didn't want him to know how much I didn't know; he's like that."

I let it pass, and she said: "Do you know what a *Cressonus* would be like, if there really were such a thing?"

"I can make a guess at it. Most plague species exist in two phases—solitary and gregarious—which is supposed to account for the so-called 'disappearance' of huge swarms under normal circumstances. I imagine this one can fly huge distances very fast, like the ordinary *migratoria*, and once on the ground its mandibles indicate that it eats everything in its path. Greenstuff, sails, mice, chicken, rats, anything that couldn't move out of the swarm's way fast enough."

"Would that include a confirmed alcoholic sleeping in a coma?"

"If he was drunk enough, old enough, sick enough—yes. You have to think in terms of several billion insects attacking at once, all hungry... But *billions* of them, swarming all over his body. At the first few thousand instantaneous bites, he'd roll over and start struggling, because they'd go for his eyes first, but it would be too late. I don't know much about the *Cressonus*, not yet, but if the mating problem was ever solved...we have to think in terms of *billions*."

They talk loosely of locusts "blocking out the sun" and it's a nice, descriptive cliché; but they do just that. Sometimes, when they are mating, the ground in Africa will be covered with them, packed *tightly* side by side two bodies deep, nose to tail and haunch to haunch for an area of fifty, even a hundred or more square miles.

Brooding on this, I remembered that the largest sighting ever recorded and confirmed was a flight of the desert locust across the Red Sea in the year 1889; it was estimated to be an unbelievable *two thousand* square miles in extent.

The only other creature that travels in swarms that size is the safari ant, the subfamily *Dorylinae*, with its large, predatory jaws and an instinct that its survival depends on the use of enormous colonies. I've seen the havoc these two pests can cause, and it's terrifying.

Some years ago, when I was studying the origins of the Bante language and living among the Babangi of the Upper Congo, I saw both of them at work, at the same time, over the same area. Half a dozen sleeping children, already half dead from malnutrition, had been completely eaten.

I said, worrying about it. "They'd go through the eyeballs first, the moisture and sweetness attracts them. It's a gruesome thought."

She shuddered.

It was so quiet and *peaceful* here! There was a great temptation just to enjoy it all and to dismiss entirely the dark cloud of tragedy which had brought us to the islands. Staring out across the water at Moorea, Maite said: "Shall we go to Faatua soon?"

"There's a great deal we have to do here first. Faatua can wait."

"I'd like to examine the soil there."

"Whatever for?"

"Formic acid."

"We know it's there. And I think we can guess how it got there and why."

She raised her eyebrows at me, and I said: "First, we have to know a great deal about whatever became of Jules Cresson. If we think in terms of breeding a very special kind of insect, something like Falleron's drawing, for use as a *weapon*, there's no better place to do it than somewhere in Polynesia."

She looked a bit doubtful, sipping her Hinano and staring out across the open sea; a small sloop out there was cutting white circles in the blue water around a large white yacht.

I said: "It just couldn't be done in a back room somewhere, with a heap of cabbages for food. You'd need an island so remote that *no one* ever goes there, far enough away to insure the kind of complete secrecy that would be required even in the case of an accident—like Faatua, which I can only regard as that, an accident."

She said promptly: "We can't be sure of that."

"No, we can't. Just a guess for the moment, until someone turns it to profit. The climate is ideal out here, the vegetation is dense and varied, and—most importantly—a man can come and go as he pleases here, provided he has his own aircraft. He can fly off clandestinely with the greatest ease, and no one would even suspect that he wasn't still lying in the sun on his private beach on his private island. So—what we're looking for is an island with plenty of varied vegetation..."

"Ninety-nine percent of them, that's a great help."

I said patiently: "Uninhabited..."

"About half of them."

"And most important of all, with no overflights. Nothing, for example, lying along one of Air Polynesia's more traveled routes, or even where a charter plane might want to land for one reason or another."

Finally, she was paying attention, her head tilted back, her eyes bright.

I said: "A *private* island, probably one that's been purchased in the last few years, and one where, for one reason or another, nobody ever lands. Far enough away to discourage the day trippers and the tourists, the kind of place in which no one would take the purely *casual* kind of interest that says: let's stop on the beach for a picnic. It's got to be big enough for a plane to land comfortably, it presumably has to have enough water to support life. And, perhaps most important of all, it has to be a long way away from the main island grouping."

"Oh?"

"Because if someone is slipping out from time to time to blackmail Libyans and to visit the south of France, then he's got to be able to do it without going through the normal immigration and emigration formalities. Is the percentage dropping fast enough for you?"

She nodded. "It's looking better."

"I'll add one more thing: ocean depths are important too."

"Oh." She frowned darkly. "Why's that?"

"Ocean depths, and wind directions, have a great deal to do with the currents that take stray vessels to unexpected islands, like coconut husks washed up on the tide. The island I'm looking for would not be in the path of one of the major currents. Now, look at the charts, put all that together, and I'll be surprised if we can't put our finger on exactly the ideal place. Whether or not our man was as careful as we're being, I don't know. But logic says he probably was. Do you know anybody in the government here?"

"More cousins than you can count."

"Good. I also want to know about the man who crashed at Faatua. What do we know about him already?"

She said promptly: "His name's Hawkins, an American, and he seems to have a lot of money. A retired oil man."

"Are they looking for him?"

"I'm quite sure I told you that already. They sent a schooner to the island."

"Was that all?"

"They also had a search plane out for one day."

"A thorough search?"

She sighed. "Not in the Western sense that you're accustomed to. In Tahiti, if you do something *thoroughly*, it often means that you think about it casually for a while and then give up. A local characteristic."

"All right. We want detailed weather reports covering the Societies and the Tuamotus, including winds and currents, for the last fifteen days. I want a list of all non-Polynesians who have bought islands here during the last ten years—film stars, retired officers from the armed services, businessmen. Among them we're looking for someone who could logically insist on the kind of seclusion we know our man must have."

"A film star, you said it yourself."

"That was merely an example, simply because there are several of them who have retired out here. Our man is probably of an entirely different caliber."

"Jules Cresson?"

"Now you're jumping to conclusions. I won't have it. We'll need a charter plane at first light. I'll fly it myself."

I gave her my pilot's papers and said: "See that there's everything we need on board, food and drink, full fuel tanks, and scuba gear. You know about scuba diving?"

She laughed. "What is there to know? I can go down to fifty-five feet without it. The planes in less than thirty feet of water, no problem. We have to file a course with the charter people. Faatua direct?"

"We overfly Huahine first. Then land on Faatua. Then back and forth over the prevailing current until we find Hawkins and his rubber raft. If he hasn't already landed somewhere, which he may have done."

"No. We'd have heard. Nearly all the islands have radio communication, you know. We're not that uncivilized. Oh, yes, we'd have heard immediately."

I said: "Unless he's keeping it quiet himself. And if he is, it's the best possible sign that we're on the right track."

"And if Hawkins is the man behind all this? And if he drowned?"

I said: "No. The timing is all wrong. Now finish your beer and get going. I need some exercise."

She leaped to her feet. "All right. Where shall we meet?"

"Dinner at the Belvedere. Why don't you book us a table? And you'd better get us a car."

"What time shall I pick you up?"

"You drive the car there, I'll walk."

"Nobody walks to the Belvedere, its seven miles straight up in the air"

"You don't listen to me, do you? I told you, I need some exercise."

A deeply bronzed young man was strolling by, bare-chested and barefoot, strumming a guitar, a crown of *tiare* flowers around his black, curly hair, and she paused to watch and listen. The old Tahitian lullaby was getting to her already, its insidious charm working on her; a few hours in these islands, and you not only never want to go home again, you never want to do another day's work, either. As though reading my thoughts, she said, sighing: "What a shame we have so much to do."

I watched her move away under the bright colors of the trees; even her walk had changed now, along with her name; she was *swaying*, a marvelous articulation of her hips that was exciting in the extreme.

I paid the bill, walked quickly along the seafront, and then turned to the east toward Vaininiore, along the bustling, cheerful side streets to Pusa, on the Farii Piti. When I hit the forest and the steep climb, I began to run, jogging easily along the broken dirt road that leads on and on and up to Pirae, moving quite fast through the masses of ginger-plant, and hibiscus, and calophyllum, and the lovely lilac-colored ipomoea; the sun broke through the clouds in an unexpected burst of gold, and the mist was rising from the heavy vegetation. High up here, the evaporating waters were condensing on the summit, and the ripe profusion of the greenery was astonishing, as rich and powerfully scented as a man could wish for. (They say, and perhaps not apocryphally, that coming in from the sea to Tahiti, you can smell the island before you can see it).

Here, indeed, the scent was overpowering, and I thought there are people to whom the destruction of foliage like this serves an important and wretched end. I tried to imagine this mountain denuded of all its glory; happily, I could not.

I thought of Gerard's sad grapes for a while, and the tragedy that had struck the new millet-fields in North Africa. And I thought about Faatua, a lush and beautiful island that had become, almost overnight, a barren stretch of desert and bare rock.

I thought: where would a man go who was experimenting with a monstrous new breed of insect that would devour every living thing in sight? A louse that would get ravenous for chlorophyll? I was sure that the answer was, without a doubt, somewhere in these islands.

I clambered for a while over the steep, steep rocks, not really wasting time but letting the *feeling* of the island take hold on me, enjoying its warmth and its feeling of almost prehistoric isolation; there were no sounds up here except the gentle sounds of nature, the cries of birds, the susurration of gushing water. I found a river in a little while, and found too a good-sized pool where I swam for half an hour, six-stroking back and forth from rock-shelf to rock-shelf, and then did a couple of hundred quick push-ups because I have an extreme distaste for flabbiness.

When I felt that I had taken care of my bodily well-being, I decided to let the island do the rest.

More than an island, more than a corner of paradise. Tahiti is a state of mind, and I let it embrace me, gently, softly, comfortingly.

I sat down under a scarlet hibiscus, and looked out through a broad gap in the forest at the ocean down there where once, many years ago, the beautiful women of New Cytheria, as Tahiti was called then, came swimming out to the ships of the first navigators, enchanting them with flowers and caresses, bare-bosomed and shaped, as Gauguin had said, by sculptors.

The silent pool was empty, but there was a vision there: a young girl in the water, a *vahine* with a flower behind her ear, her long auburn hair, its color glinting with every movement of the sun and the clouds, hanging loose over her alabaster shoulders. Her breasts were soft and gently molded, small as cut lemons, and she turned her head and smiled at me, and it was Maite.

I wondered if she were Fenrek's girl. He was as secretive about his many loves as he was about his work, and I thought perhaps she was; it saddened me.

That damned euphoria was slowly, insidiously, taking hold of me.

It's fine if you're a tourist, trying to forget all the world's woes, but in the kind of work I do it's a very dangerous thing—the feeling that God's in his heaven, all's right with the world; He seldom is, and everything's mostly wrong.

I heard the soft footfall, and I swear that for the moment I didn't think twice about it, though anywhere but here I would have been diving for cover in a flash. And then I heard it again, so faint that I might almost have imagined it. Bare feet makes precious little noise on damp ground, but he'd trodden on a fallen blossom that had very lightly *plopped*.

I thought: *Jesus, someone's trying to sneak up on me*. And then, all the proper reflexes took over, and I twisted round and rolled into the pool where Maite's image had been a moment ago, and went to the bottom and swam a dozen quick strokes, and when I surfaced again, there he was, a short, fat, stubby kind of man in blue denim shorts and nothing else. He was very dark, with short, curly, black hair and a broad, flat nose; I thought he might have been a Samoan or Fiji Islander. He was right at the edge of the pool and facing me, and I saw him lift his clenched right fist up to his mouth, and I didn't wait for any more information about what he was up to.

I threw myself up and back and over, and heard the soft *phutt* as I went down again, and I came up at once and raced toward where he had been, swimming faster than I have ever swum before.

He was gone. There was no sign of him.

I climbed out of the pool, a terribly vulnerable target but quite sure that he was cutting his losses and was on his way out of the kind of danger my knowledge of his presence offered him; the enormous care with which he had stalked me presupposed that he wasn't prepared to tackle me hand to hand, under any but more favorable circumstances.

I looked, and listened, and prowled around for ten minutes, stark naked and feeling a little foolish; but no, he had definitely gone.

I found the dart that had come from his blowgun—a length of reed no more than five inches long, it had seemed—floating on the water; it took fifteen minutes of searching. It was a piece of ordinary pith from an elder berry stem, about half an inch long, into which had been fastened a long thorn from a bougainvillea plant; the red brown thorn was covered with a grayish paste. I smelled it; very faint, but obvious.

It was made from the grated kernel of the *Lecythidaceae* plant, the *Barringtonia Asiatica* which is called *hotu* in Polynesian, though it might have been mixed with an extract of the *tephrosia* root to strengthen it; the water had weakened the mixture and made it really quite hard to identify with any precision.

Anyway, these are two of the plants that the local fishermen use to poison fish—an easy way of catching the day's supply of food. It occurred to me that its damage to a full sized man would be minimal, probably not enough to cause more than an acute lessening of physical capability; but enough, presumably, to have reduced me to what he must have thought of as manageable proportions.

In other words, in spite of my size, strength, and knowledge of all the martial arts, I would quickly have become an easy victim. To be securely bound hand and foot? And carted off to where? Or perhaps to have my throat cut at his leisure.

I was wondering *who* knew *how* much? Well, time would answer that crucial question, without a doubt, I thought about it all the way home.

CHAPTER 3

The Belvedere is high up on the mountain where I'd spent most of the afternoon walking around and thinking out the problems that lay ahead of us.

It's a very open air and informal sort of place, with a huge verandah of rough-sawn planks that seems, in the darkness, to be perched on the edge of limbo, the dense forest beyond it not quite impenetrable, as though it were important, as indeed it is, to get occasional glimpses over the treetops of the shimmering moon on the sea far below. The night was warm and humid, that masterly medium temperature when you feel neither hot nor cold but just right, regardless of what you wear; it was the kind of night that makes you wonder why people ever took to wearing clothes. There were no flying insects, and they'd built the place with an eye for the old Tahiti of thatched roofs and rattan-tied beats, with no touch of modernity to intrude upon comfort.

Maite was already in the bar when I got there, and she told me, in one breath, three things. First, that we were guests for the evening of friends of hers; second, that she had all the information I'd asked for; and third, that her analysis case was missing from the hotel.

I said: "What do you mean, missing?" and she said simply: "Not there anymore, I told you."

It was a little leather satchel containing silver salts and methyl alcohol, and formaldehyde and sodium formate, and all kinds of rubbish she was never going to need anyway, and she'd left it on the bed, she was quite sure; and now it was gone.

People don't steal in Tahiti. You can leave your bankroll lying about, and no one will as much as touch it.

Perhaps I should correct that. They'll examine it carefully, and critically, and at great length until they get bored with it, because they are very curious people; but they won't steal it, ever, because stealing is an unfriendly and inhospitable aspect of human endeavor and therefore has no place in Polynesian philosophy.

I said: "You called the desk? It could have ended up in someone else's room." Confusion is part of the informality.

She shook her head. "It disappeared. I went back to my room, where I'd left it, and there it was, gone."

I didn't mind that all that useless stuff had vanished, but the implications were disturbing. It occurred to me that if we were dealing high enough up on the criminal scale for blackmail of a rather violent, unforgiving, and totally unpredictable government, then the fact that *somebody* wanted to know just how well-equipped we were was a trifle alarming. I thrust the worry to the back of my mind for future consideration.

She handed me a list of foreigners who had bought private islands in this vast ocean—a rather imposing list of them—and I was delighted to see that she had starred them all, just like cognac; one, two or three stars. There were four of them indicated as excellent vintage, and I crossed two of them off immediately, much to her chagrin.

She said indignantly: "But why? I thought they were very good possibilities."

"No. They're both directly in line with major islands that have airstrips, so there's always the possibility of overflights. You really don't pay attention to what I tell you, do you?"

She sighed. "All right, we'll give them two stars instead of three."

The other two gave me food for thought, one of them in particular, and I said: "Rangitefara, very interesting."

She held my look, challenging. "I thought so. No doubt you have a special reason for saying that?"

"Hawkins' plane was a Piper Warrior, not so? And the Warrior's range would be just about right—Rangitefara to Papeete and

42

back, so he'd be quite happy setting out for the return trip. But an adverse wind would give him a bit of a problem, since he's already stretching his fuel supply to its limit. He would have run out just about where Faatua is. Nothing more than a possibility, but worth considering. First thing in the morning, get that list off to Fentek on the Telex, will you do that for me?"

"No, I don't have to."

"Oh?"

"I did it already. I thought that's what you would want."

"Oh. You arranged for a plane?"

"I'm the perfect girl Friday."

"And the weather reports?"

She handed them to me, superimposed on a very good naval chart of the area marked in red 'restricted'. As I studied it, I said idly, not making a point of it: "Are you Mat Fenrek's girl?"

When she didn't immediately answer, I looked up at her and saw a very grave and thoughtful expression on her face that was hard to interpret. Then she smiled quickly, and said: "No, I'm not, so that makes it all right, what you are thinking; doesn't it?" Not stopping for a change of mood, she ran a finger over the chart and said: "If Hawkins had any luck at all, he would have hit this current, here, and with the twelve-knot wind that was blowing most of the time then, he would have been carried...in this direction."

I ran a finger lightly over her hand; her skin was warm ice. The barman was peering intently at the top-secret map over her shoulder, a tray of drinks held high on the flat of his hand; he was studying it with her intently, and he said cheerfully: "Very deep water there; you see? What's that figure? Four thousand meters? Very deep." He swept himself away, and I looked at Maite and sighed.

I said: "In America, in Europe, we'd be going over this in a dismal office, with security guards keeping the curious away."

"Not in Tahiti. And that's good. Everybody here knows everybody else's business, which is going to make it all a lot easier for us." She brushed it off: "It works both ways."

"What's the local government doing about Faatua, do you know that?"

She shrugged, a bare and elegant shoulder raised a trifle.

"They're wondering what happened, just like everybody else."

She was ruffling through the papers that were clipped to the chart. "And there's something else here you ought to see right away." She pulled off a slip of paper and said, tapping it with her hand: "Jules Cresson was here four years ago, trying to buy himself an island, unsuccessfully."

Well, that was an illuminating comment. I said: "What happened?"

She grimaced. "He tried, unsuccessfully, to buy an island."

I said patiently: "Any *particular* island? And why didn't it come off? And what happened to him afterward?"

She plucked the flower from her hair, examined it critically, held it under my nose for an instant, and then tucked it back into place. "He was apparently making inquiries of the authorities, and they put him on to one or two that were up for sale, but he couldn't afford to pay the price, and he disappeared."

"Disappeared? Where to?"

She grimaced again. "Disappeared. If we knew where he had gone, it would not have been a disappearance."

"Left the islands?"

"Apparently not."

"Then he's still here?"

"Apparently not. He disappeared, how many times do I have to tell you?"

I saw that I was going to need a great deal of patience with this young woman. I said: "Do we know where he lived while he was here, perhaps?"

"Yes, we do. He stayed at a hotel called the Taaone, that's a nice little place on the beach two miles to the east of the town, quite inexpensive and very charming. My cousin owns it."

"And you called, no doubt?"

"Yes, of course. They remember him quite well, largely because he left without paying his bill. He stayed there for a month, and kept asking them to be patient because he was expecting money, and they could hardly throw him out, I mean, well, could they? And then one day he went off and didn't come back."

"And what did he leave behind at the hotel? In his suitcase?"

"No suitcase. He must have sneaked it out. There was nothing left, not even a dead razor blade. He just...disappeared."

"Four years ago."

"That's what I said. Can we take our drinks to the verandah? I want to enjoy the view."

We wandered off into the night and stood at the railing, very close together, looking out over the forest, the cool night drifting around us comfortingly. There was a large yacht moving silently by down there, bright with its yellow lights against the sea, and the moon was high over the purple dragon of Moorea, a crescent poised like a scimitar. It was a remarkable saffron color, a moon of great authority, and Maite whispered: "Hina, she's up there, I can feel her presence."

Hina was the daughter of the god Tiki, and he fell in love with her; but he was caught with her by his jealous wife, Hina's mother Ahuone. To hide her shame, the young girl fled to the moon, from which point of vantage, to this day, she rules the bodies of all Earth's women.

Maite leaned close to me, and nestled her bare shoulder against my chest, a sensuous, enticing movement. I could smell the scent of her flowers; and she said: "I'm so glad I'm home again."

"I can't think why you ever left."

"No. It doesn't make much sense, does it? Do you think we'll find Hawkins? They did search, you know."

"But they'd naturally expect him to land on the island where he crashed. They wouldn't look much further."

"I wonder where he was going. Do you think he really has anything to do with all this?"

"I don't like coincidences. A plane goes down close by, the island is devastated the next day..."

"And Gerard's place? Why, do you think?"

"At a guess, the new weapon was being tested. It was successful, so they sprung it in North Africa immediately. Where next, I wonder?"

"Out here, do you think?" Her voice was terribly sad.

"No. I'm convinced that the Faatua incident was quite accidental. But it's given us the lead we require, and we take it from there."

ALAN CAILLOU

Somebody called out: "Maite!" and she swung round, delighted. A thick-set, handsome man in his sixties was approaching us, his arms outspread, a gray and grizzled man with short-cropped white hair and a deeply tanned complexion. He wore a tight, short sleeved blue sweater and linen slacks, and there were half a dozen leis around his neck, He embraced her and kissed her on both cheeks, and hugged her for a while and beamed at me, and she said, making the introductions: "Captain Vanaa, from Huahine, and Cabot Cain, from San Francisco."

A gray-haired, plump, and elderly lady with a broad, broad smile was moving in behind him, and there were others with her. Vanaa said, gesticulating broadly: "Mr. Cabot Cain; my wife Te Tua, my good friend Auguste from the ketch *Pinaa* in the harbor, and Auguste's lovely lady Vaite. Our new friend Cabot Cain."

Auguste wag a young and athletic-looking Frenchman, tall and well-built and cheerful, his yellow hair tumbling all over the place, with the kind of face that sculptors like to study, deeply etched, a broad and intelligent forehead, and a good, strong jaw. He reached up and slapped me on the shoulder and said heartily: "We're late, Mr. Cain, and it's all my fault. Vaite's my crew, and she fell overboard, she always does that, she's well named."

Vaite means Dropping Water in Tahitian, and he was enjoying the joke immensely, a boyish, charming grin on his face, his white teeth shining. She was a delightful young woman, his Vaite, rather plump, round-faced, and very bouncy, with that long black Tahitian hair that was tied in a single knot and left to drape effectively over one shoulder. She wore a white evening gown that shimmered when she moved about, which was all the time; her eyes were marvelous, very large, and dark, and deep.

Captain Vanaa had turned back to the table that had been set for us, and was examining it critically, approving the flowers laid out at each place setting and the fine array of polished glasses. He said: "A drink, a drink for God's sake, what are we all having?"

The waiter was bustling around cheerfully, and I saw that the table had been laid for seven; there were only six of us. Captain Vanaa saw me noticing it and said expansively, a broad, broad gesture with his massive arms: "Another guest coming a little later, Mr. Cain, she's

46

modeling this evening. Her name's Tiare."

Tiare...the most fragrant of all the Tahitian flowers.

I suddenly thought, out of the blue, what a flair the Tahitians have for names; she could have been called Hortense. But no; even Vanaa's gray and elderly wife was named Te Tua, which means Beautiful Back, and that's a nice thought. And the *tiare* has a charm all its own, possibly because it has become a symbol of the island itself. It is a form of gardenia, the *tahitensis*, though it doesn't look a bit like one, and is used not only for *leis*, hats, crowns, and for personal decoration but also for a skin lotion they call *monoi*. But its main value, perhaps, lies in the fact that perfect strangers on the street, seeing you pass by and looking unhappy, will put a couple of *leis* made from them around your neck just to cheer you up.

We sat down to dinner when the drinks were poured, and they brought us a splendid dish of *oura miti*, the local spiny lobster that some people call bay prawns, four inches long and served *flambé* in cognac on skewers, which makes for a very civilized dish indeed. And I learned that Maite had been hard at work in her absence.

Captain Vanaa said: "I hear you are looking for that American who brought his plane down near Faatua, Mr. Cain. You'll never find him."

"Oh? How's that? We're studying the winds, the currents...his whereabouts ought to be totally predictable."

"Perhaps. But there are spirits at work out there. All kinds of strange things are happening. Sail north of here for weeks on end, and you'll make no landfall except Faatua, Go due west, clear across the Pacific Ocean...nothing. Only to the east of us, and to the northeast. The rest of it...an empty ocean. And yet, a few weeks ago when I was sailing out there, I came across a launch, heading due north, where there's nothing, and when I tried to approach them they put on speed and ran from me. And a month ago, I'd seen that same launch drifting, near Huahine, far out at sea but heading for shore on the current, and I waited for them to see if I could help, three men on board. They came in during the night, and I saw them from my house, but they walked off along the beach where my fish lines are, and I lost them."

"But if you were waiting to help them...?"

He was grinning ferociously, a tough, weather-beaten old man.

"It was night, Mr. Cain, and the night is for the *tupapaus*, the evil spirits, not the time for an honest man to be anywhere but in his own house. In the morning when the sun comes up, yes, I went looking for them. But by then, they had gone, and I thought: what am I doing wandering along the beach looking for people who don't need my help? I got tired of it, so I spent the rest of the day sitting under a tree and wondering about them."

"And what did you decide, Captain Vanaa?"

"I decided it was none of my business. They were Americans, by the looks of them. Forgive me, but...strange people. They had an air of...of great purpose about them, of urgency. It did not endear them to me." He shrugged. "Just men. But on a little island like Huahine, we always know who comes and who goes. From where, and where to. It is the custom."

There was mischief in his eyes, and I said: "But there's something else, isn't there, Captain?"

He laughed out loud. "Yes, there is. They were all three of them carrying guns. Rifles. I haven't seen a gun since I was in the navy, and that was a long time ago."

"And you don't know what they did on the island, while your *tupapaus* were at work?"

He was still laughing, delighted with the memory of it, something to talk about for years. "But I do. Lou How, the Chinese who keeps gasoline for the outboard motors, he lost twenty gallons of gas that night. Five four-gallon cans of it. No. I do not interest myself in men who carry guns. Or in thieves."

And then the missing guest came, and all I could do was stare.

I had turned to the young Frenchman Auguste to ask him what sort of ketch he had, wondering if it were perhaps the tall, blue-sailed beauty I'd seen that afternoon crossing over from Moorea, and I was conscious that his attention was distracted, his dark, sun-tanned face alive with pleasure. A lot of other heads had turned too, and I was suddenly aware of all the patches of light and dark on the great verandah, the pools of pale yellow glow from the hanging lamps fading into a chiaroscuro here and there, in and out of which people were moving around, brightly lit one moment and hardly seen at all the next. And coming down the steps from the entrance, her arms widespread with a mass of *leis* draped over them, her body slim and ethereal and almost wafting, was one of the most lovely women I have ever seen in a life that is fortunately filled with many such memories.

She seemed to float toward us out of the darkness, her long, long hair shining as she moved under a light and then framing her oval face in darkness as she moved out of it, a young *vahine* in her early twenties, a vision of loveliness that was so startling as to be almost unreal. That extraordinary hair hung down almost to her thighs, a splendid, cascading sweep of it, and she wore a rust-colored evening gown that hugged her body, nicely open at the breast and draping itself magnificently over her hips, a gown that was unexpectedly chic and fashionable here. She wore a dozen more *leis* around her neck, and it seemed, momentarily, that she was half-concealed under great piles of flowers, the white and amber wax of them giving out a perfume that was as overpowering as her physical perfection.

She was advancing on us laughing, her eyes alight, and holding out her arms as she placed the *leis* around our necks, one after the other of us, kissing us all on both cheeks and embracing us, and laughing to herself all the time as though there were great humor here somewhere if only it could be discovered.

Somehow, she was not quite believable. There is a legend, of course, of the *vahine's* beauty, but most of it is really a thing of the past, a memory of the discoverers who were affected more, perhaps, by the sheen of the skin and the bare breasts which the damn missionaries promptly covered up, than by the fact of beauty itself; today, the young women are charming rather than lovely, sensual rather than truly beautiful, and enticing rather than voluptuous.

But Tiare...

Her skin was flawless, the rich, soft amber that spreads from the center of the flowers after which she was named, and she held her head high, tilted back a trifle for better attention, it seemed, to all that was going on around her, and she was laughing all the time for no reason at all that was immediately apparent; the laugh intrigued me deeply. It was not inconsequential, or unreasoning, or shallow; rather, there were thoughts reflected in her dark and shining eyes that made fun of everything she saw or heard, as though everything for her, too, were unreal, a put on that was delightful because no one was expected to believe it.

There was a great deal of bustle at the table as Auguste did his damndest to get Tiare to sit next to him, and his Vaite neatly maneuvered the chairs so that she sat between them. Maite had already turned to Vanaa, and was taking up the question of the "empty" waters to the north of his island.

She said, frowning: "But there is a group of small islands out there somewhere, an atoll..."

The Captain nodded. "Yes, yes, there's a place called Rangitefara, a lagoon and a very small island, it's always been uninhabited, the kind of place that...well, you must understand about the currents here. In one or two isolated instances, there's a small landmass that no one, in the old days, ever drifted to because the currents meet and merge and finally bypass it. Yes, I remember it well..."

It was one of Maite's three-star islands. Auguste's voice boomed out suddenly: "Tell him about the Japanese, Vanaa!" and the Captain said happily: "Ah yes. Well, many years ago a team of Japanese were trying to set up a business there, diving for sponges. Only...when no sponges were being brought here for export after nearly a year, the government made some discreet inquiries and found out what they were actually up to. They were trying to set up a pearl bed, cultivating black pearls, and smuggling them out. Very properly, the government put a stop to it. We have our own cultivated pearl business here, embryonic but very promising."

Maite said casually (how easy it was to leave everything to her!): "I heard that Rangitefara had been sold recently."

Vanaa frowned. "Was it? Are you sure?"

Beside him, Te Tua was nodding her gray head, "Yes, it was, about two years ago. To one of your American film stars, I believe." She leaned toward me and said confidentially: "Personally, I never heard of him, but they say he's a very famous man in America. Retired now, but once...what do you call it? An idol? They say the women worshipped him."

Tiare was spearing a piece of rock lobster on her fork and holding it up in a delicate hand, laughing and bringing it in close to my face and then popping it carefully into my mouth. She said: "Film star my foot! He's a painter. And not a very good one, either, a man of absolutely no consequence to anyone at all. He wants to be another Gauguin, but he just doesn't have the talent, for painting, or for anything else."

I said: "So you know him, Tiare?"

She shrugged, a slight lift of those lovely shoulders. "I met him once, here in Papeete, I modeled for him, and he tried to seduce me." She corrected herself, "No. I would not in the least have minded a seduction, although he was not a very attractive man. But he offered me money, what a foolish thing to do."

"And his name?"

She hesitated. Then: "Fest. Willard Fest. To us, that sounds like a terrible name."

I looked over to Maite, and she nodded, half-smiling, meaning: yes, his name's on the list, the list that's gone to Fenrek.

Tiare held out another piece of her *oura miti* for me, and I bit into it and said: "Tell me more about him."

She gestured. "What is there to tell? A nobody."

"And what does he do on Rangitefara?"

"He does nothing. He paints."

"Have you been to his island?"

She shook her head. "He never invites anyone, and even if he asked me, I wouldn't accept, why should I? To be seduced?"

Te Tua said firmly: "A film star. He's retired, and he wants to be left alone."

She was plump, and matronly, and really quite regal. She said, smilingly: "How would you like it if every Tom, Dick, and Harry came landing on your home every day just to stare at you because you were once famous? For that, I will not blame him. When a man retires, he likes to lie on the beach and watch the world go by at his own tempo, and that does not mean being host to a lot of gaping tourists. No. Privacy...that's why people come here; they can live alone if they want to, with nothing but the sea and the sky and the trees for company, a privilege too valuable to be destroyed by stupidity."

"And he's alone? Quite alone?"

"Oh no! They say he built himself a house there, with half a dozen servants from Fiji, and three or four men as...bodyguards, I suppose you'd call them. To keep the invaders out, you understand."

Her husband grunted. "Bodyguards! In Tahiti! What the devil is the place coming to?"

I asked him if these could have been the men he saw on Huahine, and he shook his head. "Who knows? It's possible, even likely. I know everybody else on the islands, so... Yes, it's possible."

"But you've never seen Willard Fest himself?"

"No." He grinned. "Tiare feels she has to earn a living, so she constantly meets all the wrong people. I am more fortunate. I retired long ago to my own kind of privacy, with a lovely lady to keep me company, and a small boat, and enough to eat out there in the water. The idyllic life, Mr. Cain. I don't have to meet people I'm not going to like. When I come over here to Papeete, to the center of civilization, all I ever want to do is get back to my island. Too many people here. Too much going on all the time."

Too many people. The entire population of Papeete is less than twenty-five thousand souls. There are only a hundred and twenty thousand people in all of the French Polynesian islands together, spread out over an area that's mile for square mile larger than Europe.

It's part of the charm; there are no great crowds anywhere, elbowing each other out of the way. The Captain's own little island, Huahine, eighty miles from Tahiti, has only three thousand inhabitants scattered among its thirty square miles of volcanic mountain, soft yellow beach, and blue-green lakes.

It is a fascinating place, far enough off the beaten track to have been left alone in serenity to enjoy its quiet warm breezes and the astonishing golden light of its evenings, a light that lingers on the hills as though reluctant to surrender its beauty to the darkness of the night. There's only one town, and in that town, only a single street; delightful.

It was once called Matairea, the "island of little wind," though Captain Cook, on his journey there before he had all that trouble with his sextant, had called it Hermosa. They say the god Hiro (who was the god of Thieves) split the island in two with his pirogue, and thereafter it became known as Hua-Huatearu, which means "broken coral." Today, it's simply Huahine, the "Island of Gray Fruit."

The Captain was saying: "And how long will you be staying in our islands, Mr. Cain?"

I told him I didn't know, and he said: "Long enough, I hope, for you to visit us? To stay a few days, a few weeks, a few months?"

Auguste said cheerfully: "I'll run you over in the ketch whenever you want. If we leave early in the morning we'll be there in good time to catch our dinner on the rocks." He looked at Vanaa and grinned. "Cain and the three graces. Maite, Vaite, and Tiare, it rolls nicely off the tongue. What about tomorrow? The Captain can take Cain lobster fishing, and I'll show the ladies around the ruins of the temples, what do you say?"

I saw that Maite was watching me obliquely, and that Vaite was just as carefully watching Auguste; Tiare was making her presence *felt.*

We decided to leave it open. I was anxious to get aboard that plane and try and find out what had happened to Hawkins. I wanted, most of all, to find out about Jules Cresson; there are a hundred and thirty islands in that vast, multi-colored ocean, and roughly three-quarters of a million square miles of water, and that's a lot of territory for a man to hide in. I wondered, most of all, just *why* he was hiding; if he really was, of course. And if, indeed, he were still alive.

Maite had insisted that Cresson had just...disappeared. Was he lying, another skeleton as final as Villiers', on a coral bed somewhere? His bones, this time, picked clean not by his own kind of *docciostaurus*—whatever it was—but by the same *oura miti* we were having for dinner?

It was a gruesome thought.

The party broke up in the small hours of the morning.

Maite had hired a wretched little Volkswagen, much too small a car for me to fit into comfortably, and I wondered if I should invite her to walk back with me instead through the nighttime forest. But I could hardly leave the damn thing there.

I stood with Captain Vanaa, a man I had quickly grown fond of, in the darkness under the tall trees where the last few cars were parked, and thanked him for his hospitality. I said: "Would you do me a favor, Captain?"

He gestured expansively: "Anything at all, Mr. Cain. A friend of Maite's..."

"You said you know everybody in the islands."

"I do indeed."

"That kind of knowledge is very useful to me... Do you know why I am here?"

"Maite told me. She also said you'd be furious if you found that out. Are you?"

"No, of course not. Secrecy here is not quite the overpowering consideration that it always seems to be back home, is it? Would you see what you can find out about Willard Fest for me?"

"Ha! Then he's your man, is he?"

"I don't know. He doesn't seem to fit the bill, somehow. And yet...there's so much pointing in the direction of Rangitefara. I just...don't know."

The three graces all came trooping out of the ladies' room, tripping daintily down the steps, and we packed ourselves into our cars and drove off.

The night was still, and cool, and moist, and ii was good to be alive.

CHAPTER 4

There was a fine, gentle, insistent rain when we took off, and the sky was amber and gray and luminescent.

There was a silver mist hanging over Tahiti's jagged crags, with darker clouds above it as though they were letting the moisture seep down, taking its own good time, onto the forests below; it looked as though the innumerable gods of the Polynesians were delicately draping the island with a scented, permeable, leaden vapor, shielding it from all possible harm.

Maite had found us a Cessna Golden Eagle, the new 421B, a splendid, twin-engine, six-seater, geared, turbo-supercharged, injected, opposed, 520 cubic inches, with first rate pilot visibility (which might be very important, I thought), plenty of room in its cockpit and cabin, and three-bladed props that turn at only 2,275 rpm even at full power, which makes for quiet and relaxed cruising, with none of the give-em-hell sort of feeling that so many light planes suffer from. I was a bit worried about its runway requirement, which is 2,507 feet, as I felt we just might have to try for some fancy landings on very small beaches; but its handling qualities, I could tell just by looking at it, would more than make up for this. I once conducted a short course at Fort Worth on the Aerodynamics of Engine-Out Climbing, and I know about these things.

My first time with an Eagle; I was sure I was going to find it a very satisfying aircraft indeed.

The owner of the charter company was a bright young Tahitian named Teiho, a roly-poly, cheerful man who wore a green and yellow shirt in a violent flowered pattern, white shorts, plastic sandals, and a heavy crown of *tiare* blossoms for a hat.

I said to him: "What about that plane you rented to Hawkins? Are you trying for recovery?"

He grinned, and spread his arms wide. "Recovery? Far too much trouble, Mr. Cain. And even if I got it out of the water, what would I do with it? The insurance people might, one day, but I doubt it. Faatua's a long, long way, and since what happened out there...no one even wants to go near it. The night-spirits were at work; maybe they're still there, who knows? Is that where you are going?"

"Eventually, yes."

He shrugged. "Well, there's a rubber raft aboard for you to float home of if they bring you down."

"They?"

"The *tupapaus*, the dark shadows of the night." He slapped his chubby thigh and roared with laughter, and I said: "So if I don't get back in a reasonable time, will you come looking for me? Somewhere between Huahine and Faatua. If I'm not back by this evening?"

His broad, fiat face was the color of strong tea, with overtones of orpiment, and most of his teeth were gone, though he couldn't have been more than thirty years old. There's all the high-protein food in the world in the wafers of Oceania, but it's easier to pull up a taro root if you're hungry, and that's what happens, it's an island affliction. He said, grinning: "I will, Mr. Cain, I will."

Maite went off to file the flight plan, and while I was waiting for her I was surprised to see Tiare far away by the edge of the water, posing by a dugout canoe while an elderly man with a short, stubby black beard danced around her with a Nikon and a telephoto lens. I called out and waved, and she came running over, delighted, and flung her arms round my neck and kissed me, and said, laughing: "The only man I ever really loved..."

A young man was sitting on a low wall nearby, in the shade, doing nothing: bare feet, bare chest, and a rather surly expression on his face. I felt he was watching us and not liking what he saw, and I asked Tiare: "Your boyfriend? Couldn't you do better than that?"

Her laugh was open, delighted. "I never saw him before in my life. He's just jealous of the great love there is between us."

The young boy looked away when I returned his stare, and then slipped off the wall and wandered off, his hands thrust deep into his pockets, his head down. And then Maite came back, and she kissed Tiare briefly on both cheeks, a little coolly I thought, and I kissed Tiare again and watched her run back to her assignment, and we all walked over to the Cessna. Teiho gallantly helped Maite aboard with a broad hand under her tight little behind, and he said, enjoying the joke: "Try and bring it back in one piece, won't you? They are in short supply, one of my best planes."

There was a rainbow delicately arching down to touch the twin peaks of Moorea across the water on our left, and as soon as we were airborne and climbing nicely at 1,850rmp, Maite said breathlessly: "Can we take a look at Mou'a Puta on our way? Fly around it, maybe."

I said: "Mou'a Puta is a hundred and thirty-eight degrees from here. Our course is a hundred and seventy-one point three."

"Please? It's only a few miles. I want to see where Pai threw his spear, from close up."

"Oh my God."

"Please? We don't always have to do everything *now*, do we? I thought we'd left all that nonsense behind us in Europe. Please."

It was impossible to deny her the little pleasures. I took the plane up to twenty-seven hundred, to bring us directly in line with the small round hole that goes clear through the tip of the mountain. It was formed, eons ago, by volcanic explosion and erosion which left a remnant of lava tube exposed, a dead-straight borehole like a miniature, manmade tunnel high up in the sky. That, at least, is the geological explanation for it.

But Maite is Polynesian, and so she knows better. The hole was actually cut by the spear of the great warrior Pai.

They say that the god Hiro paddled his band of thieves over to Moorea one dark might (it was called Aimeo in those days) to steal the central mountain they call Rotui; he wanted to haul it away and set it up on his own island, Raiatea, a hundred sea kilometers to the northwest. He tied *pohue* vines to it, and began dragging it out to sea, but made such a commotion over it that he woke up Pai, who was fast asleep on Tahiti itself. Angered by this impudence, Pai climbed to the top of Tataa Hill, the "Tail of the Fish," and hurled his spear across the water at Hiro in a fine fit of indignation and rage.

But he missed. Instead, his spear went hurtling over Hiro's head, high in the night sky, and made the famous hole through the mountaintop, finally coming down to Earth again on Raiatea itself, where it left a deep imprint which remains, as does the neat round hole in the rock, to this day.

It's nice to reflect, however, that Hiro's ambitious efforts were not entirely in vain; he did succeed in tearing away a small hill from Moorea (thereby creating Cook's Bay, the most splendid piece of geography in the world), which he dragged across the ocean and set up just where he wanted it, and where it still stands, in the southeast corner of Raiatea.

It's also nice to reflect that this little Raiatean hill, geographically and academically, is precisely Moorean in aspect—the same soil, the same rock, and the same vegetation, quite markedly dissimilar from the rest of Raiatea. Obviously, this is the only way it could have gotten there, in spite of what all the savants might have to say about it.

Thirty-two minutes later we passed over Huahine's central massif, dropping down to twenty-five hundred to skim over Mount Turi and slide down over the treetops to dip our wings over the little seashore village of Fare, where Captain Vanaa lived. We skimmed out to the break in the coral they call Avamos, the "Terrifying Passage," circled the enclosing line of the reef, and took a new course of thirty-one, heading toward Faatua now, but flying low and at minimum throttle.

Hands-off stability is very good on the Eagle, so we were able to relax as we watched the water, with the engines purring gently like two contented cats. There was a single pirogue down there, of the type they call *Va'a Hoe*, with no sail, just a single paddle to propel it along. A bronzed young Polynesian with the inevitable flowers in his hair looked up and waved as we flew over. It was impossibly restful and lethargic.

And then, forty-two sea kilometers out—and just where it was supposed to be—we found the rubber raft from Hawkins aircraft.

It was high and dry on a long, thin strip of sandbar; not really big enough to be called even an islet, though there was a solitary coconut palm growing on it, brought in by the tides and self-seeded, no doubt, and a tiny cluster of greenery. It was about twelve feet wide at one end, narrowing to about six in the center, where it also disappeared under water for a matter of forty feet or so, and then broadened out again to some twenty feet at its widest point.

I flew over it three times before I satisfied myself that it was almost six hundred yards long, or about seven hundred feet less than the Eagle's minimum runway requirement, but I figured that the water in the center, which only looked about three or four feet deep, would slow us down enough to stop us from running away and into the coral that formed a brittle necklace around it, the waves gently lapping away in an almost imperceptible cadence.

I said to Maite: "Just hold on tight, and close your eyes."

She was staring down at it in acute alarm. "My God, we're not going to land on that, are we?"

"I assume you brought along some cognac?"

She reached under the seat and brought out a bottle. She took a very long swig indeed and said resignedly: "We'll never make it. No way."

"The soft sand will slow us down."

"And even if we do, we'll never get off again. We'll have to spend the rest of our lives feeding off one coconut tree."

"Plenty of fish, don't worry about it. Hold on, we're going down."

I throttled back to 175 knots, put out 15 degrees of flap as a speed brake, took the plane back to 145, and gave her thirty degrees, and pushed them to maximum, which is forty-five, and let her down with twenty inches of power; she settled as gently as a bird, splashed through the water-gap nicely, and came to a stop with a full three feet of runway left to play with. The sand was somewhat harder than it had appeared to be.

Maite was out like a flash, with her feet on terra firma, looking up at me, sighing, and saying: "Well, we did it after all."

She wore a green-and-white *pareu* in a flowered design today, and she looked very, very attractive as she stood there with her bare feet in the surf and a single flower behind her ear, her long hair trailing; I found it hard to tear my interest away from her.

We walked back to where the rubber raft was, an ordinary emergency raft with a single plastic paddle still aboard, a water bottle with a few drops of water still in it, but not very many, an opened packet of flares, two of them missing, and a small compass with its glass broken but still working adequately.

Maite was studying the patch of greenery, and she called me over and said, pointing: "Taro, he's been eating it."

It's a nothing plant, the taro, or the *Colocasia Esculenta* to give it its proper name, with large rhizomes and leaves which are both edible if you have little respect for your stomach and less for your palate. Some of them had been pulled up, and the leaves eaten raw. There was not enough water to cook them in, no doubt. But we found the remnants of a tiny fire as well, with a piece of half-baked taro-root beside it, half-eaten too and wholly unappetizing to look at. There were footprints all over, made with rubber-soled shoes, and at one point where the sand was of just the right consistency there was even the faintest imprint of a word left there, a word that looked like "Keds," the embossed rubber marking on the sole of the American casual footwear. Not conclusive, by any means, but the connotation, if it meant anything at all, was correct.

More importantly, there was a deep rut in the sand at the water's edge, cuneiform and coming to an abrupt stop ten feet or so up the beach.

We stared at it, and Maite said: "A boat?"

"Yes. A motor launch by the looks of it. Quite a big one."

"I wonder when?"

"Not much of a tide here, but it's at maximum ebb now, so..."

I walked into the water and studied the beginnings of the furrow. I said: "At a guess, and it can't be much more than that, the tide's been in twice since the launch came in. So, if he's been found, why haven't we heard about it?"

"Is that bad?"

"I like it. It means we're on the right track. Somebody picked him up, and that someone is keeping quite quiet about it. It's an added fascination to our Mr. Hawkins?"

We went back to the plane. I hefted up her tail and swung her round slowly, and wondered if I should jettison some of the fuel to make the takeoff less of a problem; we had the 48-gallon auxiliary tanks in the wings as well as the 26-gallon wing-locker tanks in the engine nacelles. I decided against it and helped Maite aboard and strapped her in tight, and looked at the long thin strip of sand and wondered if we'd make it. And I also wondered what might happen if one of the engines as much as coughed on takeoff; but they were in fine shape, and the craft was evidently very well maintained, so I didn't feel I had to worry too much about it.

I ran the engines up till the locked brakes wouldn't hold any more, pushing the throttle hard forward (you can do that with the Eagle without any danger of overboost), and then let her have her head, and we clawed our way off the sand in less than a thousand feet, which is pretty impressive when you think of all the fuel we were carrying. I swung her back on course and headed for Faatua, and when the tiny island came at us over the deep blue, green, and purple sea, I found a long stretch of white beach and put her down again, taxiing over where, hard by the coral of the reef, the tailfin of Hawkins' sunken plane, a brilliant scarlet, was a knifeblade in twenty feet or so of water.

The Piper Warrior, with its tapered wing, is an extremely easy plane to fly, and I wondered what had happened to bring it down; it's reliable and airworthy, with a solid Lycoming 150hp engine, fairly new on the market.

There was a strange and eerie feeling here on the beach; we were in the middle of all that terrible devastation, Gerard's vineyard all over again, on a much larger and more formidable scale. The desolation spread for more than a thousand yards up from the surf, and then the greenery of the high mountain began again, as lush as it had always been. There were light clouds overhead; it looked as though they were moving in slowly to wonder at the sorry state of the island's southern aspect.

Maite said: "This is where I need my analysis case, what a nuisance." There was that studious look on her face again.

I said: "What for, for God's sake? All you'd find is a massive concentration of formic acid. I'm more interested in that plane. I'm going down there."

She had plucked a bare stem of coralline from the soil and was peering at it intently. "I think I'll collect a few of these to take back with us, all the same. We might learn something from them."

"Nothing we don't know already."

She was a very stubborn young woman. She said: "Just to put under the microscope. I'll join you soon. What are we looking for down there?"

"For whatever there is to see, what else?"

I took the scuba gear from the Eagle while she wandered off, and splashed my way down to the bottom. It was fifty feet offshore and thirty-two feet down, and I saw that its door had been wrenched open, almost off its hinges; a very strong or very desperate man. I swam into the cockpit and looked over the instrumentation, and examined the cabin carefully. There was nothing at all to suggest just why he had crashed. Had he tried for a landing and fouled it up? I wondered how good a pilot he was.

I did find an empty Bourbon bottle, its cork gone and filled now with sea water, which made me think. The only other article which seemed to have no reason for being there was a cardboard box about the size of an orange crate which had been sent by registered post from the U.S.A. to Papeete; there wasn't much left of the packaging, though the stamps were still visible and so, to a lesser extent, was the label. I cut the string around it with my fishing knife, opened it up, and found that it contained a bundle of nylon bags of very fine mesh, each about a foot square and fastened with a zipper along one side—the sort of thing women use to wash their pantyhose in. There were fifty of them, and the invoice for them enclosed in the package was still clear and easy to read: *Arthur P. Hawkins, P.O. Box 156, Papeete, Tahiti.*

Well, that was nice. Everything was falling neatly into place, just as it was expected to.

I was carrying on with my search of the cabin, looking mostly for a map which might have shown where he was going—there was none—when suddenly a shadow passed outside the cabin's window, a mere ripple in the water that meant something was out there, and then Maite, long and slim and brown and quite naked, shot into the cabin with me. She wrapped a long leg round one of the seat supports, and gestured, twisting a hand round and round in that universal gesture which means: "Anything?"

I shook my head, pulled out one of the bags, and showed it to her, and she opened it up and frowned at it, and took the packaging and studied it intently as though she had all the time in the world; I couldn't believe that she could stay so long and so easily under water without air. I watched her for an impossibly long time, till my own lungs seemed, vicariously, to be bursting for her, and then took out my mouthpiece and offered it to her; she seemed quite surprised, but took a long deep breath and handed it back to me. And there she was, so to speak, all set for the rest of the day.

The water was incredibly clear. The sand was brightly white, and there was a lot of black coral a little way from the plane, the *antipathes abies*, as well as the lovely *rubrum* which is more common in the Mediterranean. They were fish swimming around us by the hundreds, and in the first few minutes I spotted grouper, billfish, barracuda, three thresher sharks, and some *mahimahi*. A small sailfish swam into the cockpit, stared at us for a moment, and then darted quickly out again.

I was wondering if I should give Maite some more air, and then I thought: No, let's see just how long she can manage... I sneaked a look at my watch and waited.

Her hair was floating all around her long amber body, wafting like seaweed, a heavy mass of the fern-like *desmarestia*. I thought of the poet Richard Lovelace: "*When I lie tangled in her hair...*"

And then she was lifting her head up and staring toward the surface of the water, thirty feet above us and crystal clear; a shadow was passing overhead, in the sky, and we could very faintly hear the staccato note of a helicopter as it swept over us.

She gestured again: let's go and see...

I shook my head and put an arm around her waist, restraining her, and finally gave her my mouthpiece again, and she looked at me, puzzled, and I signaled her: let's wait.

I saw it make a second pass, and then it was gone, wheeling high up into the air and out of our sight, and we surfaced, very carefully, and trod water there for a moment, looking for it. There was an unaccountable feeling of menace suddenly, and I was about to swim fast to shore and run to the plane for the other scuba outfit when Maite said, squinting into the sun: "There, it's coming back..."

It was, very fast, swooping down on us out of the sun like a bird of prey after a couple of helpless animals.

I yelled at her: "Down!" and watched her body arch beautifully as she dove, and then followed her down deep to the floor of the ocean again.

This time, it came in close, and I thought for a moment it was landing on the beach; but instead it hovered above our heads and just hung there, as though waiting for us to come up again. And then, all around us, the water was churned up in a strange and quite terrifying fashion, slim rivulets like comets appearing all round us and sending up little spurts of sand from the seabed; I saw the cockpit window shatter, the shards of Perspex bursting out like rapidly blooming flowers.

It was a machine gun.

I slung an arm round Maite's stim waist again, and swam with her under the body of the plane, seeking out its flimsy protection, holding her tight to me; and then there was a massive roar above us, and the ground shook and the water churned up, and I thought: My God, they've got bombs too. A scarred and bubbling piece of twisted metal came sliding down beside us, and then another and another, and the helicopter was still hovering up there.

I gave Maite some more air; she was trembling now under my grasp. I looked at the dial on my gear; fifteen minutes of air left, seven and a half minutes each if we shared it carefully.

For five minutes we waited, keeping quite still and hoping that even in the clear, clear water we could not be seen. And the chopper's note changed and it was wheeling away, and there were only two minutes or so left for us. We waited, and when the needle was close to zero I gave Maite a final breath and we eased our way up to the surface again; the helicopter had gone.

And so, in a different fashion had our beautiful Golden Eagle. It was still burning, and the sand around it was blackened where the exploding gas tanks had wrecked further devastation on an island that was already half-dead. We stared at it in dismay for a while, knowing it wouldn't help very much. Maite found her *pareu*, a torn and smoldering piece of rag now, and held it up at arm's length and said wistfully: "It was such a pretty one..."

I'd folded my slacks and shirt neatly, and had placed them on a rock a little distance from the plane, and they were still all right, so I said: "Which do you want, shirt or stacks? Or both?"

She grimaced: "I'll settle for a shirt, what do you think?"

I said gravely: "I think it might be better."

Her body was unbelievably lovely, long and smooth and well-sculptured, if a trifle skinny, with tight, upstanding breasts that were now half-covered with that dark auburn hair that picked up the highlights of the bright, hot sun. She seemed not in the least concerned about her nakedness, as though it were the most natural thing in the world. I thought: Well, why should she be?

She slipped into the shirt, stretching out her arms languorously and the idea that was half-forming in my mind slipped-away from me. I turned away and changed into my slacks.

She sat down on the hot sand, tucked her feet under her behind, tossed the long hair away from her face, and said: "Well? What now?"

She seemed quite unconcerned about the long moment of danger, and I knew why—it had *gone*. If it came again, then she'd worry again; but for now, all was well.

I wished I could answer the question for her, but I couldn't. There was no great problem involved in being marooned on a half-dead island a million miles from anywhere. There was dead wood enough on the island to have made a raft with wire from the plane. We could have floated on the current just as Hawkins had done, and finished up, perhaps, on Huahine or Tahaa. But it didn't seem necessary; Teiho was coming to look for us if we didn't get back on time.

I wandered around the charred wreck of the plane, still burning fiercely, and said to Maite: "Poor Fenrek."

She'd found a comb from somewhere, and was doing her hair. "Mat Fenrek? Why?"

"He's going to have to pay for that aircraft."

"Oh dear. It must be quite expensive."

"Around a couple of hundred thousand dollars."

"Oh my God." Not caring much about it, she said inconsequentially: "Do you think Tiare is beautiful?"

"The woman? Or the flower?"

"She was making cow's eyes at you all last night."

"I think she was more interested in Auguste."

She laughed. "Only to make Vaite mad. Poor Vaite! But it was your blood she was after. I know."

"To make *you* mad, no doubt."

"I don't think so." She was very serious all of a sudden.

"I wonder if it's just a natural...jealousy. She really is very lovely. But whenever she thought you weren't looking, she was...sizing you up. Sort of...checking out the opposition. What time is it?"

"Nearly noon. Why?"

"I'm hungry."

"All right. If you'll make up a fire, I'll go and find us some lunch."

"My God, another fire is all we want."

We had moved far away from the burning aircraft; its heat was intense, a funeral pyre. I told her: "Find a piece of dead wood, toss it at the plane, drag it out again, start a nice little cooking fire going, over in the rocks there."

The long, slow motions with the comb did not stop, a ritual of hyper-femininity. She said: "I can't think why there's always so much that has to be *done*. One of the reasons that I agreed to come back here was that I thought I'd be able to lie in the sun for a couple of weeks and do *nothing*. They've lost the art in France, everyone's in a rush to get something or other done. As though the advent of tomorrow were problematical, and even if it were to come, there'd be no time for anything then either."

"That was a bit garbled, but I know what you mean."

She went on combing her hair, so I walked up the slope of the beach for a couple of hundred feet, uprooted a dead tree, and dragged it back. She watched me.

She said, sighing: "I really will do that if you want we to."

"Lie in the sun. There's time on our hands now. Go to sleep and improve your tan."

"You're sure you don't mind?"

"I think I'd like it."

"All right then. But I'll do the cooking. That's woman's work."

She stripped off my shirt and draped it modestly over her middle, and stretched out full length on the sand and closed her eyes. I watched her for a moment or two and wondered what I was going to do about her, and if it was really inevitable. And then I got the fire going among the rocks. When it was smoldering nicely, I swam out to the coral reef and dove down deep, and found two fat crayfish and brought them back and tossed them among the embers where the fire was not too fierce.

I went and sat down beside her, admiring the symmetry of her body, the smooth amber already turning a little darker, I touched her very lightly on the breast, running one finger around a tiny pink nipple, and she opened her eyes and looked at me very gravely, not moving.

I said: "Lunch in half an hour, and I think you'd better put your shirt back on."

She held my look for a moment and said nothing, and then she smiled and said: "Half an hour?"

"A little more perhaps. Baked lobster. *Oura miti.*"

Her hand came up to my chin and stroked it, and she said: "It's perfectly all right, you know, if you want to make love to me. Do you feel like it?"

I thought it was a strange way of putting it, but I nodded and said: "I feel like it."

"Good. So do I. That's exactly what I feel like."

She reached up and pulled me down on top of her, and we made love till the lobsters were burned into charcoal, and then we picked at what was left of them with our fingers, laughing like a couple of kids, and then making love again and not giving a damn for anything else in the world.

And then, as we lay together peacefully side by side and slept and waited, there in the distance was the sound of that damned helicopter again. Once more, it was coming in from the sun.

I put my trousers back on in a hurry, and grabbed her arm, and we ran fast away from the beach and up into the ravines where there was cover. It was coming in fast and low, and when it came close to the beach, it hovered there for a while and then wheeled over and started climbing again, and we lay under an overhang of rock and watched it pass over our heads. I knew that even if they had not seen us, they had at least seen the footprints we had left behind us.

Maite whispered: "If they land..."

"They will. But not here, it's too rough. They'll have to go back to the beach. That's when we move."

I had already chosen our hiding place. Away to our left a long tongue of brilliant greenery snaked down from the mountain, as though probing into the barren patch of devastation and testing its quality. It was a hundred feet wide or so, and its closest point was half a mile away.

I watched the helicopter. It circled round twice, and then slid slowly down to the beach; I took Maite's arm and said: "Now!"

We ran fast together along the ravine, then climbed out of it when it began to wind in the wrong direction, and raced over broken, uneven sand and rock to where the trees were. I heard a shout from behind us, a long way off, and yelled at Maite: "Keep going!"

I dropped to the ground and rolled over under a boulder, and eased my head round it to watch them down there.

One of them was pointing in our direction, and the others were climbing out of the chopper and staring toward us. I saw that Maite had reached the cover of the trees already, and knew that she would be waiting there for me. I crawled carefully toward her, turning once in a while to watch them as they began the climb, taking their time and spreading out correctly in wide open formation.

There were five of them, and they all carried rifles that looked like Browning automatics, though at this distance it was hard to be sure. But it was their dress which intrigued me the most. There were no brilliant shirts, or flowers in their hair; instead, they wore dark green trousers, jungle boots, and olive-drab shirts, with web pouches at their sides; they were in paramilitary uniform, and somehow, it seemed out of place in these gentle islands—out of place, and ominous.

Two of them did not live long enough for me to discover their names; they got careless when they began to stalk us in the forest at the top of the mountain. But I found out, in the course of time, that the others were called Ulricson, Peabody, and Santos, and that they had been sent to wipe us out by Willard Fest.

Fest, which was not his real name, was the man I was later to know as Aimata.

It's a strange and historic name, Aimata, a dynastic name which can be given to women as well as to men, and in the last century, the islands were ruled for more than fifty years by a famous beauty whom the poets of the time called Aimata—the Queen with the Beautiful Eyes. Her name was Pomara Vahine, and she was crowned at the age of fourteen (the last king, her brother, had died at the age of six, after a reign of three years). She was much disliked by the intrusive and ubiquitous missionaries, largely on account of what they considered her loose morals; as a young woman, she had a charming penchant for naked dancing.

However, the word has another meaning, still fascinating but not so favorable; in this other interpretation, it means, quite simply, "Eyeball Eater."

CHAPTER 5

My first thought was that my interest in Maite's splendid young physique had blunted my awareness; I should have known they'd be back.

They'd begun a game with us, and the opening gambit was an underwater fusillade of machine gun fire which might, or might not, have been effective. Their next step then? To fake a retreat to bring us out from under cover.

I should have foreseen it. I'd simply been too busy thrashing around on the hot sand to think clearly; but maybe that's the way it should be, the emotions can't always be subjugated to the intellect, or we'd become robots.

My second thought was that they had left their helicopter unguarded—or so it seemed. Was another man hidden on hoard? Or were they sure they could, with their rifles, effectively cover the long stretch of devastated open ground I'd have to cover to get to it? I tucked the alternatives away at the back of my mind; there were more important things to worry about at this moment, and the first was to get the hell out of that snaking tongue of forest, which was good enough for purely temporary cover, but still would leave us much too vulnerable if they chose to move along both sides of it.

I saw that this was what they were going to do. Two of them were already moving far to our right, while the others kept their direction, heading steadily toward us, not hurrying at all; they were exchanging a few words with each other, too far away to be heard, moving easily over the barren, broken ground and around the ugly stumps of the denuded plants. The sight of that withered and spoiled expanse, from up here among the trees, was distressing.

But all was not entirely bleak. As we had run for cover, and particularly when I had lain there under the rocks watching them land, I had seen tiny green shoots coming out of the soil—coralline and arrowroot, and the hardy cassava and yams were beginning to struggle through the sand again. I knew that whatever had been so cruelly done to the land, it was beginning to recover, as it always will. Soon, in a matter of months, perhaps, all this would be green and lovely once more.

Provided I could find out who was up to what. It had become a matter of personal principle now; it was no longer merely a matter for all humankind to worry about, but a deliberate affront to two peoples who were wandering here, alone, very close to each other and looking for all that is good in the islands. The presence of those armed men down there on the sand made the problem no longer intangible; they were the first link to whoever was behind it all. There had been at least a moment of doubt, back there in Papeete, when I had thought that perhaps, after all, I had been too sure that Polynesia was indeed the source of all this trouble; that my fondness for likelihoods had carried me out of the reach of reason; that *someone* had, perhaps, merely stopped off at Tahiti on his way to, say, Australia? And merely met with his Faatua accident by chance? Only a long shot, but it had worried me. And now, I was sure. This indeed was the lead we wanted.

We were running fast together, hand in hand like lovers, barefoot over the warm soft soil, and Maite said, gasping: "We're leaving footprints everywhere, does it matter?"

I said: "No. We need them."

Five men on their own could never search the whole island thoroughly; I wanted them to know which way we were moving, so that we, in turn, would know where they could be expected to appear. Meanwhile, there was the question of a more lasting hideout than the forest could afford us, in case the siege turned out to be a long one. I wondered what kind of caves there might be up there on the mountain.

I had studied the rocks here on my previous visit, but only casually; I had been quite seduced by the Tahitian languor, with what

Maite expressed as a desire to lie in the sun and do nothing all day. But I remembered that there was a lot of igneous rock there, mostly extrusive, with great patches of trachyte, a lesser amount of andesite and basalt, and even some traces of obsidian with its related spilite.

In other words, lava.

Lava cools from the top, quite understandably, while the lower areas, still liquid and molten, swirl around and leave caves. As soon as a break in the forest gave us a clear view of the slopes above us, I studied the conformation of the purple strata there for a few moments while Maite rested and got her breath back, I found what I was looking for very quickly—a broad vein of hypabyssal intrusive rock that might easily have been porphyry or even lamprophyre.

I pointed to it and said quietly: "There. That's where we might find the kind of cave we need, large enough to be intriguing, with a small, overhanging entrance. With any luck at all, it might go deep into the mountain."

And then, quite unexpectedly, there was sudden firing not too far away from us, eight shots in rapid succession. It was not easy to tell, in the confines of all that greenery, precisely where they had come from, but it seemed to be ahead of us.

Ahead? I thought I knew what they were up to. One man, or perhaps two, had run on in front of the others, and was trying to give the impression that we'd already been headed off, trying to drive us back into that narrow strip of cover. A nice gambit, but it wasn't going to work. We went on slowly and carefully now in the direction of the silence that had followed the shooting, bent low and almost crawling along. I found a depression in the ground, a small ditch, and we followed it to one side until we came to a pool of water, cool and inviting and overhung with trailing flowers in a brilliant yellow—a lantana grown wild. This is not a local plant in Tahiti, but was introduced there not much more than a hundred years ago. There was a lot of beautiful pink hibiscus, bent and twisted and rising up everywhere out of the wet ground, and a clump of *inocaprus* trees which the local people call *"mape"* and use as a source for dyes and embrocations.

And now, the shooting started again, and it was all around us; a few bullets even went clipping incisively through the foliage above our heads, and Maite whispered, suddenly alarmed again: "They've seen us..."

I whispered back: "No, we're deep under cover, they're guessing."

More, I knew, they were frying to panic us into running and so betraying our whereabouts. I thought: The cave will have to wait until we've lessened the odds a bit.

The pool looked very promising. It was sixty feet or so across, and all around its banks the vegetation was thick and tangled.

I whispered to Maite: "There, under the water, your head behind the plants on the other side. And keep absolutely quiet, not a breath of a sound."

She whispered again, urgently: "Footprints..."

"I know. Don't worry about them."

I entered the water with her, standing up to my waist and watching her swim quickly across to the other side, lithe and sensuous movement, her long hair trailing on top of the dark green water. She dove and seemed not to come up, and knew that she was well hidden there somewhere.

Now was the time to leave no more traces in the wet mud. I examined the spread roots of a *mape* tree which reached out from the heavy trunk like long, blunt, knife-edges, lying on top of the soil and humped up thinly, two, three, and even four feet high but still very narrow; it was as if long, irregular planks had been laid on edge stretching out from the base of the tree itself. I clambered carefully over them and climbed up, using as handholds the solid round knobs which are another characteristic of this highly interesting tree. The upper reaches of it, where the long green leaves fanned out, were leaning into a dense clump of bamboo, the *dendrocalamus giganteus*, also introduced here comparatively recently. It occurred to me that it was not very long ago that the exploring botanists had made a point of the fact that the vegetation in the Polynesian Islands though luxuriant, was very limited; they had listed a mere five hundred species and varieties of the higher plants, which is very poor indeed. A huge proportion of its present wealth of flora is of recent introduction.

I was musing about this as I climbed, and almost decided to go down again and ask if Maite realized this, when far below me, in the direction we had come from, I heard a soft whistle.

It was he kind of whistle that is meant to imitate the cry of a bird, but rarely does. I draped myself along a heavy *mape* branch, hidden from sight by the enclosing bamboo, and waited.

I checked the pool again; no sign of Maite's presence. Good.

I waited a long time. And then, at last, I heard the faint sounds of them moving among the bushes—two of them, by the sound of it, and moving very cautiously indeed. Their footfalls made no noise in the damp soft ground, but there was the occasional rustle of a fern as they brushed by.

Then the first of them came in sight, his gun—it was indeed a BAR, as I had believed—at the ready, his finger on the trigger. But his eyes were on the ground, and he was following the telltale footprints, peering at them as though they were hard to see, which they were not. This was an indication of his poor ability.

Now the silence was acute.

His companion, the cover man, was a lot smarter. He was inching along behind, fifty paces or so back, his head moving rhythmically from side to side, and up and down as well, studying every bush, every tree, every cluster of ferns; he moved forward in little hops, frequently stopping to look around and then moving on again, the gun always ready. Somehow, he gave the impression that he knew how to use it skillfully.

The first man had stopped at the water's edge, a tall, lank man with very blond hair, and when he spoke, his accent was pure Pennsylvania Dutch. He said, very softly: "They're in the water, both of them."

The sleeves of his shirt were rolled halfway up the forearm, and he wore leather straps on both his wrists; I could see part of a tattoo on one of them. He was very thin, but he moved well on the balls of his feet.

The other man, smaller, thick-set, and much more powerful looking, was close behind him now, still watchful, his eyes always searching. They came to rest on the footprints in the deep mud, and he said, whispering: "One heavy man, one lightweight woman. Like reading a book, they're not very bright, are they?"

The Dutchman said: "I dunno. They say he is." The other man

answered him: "Well, go round. See if they came out on the other side."

A bird fluttered close behind me, and he looked up, startled. I could see his face clearly now; he was staring into the bamboo five feet to my left. Dark brows, the stubble of a beard, a cruel, unrelenting mouth, and a nose that had been broken long ago; there were small pockmarks on his cheeks. The bird fluttered again, and flew off, and the man stared hack at the pool.

The Dutchman was making the circuit of the pool, and when he came back he shook his head. The other man reached out and touched the bamboo, running his hand along a stem and beginning to laugh softly to himself.

For one horrifying minute, I wondered if they would start raking the water with their rifles, and I almost went into action at once. But then I realized that they would not; they'd used a machine gun for that before, and it had not paid off.

And where was that machine gun now, I wondered? It had sounded like a very heavy one, though from under water it was hard to be certain.

He said: "Look for bamboo tubes sticking up out of the water, they're under there somewhere." He grunted, and added: "Who the hell do they think they're fooling?"

And then both of them stuck their necks out, craning for a good look at the surface of the pool, all three thousand square feet of it. They were invitingly close together.

I jumped.

I was perhaps thirty feet off the ground, and I weigh just over two hundred and ten pounds. I was wondering, on the way down, at what speed I would hit the backs of their necks with my feet.

Of course, Galileo and Newton, among others, worked all this out in erudite terms of mass comparison by inertia, the collision of hard bodies, very interesting stuff though their deductions were somewhat limited and not even always correct; but there really wasn't time for much reflection on the subject. My left foot struck the Dutchman squarely on the nape of the neck and sent him sprawling on his spine over the knife-edge of one of the *mape* tree's abutting roots; I had pulled my right leg back, and I struck out with my foot at the heavy-set man, my instep ramming into his throat and sending him into the water. Continuing the motion, I fell with both knees onto the Dutchman, one at his groin and one at his chest, and heard his back snap in two as it bent sharply over that upstanding razorback of root.

The other man was trying to clamber out of the water, to get his rifle lifted up and aim, and to control his vomiting all at the same time, but suddenly he thrust he weapon forward as though it were armed with a bayonet, a skilled and highly competent movement. The tip of the barrel rammed into my solar plexus, rather surprisingly, and, as I doubled up I saw that Maite had left her hiding place and was swimming across the pool toward us at an alarming speed, thrashing at the water in a powerful six-stroke that would have done credit to an Olympic champion.

My adversary heard her, and he swung round, almost his old self again though his breath and vomit were fighting each other in his throat. He was holding his breath, forcing an absolute control on himself, and he didn't even look back to see what had happened to me after I'd gone down.

It was understandable. The hard steel of the rifle barrel had struck home exactly where it was intended to, and that's not only extremely painful, it's also incapacitating; he must have been sure that I was out at least for a moment or two.

He was quite wrong. I saw his shot hit no more than an inch from her head, and I suppose I was swayed beyond reason by my fear for her. I heard myself yell, and I rammed my shoulder into his side, and then hit him as he swung round, a very angry chop across the nape of the neck, only once, but so hard that I felt the second and third cervical vertebrae shoot out of position; I could even feel the odontoid snap neatly off the epistropheus, and I knew that we'd have no more trouble from him either.

He fell forward into the water, his legs sprawled out on the muddy bank with a beautiful coralline plant, all emerald and red and gold, sticking up incongruously between them, its furled leaves looking like an outgrowth of his body.

Maite had reached the bank, and was grabbing at his belt to pull him down under, showing a surprising anger. I said: "You're trying to drown a dead man, and I told you to stay under cover. Don't you ever do as you're told?"

She looked from one to the other of them, and it occurred to me that she'd probably never seen a dead body before. She shook her head blankly and mumbled: "I thought...I thought you might need help."

I took her thin wrist and hauled her up out of there, and she watched, shaking a little, as I pulled the bodies out of her sight and hid them under the overhang. There was a sad and terrible look on her face, as though a problem that had been merely an academic one before had suddenly become subjective and very frightening. I said to her gently: "We knew all along that *someone* was causing this. We knew it wasn't just an insect we were fighting."

She nodded miserably. "I know. It's just that...what I always knew has suddenly been...brought closer."

It's something to do with the Polynesian aspect of life; it's a hundred and thirty years since they had their last little war in the islands, and they've forgotten what violence is.

She said, shuddering: "The others?"

"Three, possibly four more. We'd better move on, we need time now. Help me with the tracks, can you do that?"

It seemed essential to find her some useful work, quickly, to take her mind off what had happened. Together, we found branches and ferns and dragged them over the marks we had all left in the mud, which, to anyone with any sense, would have told the precise story of what had gone on. That purple vein of rock I had seen was high above us on the west now, slicing through a dark patch of green forest, and we climbed up as fast as possible, stopping every now and then to listen; there were very few alien sounds, though once I thought I heard a distant voice calling softly.

There were highly scented *Pandanus* trees growing here, rather shorter than usual because we were more than two thousand feet above the beach now; their aerial roots were shooting out from their trunks and reaching down to the ground like the ribs of inverted umbrellas, their fruit already taking on that brilliant red sheen.

The sun was halfway down to the horizon, and the mountain was taking on a strange and eerie golden light when we found a suitable cave, the third of a series that I examined. It had an oval-shaped mouth half-hidden behind a shelf of granite. The rock was rich in lime and magnesia, and I scratched at a piece with my thumbnail, breaking off the tiny rhombohedral crystals. I said: "That's very satisfying."

She blinked her eyes at me, her spirits returning now, and I said: "Dolomite. That means that this was once a subterranean watercourse, and that, in turn, means that it will be long and winding, with plenty of auxiliaries, precisely what we need now. In the open, perhaps they'd find us. In here...never."

The cave was less than three feet high at the opening, but after we had crawled on our hands and knees for fifty feet or so, it widened out and began to curve gently down. Here, there was still plenty of light, and I was delighted to find a petroglyph (they are very rare in Tahiti) depicting a line of six turtles and a single, headless body of a man; human representations are even more rare here, and it was fascinating. We counted seven side passages, and went back to the third and followed it, and then crawled into another auxiliary which sloped sharply up toward a wide, broken shelf where a fissure had split the wall wide open. There were heavy boulders of porphyritic rock, and smaller masses of basanite and obsidian. It was perfect.

I climbed up and lay on my belly there, and reached down to hoist Maite up, and then spent fifteen minutes rolling heavy rocks all round her until a tiny personal shelter was formed, and she was completely hidden from anywhere below.

I said: "This time, you stay put, whatever happens."

She nodded, her eyes wide and shining in the half-light. "And you?"

"I'll be back before its dark."

"Will they be able to follow us here, do you think?"

"I imagine they will. In fact, I'm counting on it. We have to convince them that it's an unequal battle—in our favor, not theirs. That's the only way we'll get off this island alive."

She was puzzled, and I explained: "Two or three of them in here searching for you, that's going to even up the odds for me. Does that sound unkind?"

She reached out and touched me, her hand on my arm. "No. I'm glad."

"Don't worry. They can spend a month in here looking for you and not find you." There was a faint and pleasant draft around us, a shaft above us somewhere, and I said: "They may try and smoke you out. If they do, stay put anyway, there's a shaft right above us, it'll take the smoke right out. If they start tossing in explosives, don't worry about that either, you're well protected. Absolute silence, and not the breath of a movement till I get back. Are you warm enough?"

She nodded.

I left her there and went quickly back to the entrance. Far in the distance, I could see the helicopter down there, twenty-five hundred feet or so below us and a little over a mile away. I pulled myself up and around the overhang, climbed a matter of fifty feet or so higher to hide my tracks, and then took a course that would lead me down to the beach about half a mile from the machine.

It was easier going down than climbing up. I ran, and jumped, and slid, and reached the shoreline in a little over fifteen minutes, only a few hundred feet from where the greenery came to an abrupt halt at the edge of the awful devastation. I swam under water as far as the reef, coming up four times briefly for air, followed the broken line of the reef for half a mile; then went under again till I found a suitable hiding place where I could wait for dark.

The sun was low, a scarlet ball of fire just touching the water, and I sheltered under the coral rocks till it had gone, and waited another half-hour for darkness to fall. The moon was a slender crescent high in a cloudless sky that was far too bright for comfort. Then I swam carefully and silently to the beach.

I crouched in the warm and shallow water for a while, watching the helicopter. This was the moment of danger; there was still a modicum of light, and there would be until the moon went down in three and a quarter hours; I was half-expecting a fusillade of machine gun fire.

At last, I saw the flare of a match from inside—a good sign. He was careless.

I ran to the helicopter, very quickly, and crouched underneath it for a few moments and listened; nothing except his heavy breathing. I reached up and flung open the door, and he gasped and swung round, the cigarette falling from his lips. He was a lightweight, skinny sort of man, with almost no waist at all, but as I grabbed hold of his wrist and tugged, I could feel muscles like steel in his arms. I brought my right knee up under his ear as he tumbled out, then drove my fattened hand hard into the posterior scapula. He would be out cold for quite a while, bit for good measure I picked him up easily and tossed him into the surf to take his chances there.

I pulled out the machine gun he had been cradling in his arms. It was a Bren .303, which cycles at 500rpm, not the best weapon in the world but very deadly at a range of five hundred yards or so; it could have made a terrible mess of us as we lay crouched under the Piper at the bottom of the lagoon, and I had to fight hard to drive away the image of Maite with het guts spilling out there in the water.

I checked its thirty-round clip, which was full. I found three bandoliers of clips, and threw them far out into the ocean, just on principle, and then fired two rapid bursts out to sea. I waited a moment or two, and then fired a long, sustained burst, emptying the magazine. When it was finished, I threw the gun out into the water too.

I wondered how long it would take them, up there, to come charging down the mountain again, sure that their guard had at last scored a kill.

There was the problem of the helicopter to be solved. I could easily have burned it, and so put them in a very uncomfortable position. But it occurred to me that if Teiho were to come looking for us in the morning, as I was sure he would, then we'd all present a sure and easy target for them, and I didn't want to drag outsiders into this. It's very hard to assess the merits of an opponent you haven't yet met, but it seemed clear that we were dealing with a man of some skill and ruthlessness, and if these qualities were matched by his intelligence, then it seemed to me that the time had come for him to withdraw from this skirmish while he was still able to—provided I left him the means. There was always the chance that some governmental authority would turn up in the morning and present him with a problem he'd find hard to solve; a postponement of his assault would be preferable.

Or would it?

I gave him the benefit of my own wisdom, and decided to leave the chopper alone. I ran hard down the beach the way I had come, headed for the mountain in the darkness, and had the satisfaction of seeing two flashlights being used, far to my right among the trees, as I climbed quietly back to where I had left Maite.

I found her still in position, and she was trembling. I held her tight in my arms.

"All right?"

She nodded. "Yes, all right now. They were here."

"I was sure they would be."

"I didn't see how many, but I heard them talking and I saw their flashlights. They came very close, below me, and they shone a light all over these rocks..."

"It's all over now."

"Is it? Are you sure?"

"No, but he's taken too many casualties. It's time for him to pull back and re-plan. That'll give us a breathing spell."

"Do you know where they are now?"

"Yes, of course. They're trying to revive the guard they left on the helicopter, down on the beach. We'll wait here for them to go."

"If they do."

"They will." I squeezed myself in beside her in the tiny rock shelter, and lay on my back and let her rest her head on my chest, and neither of us spoke for a long while.

Thirty minutes later, we heard the helicopter taking off, and we went out and watched it against the night sky as it wheeled away to the northwest; the island was ours for the rest of the night.

I was tempted to take advantage of this, and when Maite said gravely: "Love me again, please?" I almost succumbed. But I thought perhaps they might have some other tricks up their sleeves, like faking a retreat to bring us out of hiding, so I merely kissed her for a moment or two, and then made her sleep in the soft sand by the entrance while I squatted on the rocks above her and kept watch.

As the sun came up, the bright blue sails of Auguste's ketch could be clearly seen out there on the water, some five miles from Faatua and heading breezily for us.

I woke her up in a fashion that was extremely satisfying to both of us, and then said: "Now, just in case there's still someone prowling about, we have to swim out and meet them. Are you good for two or three miles?"

She laughed, her eyes bright, her teeth shining, her long hair flowing as she tossed her head back. We ran down the mountainside together, and raced out through the warm blue water, swimming easily and lazily, and wishing that the day would never end.

CHAPTER 6

The South Pacific Ocean was calm and quiet...and immense. With the little island and its reef behind us, and scarcely a ripple to disturb the surface, it seemed as if there were nothing else on the face of the Earth but water, water, everywhere.

There was no need to race; it was merely a question of not allowing the ketch ashore, or even too close in, just in case the island were not as indisputably ours as it had seemed. The *Pinaa* was still two miles out when we met her, and Auguste's crew, the pretty young Dropping Water, promptly fell overboard as she leaned over the railing to throw us the rope ladder.

We all swarmed aboard, and Auguste slapped me on the back and said, his voice booming: "Teiho was worried about you, so we came to take a look. We've been sailing all night, it was marvelous."

Vanaa was there in the prow, standing firm on the deck with his bare feet widely spaced, staring at the island through his binoculars. All that was left of the aircraft on the beach was a charred and miserable-looking skeleton, now part of all the other devastation.

He said: "I knew something like this was going to happen. I was sure of it."

I said: "Oh? How's that?"

He waved a virile arm up at the immensity of the ocean behind him. "You know the Temple of Aralu Raha?"

"I know it."

"Right between the two wooden idols at the entrance, they

found a dead seagull. Its gullet had been pierced by the beak of a hawk. I knew at once. I said: 'Someone has shot down Cain's aircraft.' To a thinking man, it was obvious. But there were two other gulls copulating at the base of the altar there, so I knew that you had not been harmed. Tane, the god of war and the son of the great Taaroa, was keeping a careful eye on you up in his sever skies."

"Three gulls told you all that?"

He said gravely: "They did indeed."

It was good to be with friends again; I wondered if the lovely Tiare might be on board somewhere. I said: "The *tupapaus* got the aircraft, I'm afraid. And Teiho's going to be madder than hell."

"Teiho?" The Captain grunted. "He lives on insurance, he thrives on it. Why should he worry? Was anybody hurt?"

"No one of any importance. It was good of you to come."

"I promised Maite I'd keep an eye on you. And Teiho can be very persuasive when he thinks there's some insurance money in the offing." He glared at me. "Who was it of no importance?"

"Two or three armed men. They tried to machine gun us to hell and gone, among other things."

He glowered. "Machine guns? In the islands? I won't have it! You need help, Cain. Count me in."

"I will indeed."

There was a charcoal brazier flaming on the deck, with a half-dozen fillets of fish on it, scenting the air with the smell of breakfast, and Auguste grinned and produced a bottle of cognac and passed it around; cognac and barbecued fish at six-thirty in the morning, with the wind billowing the sails and ruffling your hair, and the gentle sound of water lapping against the hull, with cotton puffs of cloud in the bright sky—it's a splendid combination.

Auguste, bare-chested, bronzed, and muscular, was a young god at the helm, a modern Raa the sun deity, his blond hair shining like gold. He said: "Where to, Cain? The ship's all yours."

Captain Vanaa said darkly: "Rangitefara, where else? That's where the mischief is."

"Aha! So you found out about Willard Fest."

"I did indeed."

He was hauling on the sheets, trimming the sails just so with a reproving glance for Auguste, the old teaching the young, staring up at the burgee and checking the wind for the slightest change. When he was quite satisfied, he fastened a hitch methodically, and turned to me, his dark face grizzled and weather-beaten, a tough old man of the sea in his favorite element.

He said: "His name is not Willard Fest at all. It's Utter, William Jerome Utter. Whether he's truly a film star, as my wife insists...who knows? And he's a very rich man, keeps to himself most of the time, goes to Papeete once in a while, spends a lot of money there. Provisions, mostly."

He held his baked fish on a palm leaf in a stubby, muscular hand, nibbling at it. "He bought his island just over four years ago, paid a very high price for it, too. But Lou How, our Chinese trader, remembers him from a previous visit, two years before that. He was island hopping, like any other tourist, and while he was on Huahine he lost his passport, dropped it somewhere. One of the kids found it on the street a few days later, and took it to Lou How. Where else would he take it? We have almost no police on the island. So, Lou How sent a note to Papeete, where he'd come from, saying it had been found, and eventually sent it over there. He's a very cautious and methodical man, our trader, and he keeps copies of all his correspondence, which he showed me. William Jerome Utter, an American, born in a place called..." He wiped his fingers on his shorts and reached into a pocket, and said: "I cannot even pronounce the name. It's called Patagumpus, Maine."

He pronounced it Patagoompus, in the French fashion, and said: "How can a man live in a place called Patagoompus? Does it even exist?"

I said: "It's a few miles from a place called Mattawamkeag, do you like that better?"

He grimaced, and squinted at the writing on the paper. "He writes like a spider crawling all over the place. Height, five feet ten, weight, a hundred and sixty-two pounds, profession, impresario." He handed me the slip. "A lot more there, if you can make it out."

"And this is the same man?"

"Without a doubt. Lou How ran into him on the second visit, and he never forgets a face or anything else. He asked about the passport, and the man just stared at him coldly and said: 'My name is Fest, Willard Fest.' Low How thought he was merely trying to evade the possibility of being obliged to pay a reward, so he just shrugged it off, what else would he do? Yes, it's the same man. No doubt about it at all."

The two women had gone below to look for a *pareu* for Maite, to replace my shirt, which was getting a bit tattered now. There were just the three of us on deck, sprawled out in the sun and enjoying the breeze, It was unbelievably serene, and yet the thoughts in the back of my head were of violence, of mayhem, and of murder.

Will Utter...it was by no means a famous name, but I recalled that a few years ago there'd been quite a bit in the papers about him. I read a lot, and make a point of never forgetting what I read, and now all the memories came flooding back.

He'd been a hired killer, a particularly brutal and vicious professional who had amassed a huge fortune by specializing in the removal of gang leaders for the benefit of other gangs. His career had been, not unexpectedly, quite short; in four or five years he had made so many deadly enemies that there was no safe haven for him anymore, anywhere in the States. He had fled to Montreal and had remained in hiding there, at a time when I happened to be at the University working on a thesis about the effects of sonar and the procreation activities of the *Clupea harerngus*, or common herring. I remembered that the name Utter had become synonymous with terror when a dozen or so assorted gangsters from the States had descended on Montreal looking for him, shooting up half of the police department in the process. There'd been a couple of very brutal murders—the victims were more gangsters—and then a whole family was found slaughtered, a middle-aged couple and their four children, in an area where the Mounties believed Utter had been hiding.

And then, at last, an elderly informant had told the police where they could find Utter; this violent, cold-blooded killer had gone to the Chateau de Ramezay, the museum in the old French part of the town, to pass an hour or two with the paintings of Gauguin and Degas, two of his favorites. But somehow, their prey slipped out from under their noses and lost himself again.

One of the problems of having a photographic memory is that

you can't forget things that are best forgotten. I recalled that the informant had been blind; it was reported that, for reasons of his own, Utter had gouged out his eyes.

Vanaa said quietly, interrupting my memories: "And so? We go to Rangitefara?"

I said: "No. Not yet. Papeete."

He gesticulated broadly: "The ladies? We'll leave them on board with Auguste, if we can trust him with them, a mile or two offshore. You and I will slip over the side, and swim to a beach I know where we can land without being seen, if we're careful."

"And then?"

He grunted. "Who knows? We'll find out what then when we get there."

I said gently: "I think a little reconnaissance first would be wise. I want to get some aerial shots of the island before anyone goes charging in there. I wonder if Teiho has another Golden Eagle?"

The Captain sighed. "One more. But he'll never let you have it, not if he knows the *tupapaus* are after you."

"What time do we hit the mainland?"

Auguste said cheerfully: "Ten o'clock tonight, if we're lucky," and the Captain looked up at the burgee again and corrected him. "Not later than nine, the wind is changing, ten degrees to the north, at least. If Auguste is as good as he thinks he is, we'll be there in time for dinner."

"If Vaite doesn't fall overboard again."

He was laughing, showing off his white teeth as the women came up the companionway. Vaite had found a red and yellow *pareu* for Maite, and the two of them hunched themselves over the fish and picked at what was left of it, laughing like two uninhibited naiads.

And then, the wind swung round and hit us hard, and Vanaa skipped around the deck like a child, letting out sail and watching the blue nylon billow out. Within minutes, the sea was rough, a boiling cauldron, and we were hurtling over the waves at a fine rate of many knots, and Vanaa yelled: "You see? I told you! If this keeps up we'll be in before dark."

The little ketch was plowing through the water, rising up and slamming down in a splendid rhythm; it was exhilarating in the extreme, and in a little over nine hours we saw the great twin mass of Mount Orobena, which the Tahitians think of as the spine of the great fish that is their island—the cliffs of Taiarapu make the head, and the promontory of Panaauia is the tail. The heavy clouds still clung there, as though determined never to be shaken free by the wind.

And two hours later, we were tying up once more at the Quai Bir Hakeim.

Captain Vanaa was quite wrong about our friend Teiho and his other Golden Eagle.

It was nine o'clock when I finally tracked down the charter man enjoying a hearty dinner at the Pitate restaurant. Maite was up the road at police headquarters, talking with one of her countless cousins when I interrupted his meal to tell him that his beautiful aircraft would never fly again.

Somehow, he did not seem in the least surprised, and he became quite philosophical about it when I told him that my company would replace it for him.

He said: "Oh no, Mr. Cain, please...I have a very good deal with the insurance company, its much better if you let me handle it myself. Just tell me...was anyone hurt? How did it happen?"

I knew he wasn't going to believe it, but it didn't really matter. I said: "Well, I'd just landed, and had started a cooking fire with some gasoline out of the nacelle tank on the starboard side, and we went swimming, a long way out, you understand, and I had quite forgotten that the vent on the tank wag still open, terribly careless of me. I suppose the wind and a few flying sparks did the rest. My fault entirely, I must admit it. But please, let my company take care of it for you. We're well insured too."

I couldn't help wondering what Fenrek would say when he got a bill for two hundred and some thousand dollars. But when I thought of the massive destruction that could, any minute, break loose all-around us, the figure seemed quite picayune.

I said: "I believe you have another one, don't you?"

He was startled. "Yes. I do. That one too?"

"I'd like to take it out tonight, if I may."

He hesitated: "You're going to leave me a little short of aircraft if you keep this up, Mr. Cain."

"Just until about an hour after daylight. I promise you I won't even attempt to land it anywhere until I get back to Fanaa."

He sighed. "May I ask you to join me for dinner, Mr. Cain?"

"You're very kind, but I have a great deal of work to do."

He held up a piece of steak on his fork and said: "It's delicious, far too good to be put aside for something that has to be *done*. Why is it that Americans are never happy unless they are *doing* something? Life is really far too short, and too beautiful, for the useless expenditure of energy. Will you have a drink with me, at least? Some beer, perhaps, it's a warm night."

"Thank you very much. What about that Eagle? Is it equipped for night flying?"

He waited a long time before answering. He ordered the beer and waited for it to be brought, and finished his plate and pushed it away, and stared glumly into his glass for a while, and said at last: "It will be a long, long time before I get paid for the first one, but...yes, I can have it ready for night flying in about three hours." He looked unhappy. "If, of course, I can find one of my men to take care of it. Do you really need it so urgently? Wouldn't tomorrow be just as good? Or the next day, perhaps?"

"Tonight."

"Ah well. All right. I have to see a lady after dinner, and after that I'll try and find someone to fit the Eagle out, let's say about two o'clock in the morning?"

"I'd like to take off at four-fifteen."

"Ah, good. Then I can stay a little longer with the lady. Are you sure you won't have some dinner?"

I finished the beer and thanked him again, and felt I had to commiserate with him once more on his loss. He waved an airy hand: "Think nothing of it, my dear friend, nothing at all."

Maite came in with a file under her arm, and I knew that Fenrek, back in the Paris rat race, had been at work. We went back to the hotel and lay naked on the bed in my room while we went over the reports which Fenrek had sent. I found the notes on Jules Cresson particularly interesting.

I lay on my back and stared up at the ceiling, and let her do the reading because I liked the sound of her voice.

She said, flipping over the pages: "He was born in Quebec, Canada, and studied mostly in Ottawa and at Harvard, but that's not important, is it?"

"Very important. Go on."

"Oh. Well, he studied biochemistry, in which he has a doctorate, and specialized in biogeny and biokinetics, that's a bit obscure, isn't it?"

"No, he's a very bright man. Go to Indochina."

She was speed reading, very fast. "Four paragraphs on Indochina. He was there for three years in the early days of the Indochina war, working on defoliating chemicals and experimenting on the side with locusts. Then, when the Americans took over, he worked with them for another four years, and this time it gets more interesting, he was working on a hybrid ant, first with the *ponerines* and then with the *dorylines*, at which time he was whisked off to the States."

"Possibly, even probably, because he was on to something."

"Could be."

I said: "You're right, it *is* interesting. The *Doralynae* are both herbivorous and carnivorous. Warriors. They'd be equally happy with grape leaves or elderly, incapacitated drunks."

She shuddered: "They kept him under wraps for five years, and then let him go..."

"Does it say why?"

"No. It just says they let him go. He turned up in France, trying to interest the military in what is referred to here as a 'radical new approach to the ancient stratagem of depriving the enemy of his food supplies'" She giggled. "That sounds a bit like Mat Fenrek talking, doesn't it?"

"It does indeed. He's dropping a gentle hint in case we're not arriving at the right conclusions."

"And are we?"

"Naturally. Go on."

Along fingernail was scratching at her navel. She said: "The French weren't interested. He disappeared altogether for a while, and then turned up here trying to buy an island."

"But couldn't afford the price. That's interesting, too."

"A poor man looking for a rich sponsor?"

"A likelihood. Any notes on his character?"

"No, not much."

"They're getting careless at Interpol. Maybe I should go back to them. What about Willard Fest?" Her body was warm and subtle beside me, her skin a delight to touch.

"Nothing at all under the name, I already checked. Almost the first thing I did, what else did you expect?"

"Try them again with Will Utter, they'll have plenty."

She sighed. "I did that too, while you were telling Teiho all kinds of lies, no doubt, about what happened to his plane. I asked him to send us whatever he has on the Telex in the police commissioner's office."

"Another cousin?"

"The night duty clerk. Do we need anything special for the trip to Rangitefara?"

"Not we. Me. You're staying behind."

She turned her head to stare at me, her eyes very solemn. "I'd rather come with you. Please?"

"No. We can't get a low-light camera in time, so I have to fly over at least once in daylight. That means a low pass or two as soon as the sun hits it. Just might run into all kinds of trouble."

"You surely don't think they'll try and shoot us down?" She sounded aghast, and she sat up suddenly and leaned over me, her hair falling over my chest. "Surely you don't think that?"

I said: "I can't think of any reason why they shouldn't. Rangitefara is far enough away from the rest of the world for a whole squadron of planes to disappear. That's a very big and empty ocean. They tried murder once when we weren't expecting it, they tried again when we were. This time, I'll take every precaution, and part of that is leaving you behind."

"Please?"

"No."

"Then take Captain Vanaa with you. He knows every inch of every island in the South Pacific."

"No."

There was a long, long silence. I was conscious that she was on the verge of tears. She threw an arm across my shoulder, and nestled her head in close, and then put a leg over my stomach and just lay there, warm, enticing, and very desirable.

And then, at a rather awkward moment, one of Maite's innumerable cousins turned up from police headquarters with a Telex from Fenrek in Paris.

He was a thin-faced, wiry sort of boy in his late teens, with a wry and twisted smile on his dark and handsome face, and large, inquiring eyes that must have driven the girls mad. He wore a bright yellow shirt and green slacks, and a half a dozen necklaces of seashells, with a broad crown of *tiare* blossoms around his forehead. His hair was long and back-combed and very mod.

He apologized profusely for the intrusion and said: "But Maite told me it was urgent, if anything came in to bring it over at once."

I said: "Please...it was good of you to come."

He grinned. "It gives me an excuse to visit the disco downstairs, a good time of night to go hunting." He patted Maite's behind affectionately, shook my hand, and left us.

The report was clear and—for Fenrek—rather chatty. We got back into bed and studied it.

...found your inquiry very interesting indeed, and am surprised: at the connection you have apparently inferred. Subject is believed dead, but FBI are of the opinion he is still alive and in hiding. He was born in Patagumpus, Maine, in 1935, height five ten, weight 175, and if the question of identification arises, we have a Portrait Parle on him. From 1956 to 1970 he was on the FBI's most wanted list, essential charges being sever separate counts of murder. He was a professional hit man for the Carlotti-Hanson group, and was reported to have been executed by his former employers in 1972. He is known to have secreted a considerable amount of money in a Lichtenstein bank just before his disappearance, but his known assets in the USA, also considerable, have been blocked by the IRS. Our information on him stops in 1970. He is known to be highly intelligent, restless, ruthless, and brutal. His DR is A plus, repeat, A plus. His hobbies

are painting and amassing money, and he was always known as having a finger in each of a dozen different pies, both legal and illegal...

There was a great deal more, seven pages of it in all, but most of it was unimportant. Maite said, very worried: "A danger rating of A plus? That's the first time I've heard them use the *plus*."

I said: "It's unofficial. A warning from Fenrek. But the essential word is *restless*."

"Oh? I must admit, I was, wondering about that. A strange word to use."

"Not in this context. The essential question is: can a rich and *restless* man stay buried forever on a distant island, cut off from everything he's ever enjoyed, when he's only reached the ripe old age of forty? A *restless* man will ignore quickly get bored with retirement. The pattern is emerging nicely."

The timing was just about perfect; I was sure now what was going on.

At four thirty in the morning, only fifteen minutes late, which isn't at all bad for Tahiti, I took off once more from the airport of Fanaa in Teiho's other Golden Eagle.

That one, too, was doomed.

CHAPTER 7

Rangitefara belongs neither to the Leeward Islands (a subdivision of the Societies) of which Raiatea is the largest and Bora Bora perhaps the most spectacular, nor to the Tuamotus, among which Rangiroa, with its astonishing forty-mile-long atoll, is the most important. It lies more or less halfway between the two groups.

Its vegetation is that of the Leewards, and its configuration that of the Tuamotus; in other words, it is an atoll, a ring-shaped reef of coral enclosing a lagoon, the entrance to which—as is almost invariably the case—is on the leeward side of the prevailing winds.

But it has a peculiarity all its own. The hard coral of the lagoon's inner ring has disintegrated over the centuries to an astonishing degree, a direct result of the abundance of fish here and the heavy concentration of their disintegrating dead bodies, which are locked within the lagoon. The strong winds that buffet the reef from time to time have broken off masses of coral which the waves have piled up to form a jagged pinnacle, a mountain more than five hundred feet high, which has become covered with dense and impenetrable vegetation, far thicker and more prolific even than on Tahiti itself. It is a non-volcanic island on the extreme western tip of the lagoon.

From this mountain, a low sand bar runs in almost a straight line to the center of the atoll, a little over a mile in length, and then, once again, the mountain appears, curving sharply round to meet the coral reef again on the northern side. I had seen the marks left by the helicopter on this sand bar, and had photographed the hangar—a small building of wooden poles covered with a *fare* roof of Pandanus fronds.

The island comes as a surprise when you first fly over it, largely because—since it belongs to neither group—you don't really expect it to be there; scattered though the islands are, and limitless miles distant from each other, there is, none the less, a logical pattern to their placement.

You wonder, too, why it's never been inhabited, until you realize that with the very peculiar pattern of cross-currents in the area, the ancient Mikiroans who first populated the islands could never have become established there; neither winds nor tides would have taken these seafaring people there from *anywhere*.

Tradition states that the original inhabitants of these islands were the descendants of hermit crabs. But the crabs on Rangitefara had been left alone, undisturbed by visitors or settlers, while the dugout canoes and outriggers, the *va'a hoe* and the *va'a ta'ie*, drifted serenely over an unending ocean and found their sheltering coves elsewhere.

Until, that is, the arrival of Willard Fest the impresario, or Will Utter the professional killer, or the man who chose to call himself...Aimata.

It was a good name for him, and on indication of a sardonic quality that sat strangely on him. It was a name to make people shudder.

As the red sun rose slowly up out of the water, I made a hard and fast turnaround the atoll, skimming over the water at zero feet, one hand clicking the camera and the other very hard at work on the controls. I was astonished at the variety of vegetation there: coconuts; pandanus; the beautiful Barringtons they call *Hotu*, with its shiny red and green leaves; casuarinas; country almonds; and the *callophylum inophyllum* which the Tahitians used for carving the idols they placed in their royal temples. There were breadfruit, banana trees, arrowroot, yarns, cassava, and a dozen other food plants growing in wild abundance. There were even time to see a line of lobster baskets, of non-Polynesian design, set out in the shallow water at the foot of the cliff. I also saw one man running fast from the tiny hangar toward the shelter of the forest, racing over the sand and then disappearing among the dense green cover of the frees and the ferns.

I was delighted to see him; it was the Fiji islander—perhaps he had been a Samoan after all—who had phutted his little blowgun at me back there on Papeete's mountain.

I flew low into the sun, and then came in for a final run dead center over the main peak, where a small clearing had been cut and the pandanus roof of a large house could be clearly seen. I climbed steeply, missing the treetops by inches, and then, as I throttled back and slid down the other side and across the smooth water, the trouble I had been expecting came at me, fast and murderously.

I saw the red flash down there in the greenery, and went immediately into a turn so tight that I could feel the fuselage shudder in protest. I stood the Cessna on its tail and went up high at full throttle, a marvelous burst of speed, well over the theoretical maximum of 1,850rpm, and saw, looking back, that the missile was still streaking toward me, a gray silhouette with a fiery scarlet plume behind it. Still gunning the engines, I waited till it was almost on me, a very scary wait for almost ten seconds, and then brought her up and over in a sickening roll that almost tore the wings off.

I held her, plunging down and shrieking like a banshee, till I was a hundred and fifty feet from the water before bringing her out of the roll and straightening up again—a maneuver I would really not recommend to even the most skillful pilot. I felt her belly touch water, a most alarming sensation; but then she was bouncing back up again and climbing steeply, screaming, and when I turned my head to look, that damned missile was on my tail again, and I knew what it was.

It was one of the SAMs, the Seven, a solid-fuel, heat-homing device 4.3 feet long—small enough to be packed into a suitcase—and deadly as a twenty-two-inch naval gun.

I suppose we can postulate that the SAM Mark Seven has caused more of an uproar in the Western world than any other weapon since the introduction of the first cannon in the early fourteenth century. Even its less sophisticated antecedents were knocking hell out of America's planes in Vietnam, and the Seven itself was the single weapon most notably responsible for the early setbacks the Israelis suffered in their last brush with the Egyptians. It is also fast becoming the ultimate terrorist weapon, not only because it is immensely deadly and still small enough to carry around easily, but also because anyone with a bit of money and the right connections can buy the damned things without any trouble at all. There always have been merchants eager to satisfy the cravings of lunatics for violence—it is a richly rewarding venture.

And there it was, not plunging into the water as it should have done, but doing a rapid U-turn to get after me with a miraculous stubbornness.

I thought: My God, fake her up fast again, and dive down hard to zero feet and pull out, and hope the damn thing overshoots this time. I pulled back and threw her upward, and rolled over again and found the water skimming over my head for a hundred feet till I completed the roll and brought her over again, and it was still on my tail. I was hoping my turns were faster than SAMs, but they weren't; there's *nothing* that can outmaneuver a Mark Seven. That's what makes them deadly.

Seventy seconds after I first spotted the launch, it hit home.

Even so, I almost made it; but almost is never enough. I had thrown the flaps to their full forty-five, and pulled hard back on the throttles and it seemed that the McCauley three-bladed props had stopped in midair, and the Eagle with them. The missile shot past me as I pulled out of the stall, and I saw it astonishingly close beside me, and a trifle ahead of me as its heat-activated fin did a double-flip; and then it spun round and came right at me from a distance of less than fifty feet.

I pushed back the flaps, and shoved on the throttles, and threw everything into a dive that was surely going to break us in two; the damn thing swerved with me and caught the massive vertical tail and blew us to hell and gone.

I was fifty feet off the water and still diving, and the Eagle twisted round and rolled over—a soul of its own, even in death, which is what good design is about—and the door popped off with the inrush of air, so I just leaned back and fell out; what else could I do?

All I could think of was: What kind of lies am I going to tell Teiho this time?

I was rolling over and over, spinning crazily and doubling myself up into a ball as I hit the water, smashing down into it with a force that seemed to thrust my knees out through the top of my head. I was conscious of twisting and turning over and over, and of wondering if I were still alive and, if I was, how long my lungs could hold out. I hit the bottom on sand which sent up a cloud of mud as I barreled into it, and there was a dull, numbing blow to my left thigh as I hit coral. The mass of it was enough to stop my onward movement, and I opened my eyes and saw, that it was the *corallium rubrum* again, the one I like so much. I reflected that in the days of the ancient Romans, it used to be hung around children's necks to preserve them from danger, and I decided that perhaps, when I had more leisure, I would come back here and get some of it to take home.

But now there were more urgent things to worry about; I was far too deep for comfort, and my ears were bursting.

I thrust out with my arms and legs, and broke the surface three hundred feet from the plane, which was still twisting and turning over in the water in slow motion, an incredible sight.

And then, it blew up.

There was just time for a quick gulp of air, and then I arched my back and went down deep to escape the fierce blast of fire which was shooting out across the water toward me. I swam deep and fast, my ears pounding, and when I finally came up with not an iota of breath left in my lungs, I was fifty feet from the curtain of fire that was settling around what was left of the plane.

I thought: Jesus, two planes in two days, it's getting to be a very expensive habit.

But there was not much time for reflection. I knew that there was no land of any sort for an infinity all around me—except the island itself. It was some two thousand yards away now; and there, no doubt, *they* would be waiting for me.

I remembered what Vanaa had said, that a careful man could land unseen on the western tip. But I realized that under the circumstances this was rather wishful thinking, a weakness I usually don't permit myself. I knew they'd be out there on the shoreline watching me even now through their binoculars.

Could I find a piece of coral to shelter behind? And wait some twelve hours till it was dark? I knew damn well they'd have a launch out here very soon if they lost me for long and although I'm a powerful swimmer, I knew I could not evade a motor launch for any appreciable length of time.

So I swam slowly toward the land and wondered how to evade, instead, what was waiting for me. I knew that I could not hope to do this either.

It took me thirty minutes to reach the coral-studded sand of the shore, but I really wasn't hurrying and had decided to conserve my energy in case I could make better use of it later on. When I clambered up onto the beach, there they were, eight of them, as angry looking a bunch of bastards as a man could ever hope to see, all lined up in a semi-circle with an assortment of rifles, pistols, and a couple of machine guns pointed at me.

They were mostly in the same kind of semi-uniform they'd worn on Faatua, but one of them, fairly obviously the only man who mattered here, was dressed in a dark blue sweatshirt and blue shorts, with blue canvas shoes like the Keds that had left their mark on the sand bar where Hawkins' rubber dingy had gone aground.

He was a very good-looking man, of medium height (which means that he came up to the middle of my chest), quite stocky and tough-looking, and rather younger than I'd expected him to be. His hair was long and black, and there was a strip of embroidered red cloth around his forehead to hold it out of the way. The lines on his face were deeply etched, his eyes very dark, and his eyebrows a very straight line above them. His nose was sharply hooked, and this, with the band around his head, gave him a faintly Aztec look. It was a very handsome and striking face indeed, but not one that inspired any confidence; the lips, tightly compressed in anger now, were far too thin. His hands, though strong and stubby, were well-kept, and there was a huge gold ring on his left little finger. He somehow gave the impression that he was part of the islands, that he'd lived here all of his life. He could have been one of the sons of the supreme god Taaroa, who was too distant a deity to concern himself with such unimpressive creatures as us mortals. I wondered how deeply he must have offended Tiare; she had described him as a nobody.

She was quite wrong; this was a tough and very impressive sonofabitch.

The others had gathered in a semi-circle around me, their guns ready, in case I might attempt to make a break for it. Two of them had even moved in behind me as though to cut off any escape by water. I thought it rather amusing, and said gently: "It would take me a month at least to swim anywhere from here, wouldn't you say?"

Nobody smiled. Nobody said anything for an intolerable length of time. I took off my shoes, tipped the water out of them, and said: "It must be Willard Fest; I imagine?"

The good-looking man nodded. "Yes, Cain, Willard Fest. You know nothing about me, and I know everything about you."

"Wrong on both counts."

"...except for a couple of details we'll get to in time."

His voice was as strong as his face, quite deep, and a little coarse. It was the voice of a rough and not too-learned man, a touch of the ghetto still in the intonation. He looked out to sea for a moment, staring at the flaming wreckage of the plane, a pall of black smoke hanging over it now. He turned back to me and said: "I'm glad you got out of that, it's very helpful."

I knew what he was thinking, but I said: "Oh, yes?"

He nodded. "Yes, I am. When a man's had a smell of death as close as that one must have been, it usually means he doesn't want another in a hurry."

I said: "That's good thinking, Mr. Fest."

He stared at me coldly, very thoughtful and calculating. "Who knows you're here, Cain? Apart from Vanaa and that broad you've been screwing?"

I said: "Everybody knows I'm here."

He grunted: "Correction."

There was a wry, sardonic look on his face. "Everybody knows you were coming here, maybe. And when they come looking for you, there'll still be enough wreckage floating around to tell them the whole story. You're kind of careless with rented aircraft, aren't you? Scratch Cabot Cain, lost at sea, the poor sonofabitch."

He peered up at me, squinting, his mouth set very firm.

"They tell me you're a very bright man, Cain, but let me paint the picture for you anyway. They'll come looking, and yes, we'll break precedent and let them come ashore. Yes, we saw the plane crash, and yes, we went looking for survivors, and no, there just weren't any. The plane broke apart in the air, no doubt through careless handling, it can happen. Or you went too low and hit the water, and that's all there is left out there, what a shame. So you're a dead man, Cain, and the sooner you get to realize that, the easier it's going to be for everyone, especially for me."

He turned away and said: "Take him up to the house. Better carry him."

Now, there's only one way anyone is ever going to carry me, and that's in a state of unconsciousness. I was aware that he must realize that, so I was ready.

I said: "Don't worry, I can walk," and without looking round he said: "Oh, we'll take care of that."

One of the men behind me moved forward as I swung round. He was moving with that kind of controlled laziness that usually means there's trouble coming, and as he brought up the stock of his automatic rifle—it was a German FG 9.92mm—to drive it into the side of my head, I reached out fast with one hand and drove my fingers into his throat, and with the other hand took hold of the gun's barrel and pulled hard.

He held onto it, of course, so I dropped to the ground, put a foot in his stomach, and threw him twenty feet into the surf. I swung the gun around at a second man, rushing stupidly in now, to catch him a fearful blow with it across the groin, doubling him up so that I could bring my knee up under his chin and knock him out.

For a moment, not really believing it, it seemed that might be able to get away with something here. But, there were just too many of them, even though it was a likelihood that nobody, just yet, wanted me dead, and that, therefore, they would not start firing unless they had to.

Three of the others had jumped on me, and another man had his rifle barrel under my throat from behind, quite expertly, and then a blow landed on the back of my skull so hard that all I could see was a blinding flash of crimson and yellow light. As I fell to the ground I heard, rather than felt, a violent thudding into my solar plexus, still bruised from that other encounter with them, that doubled me up and knocked me out cold.

When I woke up I was sitting on a hard wooden chair, highly polished and light amber in color, made of *calophyllum* wood, no doubt, with my wrists wrenched up behind me and tied there, my feet bound to the chair's legs. There was a strong nylon cord around my neck and looped over a rafter above me—not pulled too tight, but taut enough to inhibit very much movement in one way or the other.

It was a big, open-sided room, the kind of living room a man can build for himself when the weather is nearly always perfect, with bamboo walls and plaited pandanus fronds for a roof, no ceiling or glass anywhere. The floor was of red cement, highly waxed and polished, and the furniture was mostly wood and leather, with a good-looking bamboo bar tucked away in a corner, and three very big and comfortable-looking couches, also of wood and hide, under the three huge windows. We seemed to be well up on the mountain, and the view all around was spectacular, to say the least, with scarlet and purple bougainvillea hanging down everywhere; and pink and yellow hibiscus plants, and a great mass of frangipani on the windward side that filled the huge room with its perfume; under other circumstances I would have found it delightful.

Willard Fest was sitting at the bar across the room, on a high leather stool, his feet tucked under him and a snifter of cognac in his hand. He was sipping it slowly, watching me all the time, and I said: "Do you think I could have one of those? Or is that asking too much?"

He nodded slowly. "Yes, too much. You came out of that very fast, Cain. We didn't really expect you'd wake up at all."

"What time is it?"

"Does it matter?"

"No."

I was looking round for a clock, but could see no sign of one. The shadows indicated that it must be around ten thirty, and I found it hard to believe that I had been unconscious for so long. My skull seemed to be splitting in two, and there was no feeling at all in my hands or my feet.

But there were some fascinating paintings on the wall, all done by the same hand—my host. They were Post-Impressionist in style, with colors as brilliant as the local flora put on with a spatula in violent, rhythmic form that was quite extraordinary. The strokes were thick and pure, with a barbaric intensity to them, but there were unexpected touches here and there of the calculated, divisional technique of Seurat. It seemed to me that with the proper discipline—and training—he could easily have become great.

There was a gorgeous seascape in riotous purples and greens that was quite remarkable; an indifferent study of a Polynesian fisherman removing the jaws of a shark; an excellent still life showing a bowl of torch-ginger, rose of Columbia, and clerodendrum; and a full-length, very luminous study of a young *vahine* half in and half out of a pool of crystal water, the body cut neatly in two by a trick of diffusion and an unaccountable agony reflected in her eyes—it was startling.

But the picture that commanded most of my attention was a huge and very striking portrait of Tiare—the occasion, no doubt, on which he had so deeply offended her. It was distorted, but easily recognizable. Her head was turned a little to one side and tilted down, her eyes sad and reflective, her hair falling over one naked breast; the light on her skin was astonishing, and there was a peculiar blue tint to the flesh tones, a pigment I had never seen before. I thought it might have been made from the burned almonds of the candlenut, the *aleurites moluccana,* which is used locally for tattooing.

I looked at Fest and thought: What a waste of a great talent.

He said at last: "What did you expect to find here, Cain? What brought you to Rangitefara?"

I said: "I was looking for Jules Cresson, what else?"

"Oh."

He fell silent for a while, troubled. Then: "What makes you so sure that you'd find him here?"

"I wasn't sure at all. It just seemed a reasonable supposition."

"Based on what?"

"He was in the islands looking for two things: a wealthy sponsor, and some suitable place to continue his work. There was never any record that he'd left the islands, so either he's dead or hiding out here somewhere."

"So he's dead."

"Then who's carrying on with his work? Who knows enough about his damned insect to put it to work effectively? Like in Libya."

"Libya?" He laughed shortly. "They're paying off. I don't suppose you know that yet. I just got word this morning. We told them we'd do it again, there's still a few hundred thousand acres left that we didn't get the first time, and we told them..." He broke off and stared at me somberly for a while, and said: "Too much money involved, Cain. Did you really think you could stop me? Too much money."

He moved off his stool and went to the window, staring out across the mountain and the sea. A strange man; it was hard to imagine the casual violence that I knew was there. There was almost a dignity to him, the dignity of a strong man who knows what he's doing, all the time.

He turned back and said: "You worry me, Cain. I don't like the way you found me so easily. You'll have to tell me about that."

I said, offhandedly: "I suppose I will, in the course of time. Meanwhile, why don't you tell me something..."

"I don't have to tell you *anything*."

"No, but...what about Hawkins? Is he one of your men? Is he here? Just idle curiosity."

To my astonishment, he began to smile, a thin, twisted kind of a grin as though there were something that he found, secretly, to be very amusing indeed. And then he was laughing outright, an open kind of laugh I can only describe as mischievous.

He said: "Hawkins? That's funny, very funny. Yes. Hawkins *was* here. Yes, he was one of my men. Not any more though. He's gone the way of all flesh." He thought that was very funny too, and then one of the doors opened and a man was standing there with a rifle loosely held in his hand. He was out of breath and perspiring, as though he'd run up from the beach. He said briefly: "We got a plane."

Fest turned to him sharply: "Coming in?"

"I don't know. He's way out, flying at about two thousand feet, heading this way."

"Police?"

"Private. Twin prop, by the looks of it, too far off to be sure."

"Heading?"

"A hundred and seventy. Could be from Tahiti."

"All right. You know what to do. Tell Peabody."

"He knows, he's ready if they land."

"Tell him...if they want to come up here, argue for a while and then give way." He jerked a thumb at me. "Get him down to the cave, better get Ulricson to help you, carry him down the way he is. I've an idea he's a tricky sonofabitch if we don't watch out."

"Okay."

Fest came over as the man went out, and carefully took the nylon cord from around my neck. When the two men came in they stared at me for a moment, and the new man, Ulricson, said jauntily: "Why don't we pull a Hawkins on him, Will?"

He was a sly-looking bastard, and was fiddling with a long knife, tossing it in his hand, playing tricks with it. He flipped it around my eyes a couple of times and laughed.

But Fest was not amused any more. He said morosely: "No, I haven't finished with him yet, not by a long shot. Just lock him up, I'll see him when they've gone."

I could hear the plane now, a Mitsubishi by the sound of it, circling over our heads. The sound died suddenly, and I wondered if he'd throttled back and flown over the water where the plane's wreckage was. There was no way of knowing.

Fest was watching me carefully again, and there was something bothering him. He laid a finger along the side of his hooked nose and said: "Just one minute."

The body bearers waited, and Fest said to me thoughtfully: "I wonder if you know my other name?" His eyes were very alert, as though he was sure he would have to watch out for a lie, and might even perhaps see one coming.

I was too tightly trussed to shrug, but I said: "Another name?"

It made him happy. The broad smile creased his face again, and he was chuckling. He said: "I'm told you speak Polynesian, is that true?"

"I speak a lot of languages. One of my hobbies is keeping the mind busy."

"Yes, so I've heard. I took a Polynesian name. It's...Aimata." He was laughing outright now, on the surface, at least, a bright man with a sardonic sense of humor. "You know what the word means?"

I said: "I know."

"I'd been thinking about a nice, good-sounding local name for a long time. Then I heard about the drunk, what was his name? In the vineyard?"

"Villiers."

"Yes, that's right. And that's how they would have taken him. Through the eyeballs." He couldn't stop laughing. He said again, choking over the word: "Aimata. That's what they call me now. *Mister* Aimata to you. You like it, Cain?"

I said: "It suits you."

He went back to the bar and picked up his drink again, and jerked his head at the two men, and then I was being carried, clumsily and uncomfortably, in my beautiful *calophyllum* chair, out of the room and down a long, long flight of wooden steps that led, unexpectedly, into the bright cool sunshine, along a neatly tended path, into the forest, and up to the mouth of a small cave in the side of a sharply rising outcropping of coral rock.

They dumped me down here for a moment, and Ulricson wiped at the sweat on the back of his neck and growled: "Heavy sonofabitch, isn't he?"

I lay on my side like a well-tied carcass, and waited until they'd recovered their breath for the long haul down to the bottom. It was steeply sloping now, and there were bare electric bulbs strung out on a roof that seemed to have been cut more or less straight with an axe: I could see the chisel-marks everywhere. At the bottom, they dropped me again and Ulricson opened a heavy iron grill that covered what looked like a short tunnel, not much more than five feet high and about as broad; they sort of rolled the chair in, with me strapped tightly in it, and slammed the door shut. I watched them put a chain around it, and fasten it with a very heavy padlock. They tried the door once and went away; in a moment the lights were switched off and I was left alone in the silence. The only sound was the faint and distant hum of a generator. I wondered how long it would take me to get out of here. I decided to make it a point of principle to hurry it up as much as possible. I wanted another session with Aimata but under my own terms and conditions, not his.

I swung my body hard to one side, and in four or five efforts had moved the chair onto its back, so that my bound wrists were pressing tight with my own weight into the hard, sharp coral of the floor.

I figured it might take about an hour, and hoped I had all that

106

time.
The darkness was a great comfort to me. I always work well in the dark.

CHAPTER 8

It was really one of the most painful experiences I had ever encountered. Fortunately, they had bound me so tightly and the cords were biting so deeply into my wrists that there was absolutely no feeling in them at all—at first. It was rather like rubbing senseless, detached pieces of my own body over sharp and gritty coral, and just hoping that some of the cutting, at least, was being done in the right places.

I could even hear the scraping of bone on the jagged extrusions; and when I began to feel it, too, it seemed like one of the metacarpals; or possibly the extremity of the ulna, so I shifted over a half-inch, and continued rubbing. All I could do was guess about the precise positioning, knowing that my numbed wrists ought to be somewhere around the small of my back, and that, somewhere there too, there ought to be a few possibly bulky knots.

And then an intolerable pain came flooding all along my arms, and I knew that it could mean only one thing—enough of the cords had been frayed through to set my blood coursing again. In a little while, about fifteen minutes after I had started, my left arm suddenly came free. I rolled the chair over on to its side again, and felt for the knots on the other arm, and in another five minutes or so I was stretching out to ease my cramped limbs, feeling the blood coursing all over the place, both inside of me, where it belonged, and out, where it was running in great streams all over my hands and arms. I held them up in the air for a while to take the pain away and to inhibit the bleeding a little, and then tore my shirt into strips and bandaged them as best I could. That damned coral was as sharp as a higgledy-piggledy mess of razor blades, and while not exactly poisonous, being merely carbonate of lime that has been deposited in the tissues of Anthozoan polyps. (which in turn belong to the phylum, *Coelenterata*), it is not the kind of stuff an intelligent man wants rubbed into open wounds either.

But in a few minutes I felt my old self again, and wondered just how to tackle the chain around the iron bars of the door. It was very heavy to the touch, and I was quite sure that I could never break it. The bars, however, were something else again; they were too long to be of much use against a determined effort.

The "cell" was only five feet or so high, and they had made the door of half-inch iron bars set vertically, with only a single horizontal to strengthen them and prevent any bending; there should have been two. So I took hold of the top of the middle bar with both hands, walked my feet up till they were firm against the lintel, and then put my back to work.

If you use your back properly, as I always like to do, you can move mountains with it. In about three minutes of concentrated effort I felt the top of the bar come adrift from its mooring, just a trifle, but enough to permit me to change my position and start bending it down, using the horizontal as a fulcrum. Soon it was bent double, but there was still not room enough to squeeze through, so I spent another four minutes on the one next to it, got that out of the way too, and simply clambered through.

And so, a mere fifty minutes or so after they had so roughly bundled me inside there, I was free once more and left alone to my own devices—always a satisfactory state to be in.

There was hardly any light down here, and I toyed for a moment with the idea of trying to find the switch and put those ghastly bare bulbs on again, but I decided against it. I wondered also if I should creep out and steal the helicopter and simply fly back to Tahiti in it, but I decided against that, too; after all, I had gone to a great deal of trouble to reach the island, and it seemed absurd to run off again merely because they knew I was here. So I moved off deeper down the tunnel, feeling my way and keeping my eyes closed tightly so that when I at last opened them there would be some sort of minimal visibility.

The passage was widening out. I had walked, very slowly and carefully, for two hundred and twelve paces, always in the same direction, touching the wall lightly with my fingers all the way and moving in absolute silence. When at last I opened my eyes I could see that I was at the edge of a great cavern that must have been fifty or sixty feet high; there was a breath of fresh air down here now, which meant another opening somewhere. I moved on.

I came at last to a subsidiary passage, and now there was quite a lot of pale-gray light seeping down from a honeycomb sort of stratum in the rock high above me, a rather interesting formation where winds and the rain had broken through the dense coral of which this mountain was made; there was water seeping in too, and I cupped some of it in my hands and drank deeply, enjoying its fresh, cool taste, surprisingly sweet on the tongue. I found a tiny pool where the water had collected, and bathed my wrists and arms for a while, and then moved on again, wondering what I might find. There were electric wires strung out here, so wherever I was going, it was a likelihood at least that I'd find something at the end of the journey.

And I did.

Suddenly, a great yellow beam of light seemed to shoot out of the bowels of the earth, a beacon, and I pulled back tight against the wall of the cavern. There was a hole in the ground ahead of me, a neat circular hole some six feet across, and the light was coming up from an enclosure of some sort down there. I lay flat on my belly and peered over the edge; I could smell a very strong and distinctive odor, not very pleasant to the nostrils—formic acid.

What was below me was astonishing.

First, under my nose, there was the round shaft, like a fraction of a six-foot-wide well, going straight down for twelve feet or so and faced over with cement—a ventilation shaft. Then, the rock opened up in all directions, so that there was a damn great cave below me, well lit, and to my surprise very nicely furnished as living quarters. I could not see all of it, but it looked like a very large room, squared off by hand, with a smooth and flat floor and—barely in my line of vision—a big wooden door that was open and showed part of a narrow corridor outside it. And all down the side of the wall that I could see, there were wooden racks, rather like wine racks, but covered over with what looked like green nylon mesh. There was part of a long table visible also, with a lot of books on it, and a chart on the wall which was too far away for me to read.

I could see a big divan and an armchair, and part of a bookshelf, and a corner of a very good carpet, a fine Multan, I thought, though it might have been an Amritsar. A man was moving across my front, lifting up a corner of the mesh over the racks, and peering intently into them.

He moved to a switch on the wall and touched it, and there was the sound of a large and powerful fan beginning to hum; a moment later the smell of the acid increased as the gasses wafted up past my nose, and I realized that I was in the vent that kept the air down there sweet and fresh.

He disappeared from my sight for a moment, and then came back and walked out.

It was Jules Cresson.

Even from this uncomfortable point of view, there was no mistaking the stoop to the shoulders, the thin white beard—much thinner now than when I had met him before—the untidy gray hair, the gaunt stick of the neck. He was dressed in a long white gown, and seemed to be mumbling to himself, though I could not hear what he was saying.

I wondered how to get down there. The floor of the cavern was some thirty feet below me, too much to jump without risking a broken leg, which would be a nuisance now. I also wondered how long he would be out of the room, and if perhaps there might be someone else down there hidden from my sight. I thought probably not; a man doesn't normally talk to himself unless he's alone.

I reached out carefully for the opposing edge, and worked myself into the chimney, bracing my arms against one side and my legs against the other, and worked my way slowly down; it was far too wide for any degree of safety, but without ropes this was the only possible way. I reached its lower end—the ceiling of the room down there—without too much trouble. There was a half-inch pipe cemented into the roof not too far away from me, about twelve feet or so, and I wondered if it would support my weight.

And even if it could? What then?

I saw that the pipe seemed to run along the length of the ceiling, and it was a fair guess that it then turned down, rather than up, to supply fresh water down there, so I took a chance on it. I improved my hold on the walls of the shaft as best I could, braced my feet against one side, shoved hard, spun round in midair, and grabbed for the pipe.

Somewhat to my surprise, it held fast. I was also gratified to see that it did indeed go down, not up, and so I simply followed it along hand over hand until I came to the wall, and slid down it to the floor.

The first thing I looked for was some kind of cover to use in an emergency. There was the big divan that was satisfactory concealment; there was a large filing cabinet standing free from the wall which would have hidden me; there was a pile of wooden boxes in one corner I could get behind; and there were two closets, one of them full of clothes and the other empty. No problem, then.

I took a look at the wine rack. As I had thought, underneath the mesh there were a dozen or so cages, and in each one there were just a few curious-looking insects which intrigued me enormously, if only because they were almost exactly like the imaginary creature Falleron, back in France, had drawn from his well-tutored imagination.

This, I was sure, was the *Docciostaurus Cressonus* that Cresson had spent the best part of his life trying to breed.

It was tiny, no bigger than a large ant, but shaped like a praying mantis. Its jaw was relatively large, its body was small, and its wings, though closed now, seemed to be huge. It had six legs, a very long proboscis, large eyes, and two miniscule antennae sticking up out of its head. I saw that each of these cages contained one of a certain type and two or three of another, and I assumed that this was a question of male and female. The cages were all numbered, and some of them had small white cards pinned on them: *Strain #7...Strain #95...Strain #10...*

I moved to the other end of the rack and lifted up the mesh. Here, one of the cages was full of a mass af seething green insects, so tightly packed that it could not have been caused merely by cramming them in together like that. It was a remarkable sight; the mesh sides of the cage were literally bulging with the force of them in there, and I could only guess at how many there might be. A thousand? A hundred thousand? A million?

I could only stare at it. It throbbed, a ghastly, ever-moving mass of wet and shining putrescence, like green marmalade compressed and trying to break out of its confinement; seething and rolling and stinking formidably. I held my breath and examined it closely; I could see a thousand eyes glittering, and could hear the crunch of a million microscopic teeth; they were feeding on each other. It was *obscene*.

I continued my inspection of this underground living room, and I must admit that except for that pervading smell of rancid insect, it was very pleasant. There were blue velvet drapes hanging over one end of the chamber, simulating a window, with nothing but bare rock behind it; the bookshelf was long and tall and imposing, and crowded with books on entomology, biochemistry, plant anatomy, and natural history. I was pleased to see that my own translation of Rhabdanus Maurus, who tried to awaken a flagging interest in entomology in the early ninth century after nearly a thousand years of neglect, was among them. There was a small propane stove against one wall with the makings for herb tea on it, a very large desk of inlaid walnut that must have cost a fortune (inlaid marquetry, about 1820 or so, and almost certainly a James Moore—priceless) with almost nothing on it except an old-fashioned inkstand that did it no credit, a piece of quite phony Baroque, and a notebook half-filled with miniscule writing on the *Calliptimus italicus*, the ordinary southern European locust, with special reference to its digestive tract, which I glanced through and found very interesting indeed, the work of an erudite and hard-working man who had spent the last ten years or so concentrating on this one recondite aspect of entomology.

And in one corner, there was a wide-mouthed well, about ten feet across, railed off with a wrought-iron barrier just high enough to see that no one fell into it accidentally. I climbed over and peered down into it (the smell here was much stronger) but could not see the bottom, so I dropped the offending inkstand down it and counted the seconds till I heard the splash—an extraordinary three hundred and twenty feet deep, give or take an inch or two.

And then, I heard him coming back.

My first instinct was to take cover in one of the hiding places I had selected, but then I thought: Well, whatever for? He was obviously going to have a lot of answers; and certainly, I had a lot of questions.

And so, I waited.

For a very brief moment, I had the idea that he might not be alone; but it was just the sound of his footsteps playing tricks in the subterranean passages.

He stared at me as he came in, a bent and dignified old man who had let loose on the world a pest it could happily do without, having enough of its own. He was not alarmed, but rather angry.

He said, screwing up his old eyes: "What the devil are you doing here? You know you're not allowed down here..." He broke off, and the frown darkened. He said: "But...I know you, don't I?"

I said: "Yes, Professor Cresson. We met. Some years ago."

For a moment, he hesitated, his pale and watery eyes uncertain, and then he stabbed a finger at me and said: "No! Don't tell me! I'm ninety-one years old next March, and my memory is still as good as I ever was, I'll tell you... Something to do with the oligochaetes and their mandibles, an absurd theory you had that proved to be right after all, and I was very rude to you, wasn't I? You see? My memory, it's not failing at all."

I said gently: "Cabot Cain, Professor."

His face lit up. "Of course, I was just going to remember. Cabot Cain! And they proved your theory to be right after all, didn't they, and that means that I owe you an apology."

"Did they? I didn't even know. I'm afraid I lost touch with the mandibles and the oligochaetes, just a transitory interest."

"Oh really? What a terrible thing to do." He was quite severe. "One should never lose interest in academic matters, Mr. Cain, never give up on the demanding challenges of science. Where would the world be if we all just...lost interest? Will you tell me that, young man?"

I said gently: "From some point of view, it might be a much better place."

"Oh nonsense!"

He peered up at me, puzzled, "But what are you doing here?

114

I'm surprised, to say the least. And how did you get here, I didn't see you in the corridor?"

"It's more a question of what *you're* doing here, Professor Cresson. And I'm surprised, too."

"Me?" He looked surprised. "Why, I'm working, of course, that's all I've ever done; all my life."

I said: "Not very rewarding work, is it?"

"I don't think I quite understand you. I'd say it's very rewarding. Have you seen the new batch?"

"The new batch?"

"I see you haven't. Let me show you." He went to the cage that had so disgusted me, and lifted the mesh to display the heaving mass of jelly inside. He said excitedly: "Look at that! Can you believe it? A million of them I'd say, at a guess. And yesterday, there was one male and four females. They're beginning to die already, but I've got the strain annotated, and it's better than ever before." He was getting excited about it. "That's always been the problem with these dear little creatures, unless the climate is absolutely right, and really, it's quite critical, they refuse to go from the singular stage to the gregarious. But this one... Too late now to do anything with this batch, of course, but by God, I've answered that challenge, I've crossed over the Rubicon. It's all plain sailing now. I think you should congratulate me, Mr. Cain." He was beaming.

I said: "Is that the one you used in Libya?"

"Not Libya. Brazil. And not quite the same strain either, the ones I used there were not quite so exuberant. Procreatively, I mean. Each female was laying twelve thousand eggs, and they were taking four days to reach maturity, but that has been much improved now." He blinked his weak eyes at me rapidly. "Libya? No, Mr. Cain, you have your facts wrong. Brazil. And it worked. It *worked*, by God." He broke off and peered up at me. "Have we been using them in Libya? Surely not! He'd have told me."

"Who would have told you?"

"Why, Mr. Fest, of course."

He was still peering, deeply suspicious now. Maybe he remembered that my facts, much as I distrust so frangible a commodity, were seldom wrong. He said, very quietly: "Tell me about

Libya, Mr. Cain."

"Tell me about Brazil, Professor Cresson."

He held my gaze for a long while. He shrugged then, and said: "Jungle clearing, it doesn't sound like a very important occupation, does it? But in the vast new areas they're trying to plant, to feed a starving world, this is the one big headache they have. You see, they just can't, physically, clear fast enough. They put twenty or thirty bulldozers to work, and fire what's left, and they've cleared maybe ten acres of forest, and what's ten acres? The cost is enormous, and it's a slow, slow process. But the world's population is catching up with its potential for food, and there's calamity ahead of us. South America, Africa, Asia...almost a fourteenth part of the world's arable land is taken up with jungle..."

He broke off, suddenly delighted, and said: "Ha! Another thing I remember, you're a linguist, aren't you? You translated Maurus, didn't you, so you know Hindustani. Ergo, you know what the word really means."

I said: "*Jangal*, in Hindu it means land taken over by an excess of wild vegetation."

"Exactly! Taken over, that's the word exactly! And if we're to have any hope of feeding the starving millions, and there really are millions of them, we have to reclaim that land, and we need a new method, a swift and effective method. I tried my *Cressonus* out in Brazil, a minor experiment that I'm afraid didn't receive the acclaim it deserved. It was the third or fourth strain, if I remember correctly. We took a single trenching machine, and cut a drainage trench three feet wide and three feet deep around a hundred acre plot, and we filled it with water. And then..."

His eyes were shining, alight with excitement: "And then, I released ten males and forty females of my Strain Four, and within forty-eight hours, there wasn't a single piece of greenery left, everything was dead, everything. We fired the stubble, the dead stumps, and three days to the hour after we started with the trenching machine, we had one hundred acres of arable land, at a cost approximately one twentieth of what conventional methods would have cost, and in one eighth of the time. With the new strain, which propagates itself very easily, with no encouragement from me at all, anyone can handle them, we'll cut the time down to a fiftieth, and the cost down to a fifteenth. Think what that will do for the starving nations of the world, think of all those huge jungles we can turn over to food-stuffs!" Not stopping to take a breath, he said quickly: "And you were going to tell me about Libya."

"The new millet fields in Libya. Destroyed completely."

"Libya?" he said scornfully. "Libya grows nothing, Mr. Cain, it's ninety percent desert, a very backward..." He broke off again, and peered up at me, and said slowly: "No, you're right again, aren't you? I heard about it. They found great rivers under the desert, a thousand feet down, and pumped the water up to the surface, yes... But what has that to do with the *Cressonus?*"

I said: "You know, don't you, what it has to do with your dammed insect?" I didn't believe he did but I had to be sure.

He was shocked. He repeated: "*Damned* insect? Well, really!" He began to gesticulate, waving a fragile arm around. "Yes, yes, in the very early days, it all started with attempts at defoliation in Indochina. But that was a long time ago, Mr. Cain. The swords have been beaten into plowshares, the inevitable peacetime good that comes out of wartime evil..." He paused, and said quietly: "I really think you'd better tell me."

I said: "A hundred thousand acres of developing crops wiped out. Almost overnight."

He whispered. "An accident? That's always been the danger."

"No. Deliberate."

He stared at me in a shock so absolute that I was convinced it was not feigned. "A hundred thousand acres...?"

"Of millet."

"But...but...why? For God's sake, why?"

"Blackmail, Professor. If you want to harvest your crops, pay me. If not, they'll be destroyed."

He almost staggered to the desk and sat down heavily on the chair there.

I thought it was time for some precautions, and I asked him: "Are we likely to be disturbed for the next few minutes?"

He shook his head blankly, a numbed, uncomprehending look on his face. "My God..." His voice was a whisper. "No. No, one is allowed down here, no one at all."

I knew that this happy state of affairs would not last for long once they'd discovered I was no longer where they'd left me. But there was a good deal that remained to be answered. I said: "What's your relationship with Willard Fest?"

He was still shaking his head, driving away the image. "I've always known that it could be used to cause a great deal of harm, after all, that's what it was intended for in the first place, to deprive the Vietminh of food supplies. Rice, mostly. But now... The war's been over a long time, and I found other good uses, and the Americans packed me off, they said they weren't interested any more, and even the French would have nothing to do with it, only the Brazilians... And I proved to them how useful it could be, how very, very useful." He stared blankly out into space for a moment, then looked up at me and said, his voice very weak: "The transition from war to peace, the good it inevitably brings. The application of weapons to useful purposes. Some of the most impressive words I ever heard as a boy. '*They shall beat their swords into plowshares, and their spears into pruning hooks; nation shall not lift up sword against nation, neither shall they learn war any more...*' You see? I told you: Ninety years old, and my memory..."

I went to the door, closed it, and pushed home the heavy bolt, and wondered if there were another way out of there. Time was passing too damn fast, as it always does. I asked him: "How do you get out of here without using that passage, Professor?"

He shook his head. "The only way out of this room. Why do you ask?" I didn't answer, and he said, incredulously: "A hundred thousand acres of millet? Overnight, you said?"

"Almost overnight."

"That must have been the last strain."

"And in France..."

He was horrified. "France, too? But, good God, if those things are let loose in a developed country. It's only water that will stop them. That's why we used trenches of water in Brazil. They gorge themselves on any living organism..."

"Herbivorous only?" I knew, of course, but I wanted a comment from him.

He shook his head, a tired and sick old man. "No, of course not, how could they be? That's where the departure came, the ordinary locust eats only vegetation, but the *Cressonus* is like the ant, it eats *anything* that lives."

"I have to know everything there is to know about it, Professor."

He sighed. "What else is there to tell? You know about the ordinary *docciostaurus*, isn't that your field?"

"One of my fields. How do they swarm?"

"Like the warrior ant. But they fly to their food. Once they land to eat, they gorge themselves, and make for the nearest water. Only with their stomach distended to the point of bursting, and with such a tiny digestive tract—that was the secret, really—they drown from the inside out, like a rat that's been eating any of the plasticize poisons. They explode. They die by the millions, in minutes, like lemmings, only their work has been done. You have to start over again. The queen is the first to die, and that's very interesting, isn't it? Not at all true to the form you'd expect. Of course, I'm still experimenting to find out why that should be..."

"None left over at all? No workers? No warriors? No rulers?"

"No. Nothing. If they're carried away by water, there's not even any sign they've been there."

"Except their excreta."

"Oh yes, of course. Almost pure formic acid. We might be able to turn that to use one day, too, there are so many possible ramifications..."

He was talking for the sake of talking, trying to drive a nightmare away.

I said gently: "And Willard Fest? You had no idea?"

"I still...can't believe what you're suggesting. Blackmail? It's impossible!"

"He's a professional criminal. You never knew that?"

He was almost in tears. "For three years now, he's been...sponsoring me. He's so very kind to me! Only he won't let me leave the island, not that I want to particularly. And he helped me with this place down here..."

He gestured helplessly: "They need a controlled humidity in

the early stages." He broke off again, staring at my wrists. They were dripping all over the floor.

He said: "But...good God, is that blood on your wrists? My dear Mr. Cain, you must get it attended to."

"Don't worry about it. Apart from this room here...where else can we find your insects?"

"Nowhere else. Oh, a few bags of them, perhaps. He's taken, what, six sets I think, in the last week or two."

"In nylon mesh bags?"

"Yes, as a matter of fact. We put a dozen males and a hundred or so females in a bag, and they can go without any food at all for seven, eight days maximum. And then, the moment you release them, wherever there's enough food, they begin to breed, very rapidly. The incubation period now is six and a half hours, isn't that remarkable? Each female in Strain Nine—or is it Ten?—produces a virtually unending stream of offspring, up to a hundred thousand of them, and they go on breeding almost at once, as long as they can feed. And then, they head for water, drink deeply, and burst, and they're gone."

"Till the next time."

"Yes. Till the next time."

"And how many do you have down here, Professor?"

He hesitated. "Enough to...to wipe out every living piece of greenery over half the Polynesian Islands. That's why we have to be so careful with them. That's why I have to work on them underground. It slows down their development."

"Life cycle?"

"Like the *phentrum*, a matter of twelve days. As long as they don't eat. Once they eat...they have doomed themselves."

"The well in the corner there?"

"That's where I get rid of them, the ones I'm not saving for improvement to the species. It's very deep."

I said idly: "Three hundred and twenty feet deep."

"Yes, I imagine at least that. But...but..." He got to his feet and went over to the rack, and lifted a corner of the mesh and peered in at his dreadful little creatures. "But are you suggesting that Mr. Fest *knows* they're being misused?"

"Not suggesting it. Stating it."

120

"I can't believe you, Mr. Cain! This time, I really must insist, you are wrong, absolutely wrong. He's a kind, good man, he has always treated me...splendidly."

"You represent a lot of blackmail money to him. He asked the Libyans for ten million francs to lay off."

He was still shaking his head, "No, no, it just cannot be! He treats me like a...like a father."

"But won't let you leave the island."

"Well, he said...how shall I put it? He indicated he'd rather I didn't absent myself from my work, and at my age, why should I? And he has the right to do that! After all, he's providing me with my keep, with all that I need for my research."

He swept out a hand at the bookshelves. "Why, just look at those books! In Montreal, in Brazil, even with the Americans, I never had such a library. I have this place to work in, I have a little house up there very close to his own, I have everything I could possibly want. Including...peace of mind, and no responsibility for anything but my work."

I let him ramble on. I had my own worries to contend with, and when he fell silent, I said gently: "Tell me where that passage leads to, Professor."

"The passage?" He gestured vaguely. "Oh, it leads out into the forest and comes out in the hut the guards use."

"And how many guards are there, do you know?"

"Oh...a dozen or so, I imagine. Mr. Fest was a very famous man in America, something to do with films, I think, and the tourists always want to fly over, or sail here and just...stare at him. That's what he says. He likes his privacy, and he's very rich, so... He keeps a staff of men here, to insure that no one worries him." He tried a smile, a small joke. "A sort of papal guard, I suppose you'd call it. They seem very...obedient to his orders. Not very nice people, I fear, most of them."

"How many exactly, Professor?"

He thought, counted silently on his fingers, and said at last: "Fourteen. No, fifteen, I forgot Kanaka, he's a Fiji Islander, a very silent, unobtrusive sort of man who seems to live on his own in the forest somewhere."

I was prowling, inspecting, and most of all wondering how much time I had left. Professor Cresson seemed to be slowly accepting what I had told him, and he said: "You didn't explain why *you* were here, Mr. Cain. I assumed at first that you were working with Mr. Fest, but in view of what you think of him... Just why are you here?"

I told him the bare essentials, and when I had finished, he sat down, shaking, and then got up and went to his cages again and stared at his insects and said nothing. I was still only half-convinced that he believed me, but when he turned back to me I saw that his face was white as a sheet.

He said hesitantly: "I have seen them carrying guns, the bodyguards, and I always thought it was quite unnecessary. And then ...there was a man named Hawkins. I was going for a walk in the forest one day, and Hawkins was there, running, with two of the others chasing him. Not a nice man, really, very arrogant and ill-mannered, but I was close enough to see the expression on his face, he ran right past me, they all did, and all I can say is..." He frowned. "I never saw fear so clearly written in a man's eyes, Mr. Cain. Later that evening, I mentioned it to Mr. Fest, and he just laughed and told me that Hawkins had been very careless with some trifling matter or another, and that he'd been sent away."

He was almost weeping. He said, distractedly: "I met Mr. Fest in Montreal, though I never knew his name then, a rather strange incident... I was in the museum one day, and he was there too, not the kind of face you'd forget, a very handsome and striking man, really quite memorable. He was wearing, I recall, a very heavy Canadian loggers' jacket, plaid wool, and the place was full of police officers for some reason or another. And then, a few moments later, I saw him again, and he was in uniform, a policeman's uniform, so I thought perhaps he was a plainclothes man, and they were ushering us all out of the building, and Mr. Fest took my arm and guided me out. I was walking with a cane in those days, a touch of rheumatism; it's very cold and damp up there. And then, two years later, when I was trying to buy an island out here, to continue my research I met him again, on Tahiti itself, and I reminded him of the incident."

"And he denied all knowledge of it, no doubt."

"No, as a matter of fact he remembered it well. He even

laughed about it, and told me he had been working on a picture, a film or something. But in view of what you say...that wasn't true either, was it?"

"No. He was a hired killer, and the police were looking for him. And that's how he got away from under their noses."

He said again, insisting: "But he was so *kind* to me! He offered me the use of his island, all the help I might need..."

"*After* you had told him about your insects?"

"Oh yes. He was immensely interested, for a layman. He questioned me very closely about it."

"Of course. A new weapon he could turn to good account. As we've learned."

"Yes, yes."

"He has a helicopter here. What other means of transport are there?"

"Oh, there are two light planes; a small launch, and a large cruiser—very fine vessels, both of them. Mr. Fest is a very wealthy man."

"He's going to be richer still if we don't stop him. What about those six sets you said he had taken in the last week or two? Do you know where they are now? And when exactly they were taken?"

He frowned. "The first two...I think...yes, almost two weeks ago. They will be dead now, whatever happened to them."

Libya and France, without a doubt.

"And the others?"

He was groping at the back of his mind. "Then the man I was telling you about, Hawkins? He took one, I seem to remember. Mr. Fest wanted him to take it up in an aircraft; I'd run into a purely academic problem of their survival at high altitude... I wonder what really happened to Hawkins?"

"It's a likelihood he went above his ceiling and blacked out. He crashed. Somehow, the insects got out of their bag. They defoliated half the island of Faatua."

"Terrible...terrible."

"That's three of them. The others?"

"Yesterday. Three sets of Strain Fifteen. Five males and about twenty or so females in each set; I made them up for him. He said he wanted them...looked at by one of the entomological institutes. I think in America. I'm not sure."

"And they will live for how long? Before they go into action?"

"They must have food within two weeks, or they'll die."

"Then I wonder where his next target is."

He had gone to the stove, a broken old man, and was absently fixing herb tea, barely conscious of what he was doing.

I said, a critical question: "Do you believe what I have been telling you, Professor? All of it?"

He did not answer for a very long time. He turned up the propane under his tea. He said at last, turning back to me and peering myopically: "I'm afraid I must believe you. I'm an old man now, but my mind is still sharp and analytical, as a scientist's mind should be. There are so many little things that drop into place, so to speak, if I believe what you say, and so many unanswered questions if I do not. Yes, I must believe you. I have to."

"Then you know what we must do."

He took his tea over to the table and sat down, and stared at nothing for a while, and then looked at his hands, holding them up in front of his face to examine them as though they, not part of him, were guilty of some terrible atrocity. Then he began to sip from the cup, and it was shaking.

He said, very quietly: "I will not destroy my life's work, Mr. Cain."

"It's gone sour, Professor. It will always be a weapon, nothing more."

He got slowly to his feet and went over to the cages and touched them, an old man's treasured memories. He said, his voice shaking: "Number seven, and eight, and fifteen. My life's work, can you understand what that means? A lifetime..."

Only three of them? I said: "And the others?"

He shook his head. "The others are past doing any harm now, their life cycle is nearly over. But these three cages... It's taken me fifty years of study and hard work. And you want to destroy them?"

He was crying now, openly, unashamedly,

I said gently: "Would you be prepared to start over? Under better control? I don't yet know how, or where, but if it's really as valuable as you believe, perhaps I can help you."

I heard the door being tried. It was locked, and the bolt was rattling in its hasp. I picked up a chair and put it, very quietly, under the doorknob—still the best way to hold a door shut. I pulled out two of the cages he had mentioned, went quickly to the well, and dropped them down. I looked back at him and said: "There's one more, Professor."

I was almost sure I'd have to take it myself, but I wanted to give him the chance. He hesitated only a moment, and then wiped a hand over his eyes, went to the rack, and slipped out the last cage; I watched him drop it down into limbo. There were still tears in his eyes, but he was smiling now.

A muffled voice said: "Are you all right, Professor?"

He said clearly, raising his voice: "Yes. Yes, of course I am."

"Then open the door."

It was rattling furiously now, and the voice said: "Open up, Professor."

I went to the pipe and tock a grip on it, and whispered: "Don't try to hide the fact that I was here, they'll know, so just tell them. Tell them you tried to stop me, you understand?"

He nodded eagerly. "I understand. A long time since I attempted any...chicanery. Yes, I'll tell them."

They were pounding on the door; I wondered how long I would hold. I said: "Give me a moment, and then open it. They won't harm you if you tell them." I was swarming up hand over hand, dangling from the horizontal and swinging along it over to where the bottom of the wide vent was.

The Professor moved to the door, staring up at me in fascination, but they didn't want to wait. They broke it down before he could get there, and there were four of them rushing into the chamber as I swung myself up and into the shaft. I heard the vicious sounds of the machine guns, chipping out great hunks of cement as I pulled myself up and over the lip and rolled to safety.

There was a moment, no more, of silence down there, and I wondered if they were waiting to see if I'd poke my fool head back to take a look. But I knew that I had to do just that.

I peered cautiously over the edge again. I could see only the

Professor and one other man—Ulricson. They were both half turned toward the door, as though someone else were coming in and they wanted to see who it was.

But it was the expression on the Professor's face that struck me; there was a cold, angry contempt there that I had not seen before. He was twisting his body back, very slowly, a delicate, inexplicable maneuver; it puzzled me.

And then, Aimata moved into the periphery of my vision, and from high up here it seemed that he was *gliding* toward Cresson, an insidious, catlike movement. It was unreal, out of perspective; everything seemed to move intolerably slowly. The Professor continued his movement, and it was a lifting of one arm. He brought his hand down hard and slapped Aimata across the face, lashing out twice, back and forth with an astonishing fury; I heard him shout the one word: "*Murderer!*"

Aimata, rooted there, hardly moved with the blows. His hand was out too, an empty hand which somehow gave the impression, from this distorted viewpoint, that he was offering to shake hands; I knew it wasn't that.

And then, suddenly, the hand was empty no longer. Ulricson had slapped his long knife into it, a surgeon being handed a scalpel. Aimata made a lightning-quick movement and drove the knife into Professor Cresson's gut and sliced upward with it. I could even hear it going through the ribcage.

I saw the body drop, and the open eyes were staring up at me, as though drilling a way into my conscience, demanding that the account be paid in full. I saw the slow and rhythmic wiping of the bloodied blade on the Professor's white jacket. Then Aimata turned and growled: "All right. Now go find that mother."

I should have foreseen it. The moment he had said: '*the new strain, anyone can handle them*' I should have known. I should have realized that with a man like Aimata, the rest was just inevitable.

But I didn't; and the memory of those dead, still-gentle eyes, with no accusation in them at all, will live with me always.

I felt I wanted to vomit.

CHAPTER 9

I found it almost impossible to rid my mind of that terrible image.

I thrust it away with a conscious effort, and made myself a promise, and turned to the urgency of the moment. I wondered if he had really known just how many of them there were on the island.

And how many of them would be searching for me now? I thought it a likelihood that *most* of them were; the whole place, no doubt, would be in an uproar. Four of them were still down there, but moving out; and what of the others?

One man on guard at the hangar, another where the boats were moored—to cut off any possibility of my escape—and the rest?

Nine left, then; perhaps. Or twenty; perhaps. Or a hundred...who could tell?

Guessing at figures like these is both wasteful and very misleading, so I worried no more about it; it occurred to me that they would more probably be guarding the potential escape routes than wasting their time hunting through the forest. After all, if I couldn't get off the island, what harm could I do them?

And I worried about that plane. Had it landed? I had been too deep inside the mountain to hear. They had regarded it as a potential enemy, so it almost certainly wasn't full of reinforcements for them, but I didn't want to count on that too heavily, just in case I had been misled by their apparent anxiety when it was first seen coming in.

And then again, had it been someone sent, perhaps, by the

127

police? Or by Teiho? Or Vanaa? The imponderables were too constant for intelligent deduction, so I assumed that I had to worry about perhaps another ten men or so, at a likely maximum, with the probabilities, which I always prefer to deal in, allowing for as few as five or six. For the moment.

And of these, surely at least half would be in the complex of tunnels? Or would they perhaps have sealed the entrance or entrances?

Again, imponderables.

So, as I ran fast back the way I had come, I decided that one way or another I would get out into the forest, where my own superior skills would doubtless be more favorable than the lack of knowledge I had of the underground system which they must know intimately.

In a matter of three minutes, running hard and silently in the dark, I was back at the cavern with the little cell that had been my prison. The obvious entrance to keep away from was the one I had entered by, until the odds were better.

The silence, now, was uncanny. I had not exactly expected to hear the sounds of pounding feet racing through the tunnels, but it was so quiet that I anticipated, instead, a waiting marksman at every turn. I expected, momentarily, that the lights would come on, and it occurred to me that if I were caught in a sudden glare of those bare bulbs, I would make far too good a target. I found the wires by groping for them, separate wires a few inches apart, positive and negative in the French style, so I ripped them out, touched the bare ends together, and knew by the sudden flash of bright red sparks that I had fused the whole circuit.

The flash had an added advantage: as soon as it flared, there was a burst of machine gun fire from some hundred yards away. I had expected it, of course, and was already flat on my back and rolling away long before the first bullets whined over my head, the ricochets screaming as they bounced off the passage walls.

At least one man up ahead then, and presumably no one behind me, unless he was not too worried about hitting one of his friends, which I thought unlikely. So, as soon as the burst was over, I jumped to my feet and raced back to where an updraft of air indicated a possible opening high above me. A few half-hearted bullets followed me, but they only served to pinpoint my adversary's movements; he was running toward me. I heard his footsteps clearly; he was not being nearly as careful as he ought to have been. And after that first fusillade—a panic reaction, probably—he was firing very low; it could only mean that they still wanted me alive, which made sense.

I tried to insinuate myself into Aimata's mind. 'My other name,' he had said, meaning, no doubt, did I know he was really Will Utter; and he *had* to find that out, and be absolutely certain about it. Because if I knew, then someone else probably knew as well, and there'd be a good chance of a massive descent of the law on the island. He was too much of a wanted man to leave a question like that daggling. It all pointed to the necessity, for them, of my continued survival. Good.

It occurred to me that I really needed a weapon of some sort. I do not normally use guns, because they play no part in the essence of the civilized behavior I believe in, but there were just too many of them for fooling around with. So I lay on my side, in absolute silence and darkness, and listened. I squeezed myself tight up against the tunnel wall, and waited, and at last he slowed down (searching more carefully now, I thought) and I heard his soft footfall not much more than fifty feet away.

Now was the time for him to use a flashlight, and it worried me that he might. But there's no target in the world like the beam of a lantern in a dark, eerie, underground maze of tunnels, and I was well aware that he wouldn't run the risk; after all, he would not be sure that I had not, somehow and somewhere, acquired a gun myself in the short time I had been at liberty.

Would he be afraid I might have done that? Or not? I could only guess again; so I decided to roll with it. The only thing to do, under the circumstances.

He was approaching very warily indeed now; had he seen me? I had even been careful to turn the luminous dial of my Rolex Oyster away, hiding even its faint gleam with my body.

And then, quite suddenly, I was sure I knew where he was, *precisely*. I pulled my knees up under me, very slowly and quietly, and then simply hurled myself forward at a shadow in the darkness, a patch of black against a deeper black, praying that my eyes weren't playing tricks on me, and that I wasn't heading shoulder first, at high speed, into an outcrop of coral that had unaccountably become a trifle more clear than the rest.

No, it was soft and resilient flesh, with thin bone behind it; a leg, just above the knee, maybe six inches or so lower than I'd have aimed for had I been able to see anything at all.

I found his ankle, gripped it hard, sat down, and pulled upward. I heard his leg snap in two, and I rolled over on top of him, hit him very hard with the flat of my hand across where I guessed the bridge of his nose ought to be, missing by more than an inch, grabbed a handful of long hair, twisted the head around, and belted him under the ear, just once. It was enough; he was out cold.

I ran my hands over his body and found a revolver that felt like a Webley .38, a dagger in a sheath at his belt, and a switchblade knife in his hip pocket; I also found the flashlight that he'd been afraid to use, a four-battery Ever-Ready of the kind used most frequently on board ship, a watertight rubber lantern.

I held it up high in one hand, as high as I could reach, and switched it on, only half-expecting some more gunfire; after all, if there were someone else back there, he could not be sure who was holding it, because my brief assault had been very nearly silent, save for a couple of grunts and the sound of a breaking bone.

And in its light, I saw two more of them, shielding their faces now from its bright beam, looking very angry indeed some eighty or ninety feet away.

Back-up men, then, following correctly at a reasonable distance, and angry because, as I'd suspected, they could not be sure who had won that brief battle, even if they'd heard it.

One of them roared: "Peabody! Put that goddam light out, what the hell are you doing?"

All you need, if you keep your wits about you, is one brief flash of light in the darkness, and you know exactly where everything else is in relation to your own position. I had not only seen them, I had seen the open way behind them, as well as a deep depression in the side of the funnel like a tiny cave six feet or so off the ground, about three feet high at its entrance, and nearly as broad, too; it might have been a subsidiary tunnel, part of the honeycomb pattern of most coral caves; I didn't really care. It was deep enough, quite obviously, to hide me very well indeed.

I also saw, briefly, where Peabody's Bren gun had fallen. I switched off the lantern, grabbed the Bren, fired a quick burst at nothing in particular—my own war of nerves now—and yelled: "It's not Peabody!"

I fired another quick burst, threw myself forward and up, grabbed the edge of the tiny cave, hauled myself up, and curled up tight inside it.

Now their lights went on, too, two powerful beams from their lanterns not only flooding the passage with white light but also showing me exactly where they were, what they were doing, what kind of threat they represented, and a good many other things as well.

But I was already under cover, curled up in a ball and ready for action, six feet or so above ground level and watching them racing toward where I had been. I dropped on them as they ran past me, pushing myself down with my feet, head, and shoulders first, my arms outspread. I caught them round their necks, and as we all fell to the sharp coral floor with the force of my weight and momentum, I had one head in the vise of each arm; I simply brought the two skulls together hard and fast, an irresistible force meeting an immovable object, and the sound of the sharp crack that emanated from one or both of them was awesome. They both went limp, and it was obvious that neither of them was going to recover very quickly, if at all.

Now, it was time to consolidate my position a little.

I pulled all the unconscious bodies together and stripped off their belts and their bootlaces. First of all, I tied each man's thumbs and his little fingers behind his body with one of his own laces. I then bundled them up, two on the floor and one on top of them, and put a long leather bootlace around their necks, not too tightly to inhibit their breathing, but tight enough to be sure they wouldn't roll around very much. I bound their six ankles tightly with a belt, looped a second and a third through their arms and fastened them, and by the time I was finished I was quite sure that there was no possible way for them to get free without some sort of help.

I used one of the lanterns, very carefully, to find a mass of broken coral and hid them behind it, and finally stuffed torn bits of their clothing into their mouths and bound them in place with lengths of cloth torn from one of their shirts. I piled a large heap of stones around them, and knew that they could stay there till kingdom come without being found and making a nuisance of themselves again.

And then, I simply walked quietly back to the opening through which I had originally entered the honeycomb of tunnels, and waited there for ten minutes by my Rolex, listening intently for any alien sound that might betray the presence of an observer.

There was none.

But I adamantly refused to believe that there was no one there. The crudest common sense dictated an assurance that there *had* to be at least one man covering the entrance, even if there were a dozen other ways out I might or might not have found; this one, they knew, I was aware of. And this knowledge would make it mandatory to have someone there; I was merely sorry that I could not locate him before taking the obvious action.

I pinpointed a target I had to reach, a thick-trunked *inocarpus fagiferus* tree that stood, alone and majestic, close to a wide clump of bread-fruit trees, with huge fruit hanging from them, which the Tahitians call *maiore*. I remembered that the local legend, a very charming one, stated that these plants sprang, in the remote past, from the body of a man who buried himself halfway into the ground, held out his arms, and waited until the gods turned him into a fruit-bearing tree to save his tribe from famine. More prosaically, I reasoned that here was excellent cover.

I got as close to the entrance as I dared, crouched low, and sprinted out of there, running as fast as I have ever run in my life. It was a little under two hundred yards, my favorite distance for a burst of speed.

I once coached Tommie Smith, probably the greatest 220-yard man of all time, shortly before he took the world record with 19.5 on the straightaway, and I was consciously trying to get as near to that figure as I could. And, for the first six seconds or so, I was beginning to think there was no one there after all. But then two shots sounded in rapid succession, and I heard the savage clip of bullets burying themselves in the mud at my feet; he was aiming low, once again, and now I was quite sure—they had orders I was not to be killed as yet.

I threw myself to the ground on one side and rolled over into the light cover of the poinsettias there, more to confuse his aim than anything else, and picked myself up and raced on. I must have slipped around the trunk of that *maiore* no more than twenty-two seconds after I had left the cave.

I turned, then, to see if I could catch a glimpse of him, and dropped out of sight quickly when I spotted the movement of the beautiful ginger plants where he had concealed himself. I backed away slowly, keeping the *inocarpus* tree between us as a shield, and wormed my way in among the bread-fruit trees, sliding along on my belly and elbowing my way through the dense cover.

He was behind me somewhere, but I didn't really care very much now; that constant low shooting was a comfort, and although a bullet in the leg is a nasty business, it's amazing how many slugs a man can fake and not have to worry too much if he's in reasonably good physical condition.

I climbed slowly and carefully to the top of the rise, keeping an eye on the sun and the shadows, and worked around to a point from which I could see the hangar.

It was an open-sided lean-to, with a concrete base, heavy coconut-trunks all around to support the thatched roof, and no walls. Inside, the helicopter stood alone; there was no sign at all of the other plane which Cresson had mentioned, and I didn't like that.

I turned and ran fast, keeping under the densest possible cover, over toward where the big house was. I wondered if Aimata would be there, or out with his men?

I was conscious, as I ran, that there was someone close behind me all the way; I could hear nothing, but there was just a *feeling*, a very uncomfortable one. I found some hard rocks to run on, jumping from one to another and leaving no prints, and then I found a high overhanging branch and pulled myself up into it, and concealed myself and waited.

It was the Fiji Islander, the man the Professor had identified as Kanaka. He was running incredibly fast, and in absolute silence, an animal moving in the jungle, and stalking me with considerable native skill. He ran past me fast and then stopped, too far away for me to take any sensible action; I wondered if he would return the moment he realized he'd lost the tracks. But the stones, flat slabs of basalt covered with creeper and ferns, were leading off to the right, and he followed them, moving more slowly now, swinging back in a wide circle the way he had come. Throughout, there had been not the slightest vestige of sound from him; it was almost uncanny. I gave him three minutes to get clear.

I dropped down from my perch and moved on toward the house.

I was glad to see it from this point of view, approaching it with all my senses alert; it was a very attractive place.

It covered a great deal of ground and was set on the edge of a very high. cliff, up which creepers were climbing—lantana, and honeysuckle, and *ipomoea pes-caprae*, all interspersed with *tiare* and frangipani and ginger and cashew trees and bananas and avocados and coconuts in a wild and glorious profusion, a blaze of color that was startling, exciting, and very gratifying indeed. There was a well-tended lawn around the building, with neat paths of gravel bordered in red brick, and a huge clump of the brilliant scarlet torch-ginger. I was glad to see that even the tall wooden poles on which the security lights were placed (and covering the whole of the grounds, I noticed) were covered with creepers.

The house itself was rather larger than I had thought. The main room, which I had already seen from the inside, was on the southern side, and two long extensions spread out to form a suntrap. There was a bamboo ladder leading up to the roof, and a platform there which might have served as a lookout post, but there was no one on it.

Now, it seemed to me, I had a plethora of weapons. I still had the Bren, the Webley, and the dagger that I had taken in the caverns. I concealed the machine gun under a clump of *mucuna*, sometimes called Flame of the Forest, hid the long sharp blade among the fronds of an *asplenium nidus*, checked that the revolver was fully loaded, tested the weight of its trigger (it had been haired, rather too much I thought), and went quickly to the front of the house.

He was there.

I heard his voice, raised in angry comment; "Well, I want him found, and that's all there is to it."

Two men then? Or more?

I was about to charge into the room through the window when

I heard the answer, a thin, crackling, metallic voice: "He's got to be up at the top, Mr. Aimata, he hasn't gone near the hangar, we've been watching."

It was a walkie-talkie. I heard him say: "Well, get on to it, or I'll skin you alive." I also heard the faint click as he switched off and the sound of it dropping onto a hard surface.

I vaulted over the sill of the window, in silence. His back was to me, and he was at the bar. He swung round and looked at the gun in my hand; his astonishment was acute, and there was an emotion on his face which I could only assume was fear. But he recovered quickly. He said, his eyes very hard: "My God, you've got your nerve."

I said: "Put your hands in the air, and turn around. Now!"

He hesitated; then slowly raised his arms and turned around. I didn't even wait for him to complete the movement; I ran the three quick steps that took me to him, in silence, and jabbed my hand hard into the nerve that leads to the trapezius. As he began to fall, I hit him again once over the occipital nerve, and knew that he'd he giving no more trouble for approximately a quarter of an hour. I slipped the gun into my belt, picked him up bodily, and slung him over my shoulder, vaulted with him out of the window, and ran fast.

In forty seconds flat I was in the forest again and climbing with him up to the top of the hill. Three minutes later, I had reached the edge of the cliff that overlooked the beach Captain Vanas had spoken of. I set my bundle down, found some *boehmaria* leaves and split them with my thumbnail to make raffia fiber, and tied his thumbs tightly together behind his back. Then I took off his Keds and tied his two big toes together as well—just enough to keep him from pulling any tricks as soon as he came to.

I laid the Webley within easy reach, in case of surprise, and waited.

He came round remarkably quickly, once another eight minutes had gone by, and he glared at me with so much venom on his face that had he not been bound I would have thought it wiser to put a bullet into him at once.

I said nothing. I picked him up by his ankles and walked over to the edge of the cliff with him. With one hand, I held him dangling head down over the rocks, four hundred feet below us, and now was the time to tell him.

I said: "Nothing would give me greater pleasure than simply to drop you, right now. Are we going to talk?"

His voice was harsh, tight with restrained fury, and with that, fear. I thought: At heart, like most of them, he's a coward.

He said: "We'll talk."

I held him there for a moment or two longer, letting him listen to the pounding of the waves on the rock.

I said: "Four hundred feet down, and the easiest thing in the world is to toss you down there."

He said furiously: "I said we'll talk, you mother..."

I swung him back up and over, and put him down close to the edge; I could have rolled him over by reaching out with a casual foot. He was shuddering.

First things first. I said: "Where's the other plane gone?"

"Papeete. For provisions."

"In the middle of all this fuss and bother?"

"We still have to live. We need gasoline for the generator."

I still didn't believe him, but I let it pass. "How many men do you have here?"

"A dozen."

"Uh-huh. If any of them comes up here, all you have to say is *hold it*. Otherwise, you get the first bullet."

We were on a tiny promontory of basalt rock, tucked in among a cluster of defensive boulders on the very edge of the mountain. The wind, slight but sufficient, was blowing from the landward side, and there was a good view across the open spaces anyone would have to cross to get to us; even the expert Kanaka could not sneak up on us here. Soon it would be dark again, and the dangers would lessen.

Aimata was recovering his confidence; had he ever really lost it? He said, in a voice so malevolent it was almost frightening: "The things I'm going to do to you, Cain, before you get killed off."

I shook my head. "No. I told you, the first sign of danger...you get a bullet right between the eyes."

I could hear the faint, distant drumming sound of the plane. I stared out to sea and watched it, a speck on the horizon, coming from the south, then turned back to Aimata. I said: "How many more SAM missiles do you have?"

No hesitation at all: "Nine more."

"Where did you get them?"

"I bought them, in Southeast Asia. It's not hard, if you have the right kind of money."

"And where do you keep them?"

"Go look for them, dead man."

Yes, the confidence was there, all right. I said, very quietly: "That was a fine old man you murdered."

I could read his mind, very easily, and he was thinking: *Okay, if you were going to kill me for it, you'd have done it by now.* He was gloating, and I found I was trembling, and he said offhandedly: "I don't need him anymore, his job's done."

The plane was still a long way off, but his mood had changed with the sound of it. I didn't like it. I said, jerking a head seaward: "Reinforcements?"

"Something like that."

Another lie; he was getting far too sure of himself, and I said idly: "You've got a trump card up your sleeve, haven't you?"

He nodded slowly; his eyes: were gleaming, his hard mouth was twisted in a tight, wry grimace.

I said; "A few more bags of the insects lying around somewhere. Where are they?"

"En route to where they can do me the most good."

"And where's that?"

"Try beating it out of me. Let's see if you're any good at it."

"I just might."

He was grinning now, a sly and malevolent grin. "Why don't you ask me about Hawkins again? It's time you had something to laugh at."

I thought: Anything to gain time, what's he up to? I found some hibiscus growing wild; the type known as *tiliaceus* which has a long and stringy bark to it, slender and pliable and immensely strong; it's used locally for fishing lines and nets. I began stripping off the long, fibrous strands, starting at the top of the stems and pulling down to the base, the only way it can be removed. He watched me all the time; now it was his turn to wonder what was going on. I sat down again beside him, began to braid the fiber, and said: "All right, what happened to Hawkins?"

He was laughing again, in spite of everything; I could almost admire his complete control, whatever horrible little tricks he had up his sleeve. He said, very clearly and deliberately: "He made a mistake, just a simple one, not at all like the mistake you're making now. He crashed that goddam plane and gave us away, or might have done. We cut him up, Cain, into little pieces. You know what for?" He laughed out loud. "You know what *oura miti* is? Maybe you call it lobster. Eats anything, has a preference for fresh meat. So we cut him into little pieces and used him as bait, you should have seen the catch we got, twelve lobster baskets full to bursting. Still a lot of them in the freezer if you're hungry."

His eyes were on the plaited hibiscus. He said tightly: "Strangulation, is that it?"

I said: "As a second best, it might do. But it's not what I have in mind."

The laugh had gone now, and he was frightened, the kind of man who fears the unknown, who likes to know what's happening even if he can't control it. He said viciously: "By Christ, Cain, you're building yourself more trouble than you'll know what to do with."

"Then maybe I ought to throw you over the edge right now, what do you think? What was that plane that interrupted our first conversation?"

He said sullenly: "I don't know. A tourist, it flew off again."

"Came in handy, though, didn't it?"

He glared at me and said nothing.

Two, three more minutes before his Warrior would land? It was quite clear out there now, flying very low. It occurred to me that he might perhaps fly over our little promontory, so I dragged Aimata deeper under cover of the rocks and crouched down beside him. I held out the long cord I had plaited, about twenty feet of it now. I said: "You know what this stuff is?"

He said tightly: "I know."

"The fisherman use it, for their nets, their canoes. Strong as nylon rope. Exactly how strong, I've no way of knowing. What's your weight? A hundred and seventy-five?"

He wouldn't answer, and I said: "At a guess, the breaking point of this ought to be around two hundred pounds, maybe a little more. If it's much less than that...well, we'll find that out, won't we?"

He knew, now, and that fear was in his eyes again. He said, stuttering: "By Christ, Cain, I'm gonna hear you...hear you screaming your mother head off."

I tore a piece off his pretty shirt, stuffed it tightly into his mouth, and bound it in place. He tried to shout obscenities at me, but very little sound came out. I made a slipknot on one end of my improvised rope and fastened it round his ankle. I tied the other end firmly to a protruding root, and eased him gently over the edge. The rope held, as I was fairly sure it would, and he hung there, ass upward, ten feet down, gasping. I said gently: "It probably won't break unless you struggle too much, so I should keep deathly still, if I were you."

There was no sound from him. I stood up and looked across to the landing strip, five hundred yards away and four hundred feet below me. A man down there was raising a windsock; it was the Fiji Islander, out of my hair at last. Three other men, their rifles loosely held, were with him.

Now was the time to find out just what his trump card was; he had seemed too damn sure of it for my liking. I climbed slowly and carefully down the steep cliff, traversing to one side where the going was easier. I could hear the plane but not see it, and it seemed to have changed direction; it was climbing again, the roar of the motor bursting suddenly out as it rounded the point.

I heard it in time and was clinging by my fingernails under an overhang as he swept past me, and I was sure that I could not be seen. I swung myself to one side and grabbed at a ledge, and hung there, and now I could see the landing strip; the windsock had swung round, and the pilot was changing his approach direction, wheeling up high over the promontory above me and circling. He came back close to its edge, dipped his wings ones, and headed for the strip.

I wished to hell I had a rope, it would have been quicker. I was still two hundred feet up, perched like an ant over a void, and by the time I reached the bottom, the plane was just landing. I ran fast to an outcrop of coral, washed by the surf, and threw myself behind it and watched.

The plane taxied up to the hangar, and Kanaka ran to it and flung open the door. The sun was low on the horizon now, the vast stretch of water ablaze with a crimson so brilliant and universal it seemed the whole world was on fire. Every kind of red in the spectrum was there, in great livid streaks—carmine, scarlet, crimson, ruby, fuchsia, damask, and magenta, with layers of saffron, orange, cadmium red, and gold above them. The purples and the grays were beginning to blossom out as two men jumped down out of the plane, and then a third; he was the surly young Tahitian boy I had seen at Faaa airport when we'd made the trip to Faatua, and he had a huge revolver stuck into his belt now.

And in a moment a slight, elegant, and somehow helpless-seeming figure was roughly shoved out.

She fell to the ground, and one of them bent down and lugged her to her feet, and slammed his open hand across her face.

It was Tiare.

The flowers were gone from her hair now, and the ivory-colored sheath of her dress was torn. Even at this distance, she seemed to be shuddering.

One of the men from the Warrior was talking urgently with Kanaka, pointing. The Fiji Islander turned and stared up toward the top of the cliff, and then he was racing back toward the forest, an animal in rapid motion. I watched him barreling in among the trees.

CHAPTER 10

I knew at once that they had spotted Aimata.

How do you keep a man captive, on his own home ground, when you have to be someplace else? It would have been simpler, no doubt, if I had killed this dangerous and evil man when I had the chance, but I'm not ruthless enough to take the law into my own hands; I can judge, but I won't be jury, too, and certainly not the executioner. I thought: I made a mistake, well, we're all human.

And it occurred to me: What a frightening thought that is too.

But the trick is not to hope wistfully for rays of sunshine, but intelligently to seek them out and turn them to good account, so I put the minus behind me and concentrated on the plus.

They had taken Tiare as hostage.

Their mistake? I assumed so. I imagined that they really wanted Maite, and that the young Tahitian who had seen us embracing had come to quite the wrong conclusion. Even so, Tiare could hardly be sacrificed just because she wasn't as close to me as Maite, my lover.

It seemed that the plus was a considerable one, for a very simple reason. In order to turn her presence to account, they had to let me *know* that they had her captive; they could hardly be sure, or even guess, that I knew this already. And so, there was still a certain amount of time to play with, I had to be certain that they could not communicate to me the value of their trump card. Until that time, she was safe.

And how were they going to try to do that? A man is hiding, he has to be told something; ergo, he must be found, or else he's wandering around in blissful ignorance of the fact that they have an arm-twister up their sleeve. Their thinking had to be: *Once Cain knows we've got her, he'll come running, sacrificing himself for her; that's the kind of man he is.*

And they were right, of course.

I thought to myself: I must get her out before they find a way to let me know they've got her, and that might not be very long. An hour, or more, until the absolute darkness I needed so desperately. I forced myself to wait in patience.

And I still had to check to make absolutely sure, even though it was a reasonable assumption that they'd be expecting me to do just that. I worked my way up that damned cliff again, a half-mile to one side now from where I'd left him dangling in space, cursing his heart out and planning all kinds of horrible retribution for me. It wasn't an easy climb, and it took me fifteen minutes before I reached the top, half-expecting to find a foot ready for driving into my face.

But there was only silence.

I crawled on my belly among the rocks. My own planning was militating against me now—I had chosen a spot where no one could creep up on me unseen, and I couldn't get close in either. I wormed my way over to the big clump of *macuna* and found the Bren gun still there. I had left a minute piece of fiber lying across its stock, and it was also still there. They hadn't found it, then; not that I had supposed they would.

There was that fascinating golden light all over the western extremity of the island now, a soft luminescence that surely all the gods in their seven heavens were admiring; Taaroa, Oro, Tane, Ta, and Maui, and the sly Hiro, too, with his band of thieves, looking down on the gold dust that shone all over the land and envying us poor mortals our closer contact with it.

I thought: I need Pai the great warrior now, with his mighty spear and his terrible indignation.

Twenty minutes to darkness: I *had* to be sure.

I saw a hawk circling over the promontory, and I watched it carefully. It came in closer and was about to land on the very edge of the cliff when it screeched angrily and flew off, wheeling away fast.

Someone was there, then; how many?

I eased my way cautiously over, a yard, three, ten. Nothing from this point of vantage either. At a guess, then, he—or they—had decided to use ears instead of eyes. It's the old argument: if you can see a man, it's a possibility that he'll be able to see you too; but if you're *listening* instead... No one was going to risk peering around the edge of a rock; it never works except on television.

Unless... Were they behind me? In the forest?

No. The hawk had indicated otherwise. I got off my belly (a hard position to arise from if you're in a hurry) and onto all fours. I crawled carefully across the open space, watching every last shadow for any sign of an alien presence. The silence was quite unbroken, acute, out of this world; even the wash of the waves on the rocks far below seemed muted, the still time of the evening.

I found a tiny gully to crawl in, and eased myself along, infinitely slowly, not a sound of any sort. It was no more than forty inches or so wide, and perhaps a foot deep, not very regular, but widening here and there, with a deeper depression or two as well, an old watercourse, perhaps, sloping gently down toward the edge of the cliff; in heavy rains, a stream would gush over here like a torrent, a faucet turned on and off at the will of the weather.

I thought of a local characteristic—in the hotels, all the imported staff are always turning faucets off, because the Tahitians turn them on and leave them running; why should they not, indeed? Water is from the gods, and it's free, so who has to conserve it?

I tried to work out my precise position. How long was it since I had left the forest? The darkness was closing in, another five minutes, perhaps, to go. I was no more than fifty feet from where Aimata was either dangling upside down or not. Would *they* assume that I could not get so close without being detected? Would their senses be focused, so to speak, on the distance where a sound, a movement, would first betray my position? I was sure they would.

There's comfort in getting under the enemy's guard.

And then, as I snaked my way along the little gully, a hand came stealing over its lip, a matter of inches from my nose, so slowly and carefully that I could only stare at it. It was a sloth of a movement, so deliberate and silent that it startled me, just a small button of flesh creeping... But not a hand, a foot. It twisted round, very gently, slow-motion so reduced that it puzzled me. Two toes, then three, then the instep and a black and calloused sole.

The movement stopped. I knew what it was.

He was lying on his belly above me, and a foot was going to sleep, so he had eased it into activity again. How long had he been lying there, in absolute, inert silence? I could have opened my mouth and bitten into his great toe.

And then, the foot was whipped away out of my sight, and again, I knew what had happened; he had *smelled* me.

The gun was an encumbrance now; I needed silence. I leaped to my feet, wondering how many others there might be hidden there, and not having very much chance to debate what I could do if they were there in force. He was on top of me before I had fully risen; it was Kanaka. He came at me with his left arm outstretched and his fingers spread out toward my eyes, jabbing furiously; but I was watching the right arm, the hand swinging round and up and clutching a machete. He was like a ballet dancer, or a Japanese wrestler, balanced on one leg and flailing his limbs with a speed and poetry that was fascinating. I saw the blade coming up, and had time to notice that it was not even shining, the steel rubbed with onion juice, perhaps, to rob it of its sheen.

I twisted round and threw myself onto my face, my spread hands hitting the hard ground first, and kicked back with both feet, very hard. I thought: I can catch that blade right between the legs if I'm not careful. But there was little else I could do in the time I had. My feet caught him in the gut and he went sprawling, and he was on his feet, again so fast I couldn't believe it, backing off now and swinging the machete again, still underarm, a deadly way to use it; it can rip the belly open from the groin to the chest, and still—if he's competent—leave you alive and praying to be dead.

He was crouched, swinging his weapon round and round in that vertical, defensive circle; but to harm me, he'd have to come in closer. His black eyes were on mine, unwavering, waiting for me to take mine off him. I wondered why he didn't start yelling; was it a matter of personal pride? He'd run from our last encounter and had to make up for it.

He was even grinning at me, prancing and whirling his blade like a dervish. He said, his voice thick and rasping: "You move good, Mr. Cain, very quiet."

So he wanted to make conversation. I said: "You hear good, too, Kanaka."

The grin broadened. "You too good to hear. I smell the oil on your gun. You better pick it up, start shooting."

I thought: You bastard, once I take my eyes off you...

I crouched down low, patting the ground around me and behind me, seeking the touch of its cold metal. I must have been very close to finding it, because he let go the machete at just the right moment, and it came at me like an arrow, or Pai's thrown spear, so fast that it sliced through the leather of my belt and a quarter-inch into my side as I spun to avoid it. I heard it smash into the rocks behind me. And then he was on me, his immensely powerful hands at my throat, the hands of a man whose every waking moment is physical; he was taking the personal challenge at last, sure of his own strength and scorning mine. They clamped around my neck like a vise.

It's easy to talk of being strangled, and to imagine it as a painful and slow process. It's painful, all right, but it's not slow. Those thumbs were pushing my windpipe out through the cervical vertebrae, and in three seconds I would have been dead. There was only one thing I could do, and I did it.

I rolled over backward, put a foot in his stomach, and kicked, I knew I would have to kick hard; this was no amateur I was dealing with. Even so, his plump and overweight body went flying up into the air, and in theory it should have broken his grip and sent him flying over my head to break his fool neck when he landed. It didn't. Those extraordinary hands, the hands of a gorilla, were just too damn strong; they seemed permanently attached to my throat, as though no force in nature could break his hold.

I had only a moment of consciousness left. There were already blinding flashes of yellow and red in front of my eyes. I clenched my fists, arched my body back, and drove up between his arms with all the strength I had. His head snapped back as I caught his jaw, and I let my fists go on and up, and then threw my arms out wide.

That did it. The steel fingers tore out of my neck, and that's when he made his mistake. I do believe that if he had gone for my eyes again, he would have taken me, and I would never have lived it down. Instead, he threw himself to one side and slid along the ground right past me, and grabbed up the Bren. He pointed it at me and pulled the trigger, and there was a look of acute astonishment on his face when it didn't fire. Did he really believe I'd have left it there with a round in the breech? I suppose he hadn't even thought of it.

He needed both hands now, one to work the breech, and he knew he'd never make it. He swung the gun instead, a crushing blow at my head. I sidestepped it and hit him so hard on the point of his jaw that I heard a bone break; I wondered if it were mine, or his.

My God, he was indestructible. I could only admire the way he turned on his broad, flat feet, and his cunning, too. He came at me again, and he was trailing the machete once more, beginning to swing it up and hard; God alone knows how he managed to retrieve it.

I found I was on the ground again, and did not know how I'd gotten there, and he was on top of me, jabbing at my eyes once more with one hand and slicing down with his blade in the other. I twisted my head away and drove my fingers into the axillary muscles, paralyzing his arm momentarily, and heard the machete drop. I chopped him hard on the throat and tried to stagger to my feet, and I realized that he was helping me, dragging me to the edge of the cliff, and I thought: My God, this just won't do.

I brought my knee up into his balls, stepped back, and drove my fist into him, not caring now just where my blow landed and knowing this was almost the last effort I had in me, until I could drag in some air.

I felt his belly collapse under the force of my blow, heard the wind go out of him in a rush. He fell on his back and rolled over, and when he stood up, he had that damned bush-knife again and was raising it over his head for the killing blow. He was right on the edge of the cliff.

Indestructible? He was a reincarnation of the great Pai himself, and I was sorry for what I had to do. I dived down under the blow and rolled over onto my back, and shoved up with both my feet, one under his armpit and the other to the jaw; it was the last positive effort I could make.

I heard no scream; there was just the dull and final sound of his body hitting the rocks below.

And then it was dark, pitch dark. I was beginning to breathe again, and I looked at my watch and realized that I had been out cold for fifteen minutes. I thought: Well, at least one question is answered; up here on the little promontory, he was the only one.

I climbed to my feet and stretched my limbs. The pain in my throat was appalling, and I could hear my own breathing, a horrible, rasping sound, interspersed with a broken choking. But the light was coming back, not much of it to be sure, but a faint gray tinge to the night. I stumbled back into the forest, and fell down again, and then I rolled over and vomited and felt a little better.

I moved deeper in among the vegetation, and in ten minutes or so found what I was searching for—the sickly sweet scent of the *centrana lutica*, a weed growing in wild abundance here. I saw the pale luminescence of the white flowers, and tore off some leaves and chewed on them; they are rich in intocostrin, a substance somewhat similar to curare and sometimes confused with it; not exactly an anesthetic, but a muscle-relaxant of some potency. Properly, of course, it should be administered intravenously; but in another five minutes the frightening pain was going; in still another five, I spat out the bitter residue and felt capable again of facing whatever might be waiting for me.

Very slowly, my feet feeling like lead now, I worked my way back to the edge of the cliff and assured myself of what I already knew.

Aimata was gone. There was only my length of braided hibiscus there to remind me that I had goofed.

I turned away and moved on slowly toward the house.

There was a strange feeling of *emptiness*.

First, the silence of the forest gave the impression that no one had ever lived in it, that same feeling of complete solitude you have when you land on a tiny island you know to be quite uninhabited; there's an almost uncontrollable urge to yell, to shout out at the top of your voice, just to assure yourself that there is, indeed, the unaccustomed attitude of absolute isolation.

I remembered that long ago, on that first trip to the islands, I had experienced just this strange sensation.

I had been sailing with an old and half-forgotten friend, past a tiny atoll which was uninhabited, and on the spur of the moment had dived overboard and swum the seven miles or so to the beach. My friend, en route to Manihi for his own purposes—he was working with the pearl cultivators there, setting up the underwater complex for the oysters—was to pick me up on his return later on in the day. And being so completely alone, I had fallen prey to that aberrant impulse; I had undressed and had raised my voice to the heavens, shouting out inanities for no reason at all, no coherence to them, just delighting in the unaccustomed sensation that there was no one around for a million miles or more to hear me. I must have cavorted and yelled my head off for three full minutes before two astonished and quite alarmed faces popped up from behind a rock: two tourists from the Club Mediterranée over on Moorea, come here for a solitary picnic. It spoiled the whole episode.

But here, the feeling was not quite the same; there was the same loneliness, but a menace was added to it, the menace of ten, fifteen, maybe twenty people all hunting me down in the silence and the darkness, with intent for mayhem.

Even when I saw the hangar, at a distance, with its bright lights on, and no one in sight, I knew that there were hidden enemies there, too.

I ran on. I was moving fast now, slipping from cover to cover among the trees and the rocks and seeking out any possible condition I might turn to advantage.

How were they going to let me know they had Tiare?

I found the little wharf where the boats were tied up, all bathed in incandescent lights and no one in sight; how many hidden rifles were watching it? I crawled over the sharp coral and into the dark water, and swam out to sea to study it better.

There was a splendid ocean-going yacht, a Feadship 165-foot cruiser, a handsome and solid-looking craft with a range, I imagine, of something like seven thousand miles, beautifully painted and obviously maintained in the immaculate condition it served. I liked its lines—not overly fast, perhaps, but very seaworthy indeed.

There was also a gorgeous little 36-foot Laguna, the high-speed diesel sports cruiser by the looks of her, with the twin Ammarine AT-637 turbocharged V8 diesels which would ram her through the seas all day at better than twenty knots; about a 15-foot beam, and I'd say 23,000 lbs. displacement, and altogether a very attractive little speedster. There was a third boat there, too, a little Westsail 32 fiberglass double-ender. Two small dinghies were tied up at the wharf, arid there were three pirogues there as well.

Most of all, there were the lights, great blazing beacons that made it quite impossible for anyone to approach within two or three hundred feet without being seen at once. I swam out to the reef and worked my way around it to the other side on the tiny peninsula where the trees and the bushes came down to the lapping surf. I made my way stealthily toward the house, up the steep slope that led to its little plateau.

It was not easy to move in silence through the forest. There were no paths of any kind here, and I was forcing my way as quietly as possible, which meant very slowly, through great clumps of a hundred differing species of plants, some of which rustled uncomfortably as I moved among them, I stopped every few minutes and listened.

Once, I beard very soft voices, no more than a dozen yards away from me; I lay still and listened.

A whisper so low I could hardly hear it: "At the top, he's got to be at the top."

"If he is, Kanaks will find him."

"I hate it. I hate everything about it. What do you suppose happened to Peabody?"

"What the hell happened to the others?"

"Yeah, I don't like it."

"Well, if Kanaka don't get him, Ulricson will." There was a little giggle. "You ever see that guy move around in the dark?"

"You ever see him work with a blade?"

"Sshhh..."

I heard them moving cautiously away, and when the sounds had died away altogether, I climbed up a steep bank and down the other side, and knew that I was close to the house now. I crouched under a clump of yellow trumpet-vine, listening, watching, waiting.

And, I must admit, wondering what the next step was.

And then, in the silence, something hit me under the ear, a tight, hard, little object that did no damage at all. I rolled over fast, crouched down ready, and stared into the dark where it had come from. Another tiny object hit me in the face, and I caught it—a small seashell.

And then, the voice, very quiet indeed, a zephyr of a sound: "Cain?"

I did not answer. I could see the body taking shape now, detaching itself from the darkness, moving toward me. In the moonlight, the blond hair gleamed, and then the white teeth, and the whisper came again: "Cain? It's me. Auguste..."

Auguste? I should have known they'd come looking for me. I thought: My God, the odds are lessening at last.

He sat himself down beside me, put a hand on my shoulder, put his mouth very close to my ear, and said: "Vanaa is here, and Maite too...and Teiho."

I said: "Maite? You're mad!"

He grinned in the darkness, "She insisted that she's the only official authority here. Don't worry, she's well-guarded. Three of Vanaa's friends, pearl divers, tough bastards, they'll stay with her."

I said: "Where's the ketch, for God's sake?"

"Standing two miles offshore, no lights. We swam in, all of us, What goes on?"

"They've got Tiare."

"Oh my God."

"They think she's my girl."

"I see. Where is she?"

"I can only guess. Probably in the house. That's where I was heading."

"Good, good, we'll get her out."

"Any guns?"

He raised his two huge hands in front of my face, "What do we need guns for? We have these."

"The whole island's lousy with machine guns, rifles, they've even got some missiles."

"Jesus..."

"Ssshhh."

He had heard it, too: a man moving across our front, fifty feet off and swinging round away from us. When he had gone, Auguste touched my arm and whispered: "A little further back I passed a small cave, we can talk better there."

"All right."

He crept off, moving admirably well, and I followed him. It was not a cave, merely a deep depression in the side of a small knoll, but well-shielded. We eased ourselves in, and I said; "All right, where are the rest of them?"

"Maite and the pearl divers are at the foot of the cliff on the west, waiting. Vanaa and I were making a tour of the island, hoping we might find something interesting."

"Like what?"

He grinned. "I found you, didn't I? I guessed you'd be at the house, a prisoner. What do we do now?"

They answered the question for us. Out of the darkness came a clear, loud, and metallic voice, booming at us out of the night. It was Aimata. Auguste gripped my wrist and we listened.

"*Cain? This is Aimata, I have a young woman with me. She needs your help. We are at the house.*" It was followed by another voice, high-pitched and terrified: "*Please...please...help me...*" And then a terrifying scream that tore through my guts like a sharp knife. I felt Auguste's grip tighten. He said harshly: "Tiare."

"I know. That's what I've been waiting for."

The voice came booming at us again, from another direction now, farther away: "*Cain? This is Aimata. I have a young woman with me...*"

Another voice, another direction: "*Cain? This is Aimata, I have...*"

Another, and another, and another. From all over the island, crisscrossing the forest and the beach and the mountain, the voices were at odds with one another, a dozen speakers set up on the intercom and blaring out their threats. They bounced back off each other, a monstrous cacophony of electronic sound.

"*Cain?... I have...Aimata... She needs... Cain?... Your help... young woman... Cain?... A young woman...*" And interspersed with it all, that terrible, helpless screaming.

I think it was the scream that became the turning point. What they had done to her, I could only guess. They had held her in front of the mike, and had taped a scream that was livid and horrifying...and urgent. How had they forced it out of her? I found I was trembling.

But now was the time to put all emotion behind me. I forced myself to be calm, and calculating, and careful, and all the time that terrible noise went on, and on, and on... It boomed at us from the darkness, the *tupapaus* finally at work.

I said urgently to Auguste: "How long to get to Vanaa?"

"This will bring him back to the rendezvous at once. Fifteen minutes."

"Then on to the house?"

"Another five."

"We'll need every weapon we have. A diversion in twenty minutes."

The voices were hurling themselves at us, triumphantly, from all directions, the sounds reverberating back and forth, every speaker on the island dragged out at the end of cables, the amplifier turned up to maximum. "*Cain?... She needs your help...*" The screaming. "*Please help me... I have a young woman with me... This is Aimata...*" The screaming again.

Well, they'd found a way to let me know.

I gave Auguste the Bren gun and the revolver, and he slipped away; then I was running fast, quite openly, down to the house, making no attempt now—why should I?—to hide my movements.

I leaped over the hedge and ran across the neat lawn, and ran around to the front of the house, and threw myself over the sill of the open window.

And there they were, waiting for me, a roomful of them, all armed to the teeth and looking as though they knew, at last, that all their troubles were over. Ulricson, the surly young Tahitian, and four others.

And Aimata.

CHAPTER 11

I knew all that it was necessary to know about Willard Fest, and Will Utter, and even about Aimata.

Nonetheless, the sight of the venom on his face shocked me beyond imagining. The darkly handsome, rugged face, with its lines of pain and violence deeply cut, was a smoldering cancer of fury. He was trembling.

Two men were behind me, moving like cats, with their rifles pointed and their fingers on the triggers; Ulricson was close by Aimata, his revolver, a Colt .45, pointed straight at my gut, low down where a bullet could do the most harm. A fourth gunman was in a very sensible place indeed—high up in the rafters where I could not possibly get to him quickly. For a moment, the picture held, and then Aimata said, his voice shaking: "Jason...now."

Behind him a door opened, and a fifth man was there, a tall, well-built man in his early thirties, very straight-backed and military-looking, with a shaven head and cold, pale, blue eyes.

He was holding Tiare. One of her wrists was twisted up behind her back, and he was gripping it, his own fist twisted in her long hair so that her arm was tied in position; his other hand held a Smith and Wesson revolver, a .38, under her chin. The hammer was cocked back; I kept perfectly still.

Outside, the booming of the sound system was still thundering out its message, and that fearful scream had an added potency now; I could not see her eyes, because her head was pulled far back, but I

153

could sense the terror in her.

As quietly as I could manage, I said: "I've got the message."

Two more men slipped into the room, youngsters, both of them. One was tall and thin-hipped but with a very creditable chest on him and excellent biceps under his bulging denim shirt; he looked sullen, a chip on his shoulder, the kind of kid who thinks he can take on the world armed with nothing but arrogance and callousness. The other was big too, heavier built, with a prematurely half-bald head and hair around its sides that ruffled over his ears. They were both armed with revolvers, and they knew what to do; they'd already been drilled. Not saying a word, they handed their guns to Aimata, who held them both steadily on me. These two moved toward me, very cautiously, one on each side each took hold of an arm, and I went with them. What else could I do? I did not take my eyes off Tiare, nor off Jason's finger on the trigger; I wondered if the spring had been overhaired as it was on the one I'd given Auguste. Incongruously, I wondered if I should have told him about it.

The booming sounds of the speakers went on, and Aimata said to no one in particular: "Turn that mother off, for Christ's sake." The young Tahitian ran quickly to a switch over the bar and flipped it, and thank God, it stopped.

I was pushed up against the central pillar that held up the wide roof, a smooth pole of polished wood. I felt my arms being pulled back, a rope around my wrists, and I said: "It's not really necessary, you know. After all, I came here of my own free will."

Aimata looked at Jason. "There, where he can see her clearly."

Jason moved over with Tiare, a few feet to one side, a spectacle for me, and Aimata said: "First, a personal pleasure. Just keep your eyes on the girl."

He moved up in front of me, studied my face for a moment, and then pulled back his fist and drove it hard into my solar plexus. I tensed all my muscles, and took it. He pounded at me for three minutes without stopping, the sweat pouring down his face, raining blow after blow with fists like iron anvils, at my chest, my groin, my face, choosing one spot and hammering away at it, and then moving on to another. And he was still trembling when he stopped.

I had slumped down to the floor, and the pains were shooting from the soles of my feet to the top of my head, and I heard him say: "Now we can talk, and decide which way you'd like to die."

He looked across at Tiare, glowering, and turned back to me and said: "No sound from you, Cain? I want to hear you yelling, I want to see the pain on your face. I want to settle a score." He corrected himself: "No. *Begin* to settle it. It'll take a long, long time, and this is just for my personal pleasure."

He went to the bar, picked up a drink, and gulped it down, and turned to Jason again. "Give her to me."

Stolidly obedient, his brutal face unchanging, Jason slipped his thumb onto the hammer, his trigger finger tightening, and let it down on the chamber. He tucked the gun into his belt and shoved hard with his other hand. Tiare went sprawling into Aimata's open arms, and fell at his feet; there was just time for her to throw me an anguished glance, her eyes wide with terror, and then he picked her up and gave her the same treatment he had just given me, slapping her hard across the face, the breasts, the shoulders, anywhere that his blows happened to land, driving her into the bar and pounding at her relentlessly, and not stopping until she had fallen to the floor, unconscious, lying there with her legs tucked under her, the pale ivory of her dress a torn rag now. There was blood on her face, coming from a corner of her mouth, and the amber of her skin was a solid mass of livid bruises. And then he kicked her, three times, savagely.

Panting, he pulled up a chair and sat in it heavily, facing me. For a long time, he just stared at me, and he said at last: "A meat hook, I'm gonna sling you up on a meat hook. I figure it will take you three days to die. Maybe more. We'll see how long it takes."

He pointed a finger at Tiare's still body. "She's still alive, Cain. There's maybe a chance she'll stay alive, if you talk."

I said: "Make me a promise you'll let her go."

He laughed shortly, a dry, incisive sort of sound with no humor in it at all. "A promise? You expect me to believe you'll take my word? A promise? I can't remember the last time I kept a promise."

I put the words into his mouth. "I have no choice. It's a chance I have to take."

"Yeah, a chance, that's what it is. It's a hope you can't pass up, isn't it? Because otherwise...she's gonna be right there beside yon, slung up on a tree with a hook through her leg, right here, that nice soft inside bit of her thigh. Okay, take it or leave it, and there's nothing else you can do, I'll make you one of my famous promises. I promise you I'll maybe, just *maybe, think* about letting her go when I've finished with her. If I feel like it. If you really tell me everything I want to know. Take it, or leave it. You want better than that?"

"Yes, I do."

"You won't get it. And then, we'll go get the other one, what's her name? Maite? And we'll do the same to her. But there's still a chance that we won't, if you talk. So let's watch a dying man clutch at a straw. Because that's all it is, Cain—a straw. Just a chance I'll lay off both of them."

Tiare was groaning faintly now, coming around. He said: "You want to watch me go to work on her again? A few other things you can watch me do, too. She turned me down once, did you know that? Now she don't have much choice. You want to watch?"

It was hard to fight the coma. I wondered how much time had already gone by. I said: "All right, I'll take the straw. What is it you want to know?"

There was just a moment of hesitation. I knew what was coming, beyond any doubt, the one thing he had to know. He said: "Ever hear of a guy named Utter?"

I didn't want to answer too fast, not too deliberately. I frowned, took a deep breath, and said: "Utter?"

He was studying my face intently. "Will Utter. The name mean anything to you?"

I thought again, a long time, and he said: "Well?"

I said: "Yes, I remember. Will Utter, back in... In eighteen hundred and something, he was...the man who got killed on the Matterhorn...a climbing accident."

He said impatiently: "No, another one."

I shook my head. "The only Utter I ever heard of...what the hell does he...have to do...with all this?"

He said again: "Another one. Same name."

"No."

"You're lying, Cain. I'll have to go to work on her."

I said: "For Christ's sake! If I knew him, I'd tell you!"

"Yes. Maybe."

He stared at me for a long time, the effort of a man who's sure he knows the truth when he sees it; it's a common enough failing, in all of us. And I think he was convinced. He said: "All right, you don't know him. Who else knows about my island?"

"I didn't know myself until I crashed here."

"But you suspected."

"Sure I did."

"Why?"

Now it was my turn to play tricks. My head was pounding, my chest felt caved in, and I wondered if the damage to my throat would be permanent. There was caked blood at my waist from the Fiji Islanders machete, and Aimata's savagery had opened up the wound again; I could feel warm blood running down over my hip.

Incongruously, the image of my first brush with Kanaka on Tahiti came back to me, a vivid picture of brilliant flowers and greenery, and a deadly little blowgun. A man from the jungle in his own element, moving like a predator in uncanny silence, stalking his prey on orders from this man.

Aimata shoved a foot into my groin again and shouted: "Well?"

I said, mumbling and feeling a little surprised at how easy it was to feign incoherence: "Kanaka told me."

His astonishment was a sight for sore eyes, and a source of great gratification. It was a new trend in the conversation, and I wondered how long I could make it last. That fine, chiseled Aztec face was a study in bewilderment and anger, a strange combination. His lips were very tight. "Kanaka?"

"Sure. He tried a comic little blowgun on me, the kind they used over in...the Fiji Islands once. I held his head under water a couple of times...and finally, he told me."

It was an explosion. "Told you *what?*"

"He told me...his name. Kanaka."

"And?"

I mumbled again, and groaned, and found it easy, and be shouted: "What else?"

"I asked him...who had sent him to get me, and he said...he

157

said...he said..." I let it trail away, dropped my head on my chest, and waited for the blow. But it didn't come; I wondered if he were thinking: *I have to keep this man alive a little longer.*

He moved his chair a trifle closer, and leaned forward, and said very quietly: "You're gonna tell me, sooner or later. All I got to do is start on the girl again. Any time you say, Cain."

"Okay, okay. He tried to act tough, till he was sure I was going to drown him. He said a man named Fest had sent him, Willard Fest."

"He gave in pretty easy." He still wasn't convinced but he was wondering.

I said: "No. It took a long time, a long time...I had to pump the water out of his lungs, twice, and then...threaten to do it again. He said...he said Willard Fest had sent him, and I asked him about Professor Cresson." He was a beaten man, Kanaka, and he knew it, he knew there was only one way to save his hide, and he told me. He said you were backing Cresson, financially, in some experiments with insects that...that Kanaka didn't know too much about. He said: 'Go to Rangitefara if you don't believe me, find out for yourself.' And that's what I was doing when...when you shot my plane down."

He muttered: "It checks, it checks."

But he refused to admit it, like a mirror that accepts an image but can't hold it once the object has gone—a convex mirror that magnifies out of all proportion and then loses everything once it is turned away. He was fighting the belief, knowing, that there was no other explanation at all, and when it overcame him he leaped up and slammed a foot into me again. He shouted: "I don't believe you! I won't believe you! It's a lie!"

I gasped and said: "So ask him. You'll soon find out."

He swore and shouted at Jason: "Get that goddam savage in here!"

Good. So they hadn't found his body. How could they? It was almost dark when he went over the edge. I thought about the tide; he had probably been carried way out to sea by now.

Jason ran quickly from the room, and Aimata sat down again and said: "All right, we'll find out soon enough."

I said: "That's how I knew Jules Cresson was here. You wondered about that, didn't you?"

"Yes. Yes, I wondered about that. You're a smart sonofabitch, Cain, aren't you?"

Tiare was coming round now. She hunched up into a sitting position and tried to cover herself; she was sobbing her heart out, looking at me with an expression of the most appalling helplessness. Aimata turned to her and pointed a finger. He said: "You stay right there, I'll get to you when I'm good and ready."

He turned back to me. "How come you came to Polynesia in the first place?"

"Faatua."

"Y-e-s... And the other broad? Maite?"

I wondered how much he knew about her; he had her analysis case, so I took a chance on the rest. I said: "She is a botanist, and a local; she was living in France. I thought she might be useful, so I hired her to help me."

"And balled the ass off her."

"None of your damn business."

He grunted, and I thought: *Time, time, I need all the time in the world now, keep the conversation going somehow.* I said: "You got the wrong girl, a damn fool thing to do."

He was snarling now. "Does it matter? Because if it does, we'll kill this broad off and go get the other one, what do you care?" He kicked me again, and said; "I asked you a question, you mother."

"No...no, it doesn't matter."

I let my head fall back, a natural enough movement under the circumstances, and rolled my eyes; I saw that the pillar was secured at the top with four heavy braces of black wrought iron, bolted onto the cross-members of the roof. I let my head fall back again. I said, speaking very slowly and spacing the words out, taking in great gulps of air in between: "Why did you...have to...to kill the Professor?"

He said sourly: "Cleaning out the garbage."

How much time was there to run? I said: "He told me... He said you had...some more of those...those damned insects. Where... where are they?"

For a while, he did not answer. He said at last: "You're a persistent sonofabitch, Cain, aren't you?"

"Yes. Yes...I suppose...I am."

He got to his feet and poured himself another drink. No one else in the room had moved. He took it and stood over Tiare, looking down on her. He put out a lazy foot, rested it on her shoulder for a moment, and then shoved hard, sending her back into a prone position. He said: "No, not like that, on your back, I like the view better." He put a toe under her arm and hooked her around, and kicked the protective arm from across her breasts. "Yeah, like that, I like it better."

He turned back to me again. "What did you have to say to Cresson?"

I thought I could make this trend last quite a while, too. The minutes were passing painfully slowly. I said: "We talked...about insects."

"Yeah. Go on."

"He said...they'd take care of themselves now...the new strain."

"Yeah. That's right. I can breed them whenever I like now, I know what has to be done. And I can do it."

"If they don't...all die on you."

He grunted. "Jesus, for an educated man you don't know very much, do you? I got up to two weeks, the Professor said, they can go without food for fourteen days. Only I don't have to wait no two weeks, they're going to get fed goddamn soon. *Soon*, Cain. Like tomorrow, maybe. You heard about Libya, I guess?"

"I heard."

"Okay. You heard about Iran, too? Christ, you just turn them loose, and the way they go to work, like a sonofabitch. Before they can drown themselves, all you gotta do is pick out a couple of males, a dozen females or so, and start over. Christ, that man was a genius, a goddamn genius. He tell you how many sets I got hidden away?"

Little by little, he was giving away his secrets; I didn't need them. I knew that the experimental stage was over, that now he was ready to roll along on his own. He could even afford to leave Polynesia now, and hide out...where?

Indeed, it was *essential* that he leave. I could not explain, even to myself, just why I was so sure of this. There was something in his attitude, a sort of slick watchfulness, like a lizard that slips under a second stone when you overturn the first. His old persistence came back to me: *Does the name Will Utter mean anything to you?* It seemed he had accepted my denial; but with a man of Aimata's slippery cunning, how good is *seemed*? The more I thought about it now, the more convinced I was that he would not run the slightest risk of his past catching up with him. *If* I had lied, and *if* I really knew who he was, then others would know too.

And his alternative?

An empty warehouse, a cellar, a secluded garage was all he needed now, with the pile of cabbage leaves I had chided Maite about. Where would he go? I didn't think it mattered very much.

I said, mumbling: "How many sets? Your starter sets?"

He laughed aloud, on top of everything again, getting overly confident. "Yeah, starter sets, that's a good name. A male and a few females, just like people, they keep on breeding. Christ, the way they breed."

"And how long do you think you can keep it up."

He shrugged. "Who knows? Who even cares? Two, three more strikes, big ones this time. So who else knows about me, Cain?"

He was watching me closely again, hopefully seeking out the truth by feeding me little bits of information and watching for reactions. This time, it was easy. I said: "What about Iran?"

Still studying my face. "The rice crops. Maybe you don't know about that. Maybe you haven't heard the radio in the last few hours."

He thought that was funny, and started to laugh. "Yeah, maybe you've been out of touch. The rice crop in...what do they call it? The Caspian Provinces. They tell me it feeds the starving millions. Only this year, it won't. We wiped it out, just to show them what we can do. And we told them the barley is next, and then the wheat. And you want to know? It didn't take them long to find out we meant business, they came up with the money fast, thirty million bucks. What do you think about that?"

I said: "A rich country, Aimata. Except for the starving millions you spoke of."

"Yeah, All the money in the world, oil money. It's getting to be a problem, so much money I don't know what to do with it, ain't that great?"

"And the power."

161

"Yeah. The power. It makes a man feel like a king."

He was choosing his targets well. As he had said, a lot of people needed that rice, and Iran was hardly the sort of place that could afford to fight him. Like Libya, a lot of money was concentrated in the hands of the people at the top, the leaders who could pay it out quickly, with no questions asked and no constitutional crises to worry about, a desperate effort to maintain their top-heavy economies.

Iran? Where next, I wondered? I asked him; anything to gain time: "Where next, Aimata?"

He did not answer. He was looking down on me with a cold and terrible detached expression on his face. He said slowly: "The games I'm gonna play with you, you won't believe. Hell, I still got a cattle prod tucked away someplace, I almost forgot that."

I said heavily: "And the Professor really thought...that he could do good with that damned bug."

He was suddenly laughing again, remembering, and he said: "Where next? Hey, what about Egypt? You ever read the Bible, Cain?"

"I know about the plague of locusts."

"Yeah, they used to read it to me when I was a kid, in Sunday school. Did a lot of damage then too, didn't they? Same reason too, wasn't it?"

I didn't answer, and he laughed shortly and said: "Blackmail. That sonofabitch Moses wanted his own way. So a new kind of locust they'd never seen before, isn't that how it was?" He laughed again and said: "Sonofabitch."

I said: "That's right. And they never saw that kind of locust again, either. Maybe there's a prophecy in it for you."

He grunted. He leaned down and took hold of Tiare's wrist, and pulled her to her feet. He shoved her again, and she fell into a chair, and he said to her: "Sit there, baby, you're a guest in my house, you got to be comfortable. And stop trying to cover up, else I'll take a barbed wire whip to you, just to give my good friend here the pleasure of hearing you yell."

He turned back to me. "You work for Interpol."

Another flat statement.

I said: "Sort of. They hire me once in a while."

"Yeah. That's what they told me. Who's your boss there?"

I assumed he would know that, so I told him. "A man named Fenrek. Colonel Fenrek."

"Yeah. What does he know about this operation?"

"I haven't had much of a chance to tell him anything, yet."

"Yet?" He laughed shortly. "Man, I'm going to enjoy what I do to you. Make it last, and last, and last."

Under my fingers, I could feel the base of the pillar and the concrete floor; I could slip a fingernail under the pole's edge. Not cemented in, then, but correctly fastened with a single central iron pin, the lower part of the rod in the concrete, its upper half drilled into the pillar. What would it be? Half-inch? More importantly, how far into the pillar would it have been sunk? Six inches, perhaps.

He was still talking, telling me what he was planning for me, none of it very appetizing. I wondered about the weight of the pillar; probably not more than a hundred and fifty pounds. And the roof itself? The rafters would give, to a certain extent, if enough pressure were applied correctly. I remembered that two years ago, Cassil Alexeyev, Russia's super-heavyweight, had lifted 1,401.85 pounds, to set a record at Munich. Of course, his hands were not tied behind his back, but here we were dealing with a total of some five hundred pounds or so, and the more I thought about it, the more I liked it.

I rolled my head around again, looking for something to brace my feet against: nothing. The floor itself would have to do.

I tried to find out just where all the men were, precisely; I didn't know quite what form Auguste's diversion would take, but I wanted to be ready for it.

One of the men who had been behind me when I first came in was covertly watching Tiare, gloating; I saw him moisten his lips. The second man had been throwing her a glance from time to time too. But not the man up in the rafters. His eyes had been on me all the time, the Colt steady as a rock and still aimed at me, in spite of my helplessness.

Time, time, time. Had Aimata found out all he wanted to know? I thought I'd better throw him a tidbit.

I said, a blatant lie: "Interpol's sending a team of investigators out here. Let the girl go, right now, and I'll tell you about them."

His eyes were very sharp now, with a sense of alertness. He stared hard at me and said: "You'll tell me anyway."

ALAN CAILLOU

"Let her go. Now."

"I don't have to. Interpol doesn't have any teams like that, you think I don't know?"

"Two officers from the French Sûreté, an Italian army physicist, and an FBI man from Chicago."

He believed me, and he didn't like it at all. "They are coming here?"

"Last I heard, they were to leave Paris tomorrow."

"I want their names, Cain."

I wondered how far I could push him. I said again: "Let her go then. I'll take your word if you tell me you will."

He was furious. He came and kicked out at me again, hard in the groin, and he shouted: "You know damn well that you won't take my word, and you know damn well that I know it! So don't give me all that crap!"

I yelled back at him: "It's not crap!" and he shouted: "I want their names..."

We were like a couple of angry kids squabbling over whose ball it was, and then, at last, the sound came that I had been waiting for.

It was a single shot from outside, and I knew that whether it was Vanaa or Auguste, he was going to do exactly the right thing; and he did.

I saw the man up in the rafters, the deadly, anonymous menace, the one I had been most wary of, fly backward with the force of a bullet that caught first his gun hand and then the lower part of his face. He went up and back, hit his head on the roof itself, crashed to the floor, and lay still. No wonder; the top of his head had gone, his own revolver driven through it.

I saw Aimata staring for the briefest of moments out through the window, and then, still crouching as though to kick me again, he shouted: "Lights!" and was racing across the room and throwing himself down behind a divan.

Two of the men were firing blindly out through the window, a natural enough reflex if only to keep the unseen assailant at bay, and the Tahitian boy was racing for the light switch, and then the Bren gun started chattering out there, and I could see, in the brief second before the room was plunged into darkness, that its bullets were smashing into the opposite wall. I saw one man thrown off his feet, and then they were tearing a spluttering line across Aimata's paintings. I saw the Tahitian boy crumple and fall, and then the darkness was acute, blacker than it should have been after the brightness that had preceded it.

I heard Aimata scream: "The girl, get the girl...!" and I thrust out my feet and tripped someone. And then I braced my heels against the floor and put my shoulder against the lower part of the pillar. It would not move, and I twisted my arms around it and tugged on the rope that bound my wrists; it was nylon, cutting deeply into my flesh, and I thought: My God, I'm a physical wreck.

I thudded my back into the damned pillar, twice, three times, four times; and I felt it give, just a trifle. I got my feet underneath my behind, and gripped the base of the pole with all the considerable strength I had at my disposal, and thought of Samson and the pillars, and heaved myself up, slowly and laboriously. I felt it coming free from its central spike, and still it would not clear itself. I took a deep breath and used my back, and then it slipped to one side, six inches off the ground, and I knew that I had done it. I doubled round again and thrust hard with my shoulders, and fell to the floor as it gave way and came crashing down. The roof was of woven *pandanus* fronds tied to bamboo poles, a lightweight affair, and I was not worried about its collapsing on me; but the cross members were very heavy indeed, and I felt one of them thud into the floor only inches from my head.

But I was—relatively—free. I lay on the ground and doubled myself up, and slipped my hands under my behind and into the front, where I could use them better; and then dove for the bar.

The shooting was intense now, the Bren gun outside in the darkness changing its position expertly; I could recognize the sharper sound of the Webley from time to time, over and above the constant answering fire from within the room; they were firing back at the flashes, not a very worthwhile occupation.

I reached out and groped for a bottle, any kind of bottle, and found one. I smashed it down hard and broke it, and jammed the neck in between my knees and rubbed my wrists over the broken edge of the glass; it was the second time I'd treated my bones in this murderous fashion, and I was hating every minute of it. But in a matter of seconds,

I had sliced through the nylon. In the darkness, I groped for the chair where Tiare had been, but she was no longer there. Then I heard a door opening and knew what was happening there too; I threw myself toward it, and I heard her scream, and I collided with a hulking mass of flesh—who might it have been? I didn't care—and reached for whatever I could grab.

A wrist.

I twisted it round and up and snapped the arm across my knee, and caught her as she fell, fumbling in the dark and almost dropping her, and then I had her tight in my arms and was running out through the door, not caring now about the bullets, just hoping it was reasonably possible to avoid them provided I stayed away from that deadly window. I felt one of them tear through my forearm; a flesh wound; nothing to worry about.

And then, the grass was a comfort under my feet, and I was racing across the lawn again toward the forest. The moon was high now, and there was too much light, a pale glow everywhere. But in less than a minute I had reached the friendly cover of the trees and had dropped to the ground with my fragile burden.

A bullet clipped through the foliage above my head—a stray. I heard a shrill whistle blow, three short blasts, and the Bren gun was suddenly silent. There was still a lot of shooting from the house, but now I could identify only two guns. And then they, too, stopped firing, and there was only silence.

I placed Tiare carefully on the ground, deep under the cover of a thick clump of the flowers whose name she had taken; their nighttime scent was overpowering, and a comfort. She was moaning softly, only half-conscious, and I whispered: "Tiare? It's going to be all right."

The silence was uncanny. I wondered how many of them were left, I wondered, too, how I could find Vanaa, and Auguste, and Maite, and their helpers. And then, quite close beside us, a voice whispered: "Mr. Cain?"

I froze. It came again, very soft and sibilant: "Teiho, Mr. Cain. If you have a gun, please don't use it. Please?"

It did not sound much like his voice, I thought: Am I being too suspicious?

It occurred to me that under the circumstances there was no

such thing as too much suspicion. But could they know Teiho was my friend? Or was he?

I said quietly: "I have a gun. Show yourself."

He was moving in then, and he was even laughing quietly. It was Teiho, all right, and he was beaming with delight. He whispered: "I don't suppose you really are armed, but you're wise to be careful."

He took my hand in a warm and friendly grasp, and looked at Tiare and said: "Oh *mon Dieu*. Are you all right?"

There was blood all over my arms again, and he wiped his hands on his shorts and said again: "Oh my God..."

It was good to see him, a link with all that was pleasurable. I said, "Where are the others, Teiho?"

He pointed. "We have a rendezvous on the beach, down there. Maite is waiting there now. Vanaa and Auguste are covering the house on two sides, Maite will signal as soon as we get there, a whistle."

"The battle?"

He shrugged, "Who knows? I was detailed to watch only for you. I saw you run out... We go this way." He was peering at my sympathetically. "My God, you are a mess, aren't you?"

I said: "Yes, a mess."

"Can you manage?"

I picked Tiare up in my arms and followed him, shouldering a way through the vegetation, damp now with the mist of the night, coming out of the forest and into the tiny valley that led to the beach.

I said: "The ketch?"

He was panting with the unaccustomed exertion. "Two miles offshore, we'll have to swim out to it. Do you think we all can?"

"Who? Tiare? Or you?"

He grinned. "Maybe we should bring it in closer? What do you think?"

"The moon's too bright. It's too good a target."

"Let me help you with your burden, let me carry her for a while."

"I'll manage."

She was warm and slender in my arms, and she was coming round now. She said, mumbling: "What...what's happening?" Her voice was pathetically weak; I remembered her laugh, the times we had met before.

I stopped and shifted her in my arms, making her more comfortable. I said, whispering: "It's all right now, we're on our way to Auguste's ketch. Auguste is here, and Teiho, and Captain Vanaa, some others... There's no more danger." It's a stupid question, but it's always expected, so I asked: "How do you feel? Will you be all right?"

She shook her head and shuddered. "I don't know."

She was sobbing, crying her heart out, facing for the first time in her life a part of the world she had never known even to exist. She was so slight, and slender, and light-weight that it seemed I was carrying an infant in my arms.

We ran on, moving as quietly as possible, with only the light of the moon shimmering on the water to guide us.

Behind us there was only silence. I knew that they would be regrouping their forces.

Soon we could expect the massive onslaught of their reaction.

CHAPTER 12

We crouched among the shadows on the dark beach like conspirators in crime.

The sand was black here, with a sprinkling of powdered basalt intermingled with the grains that gave it a strange and luminescent quality, like shining jet that reflected the intermittent moonlight. All around us great twisted rocks stood up in weird and startling shapes, pitted with a constant pattern of small round holes in which the nighttime crabs were scuttling, crawling over the pockmarks with a tiny, shuffling sound.

Maite, fresh and agile and lively, had flung her arms around me and was holding me tight, the tears gleaming on her smooth cheeks. Behind us, the sea was a gently moving sheet of liquid silver, the water seething softly with some strange and inexplicable under motion where the currents fought each other; the surf was lapping quietly among the coral outcrops.

She said, trembling: "I was so...so frightened for you... I was afraid..."

I held her tight. "Tiare. She needs your help now."

"Yes. Yes, of course."

I had lain her bruised and bleeding body down on the sand, on the dark wool sweater that Vanaa had put down for her bed; Auguste was dribbling seawater over her, crooning to her. I heard him whisper: "...and we'll get you out to the ketch, Vaite is there, she'll take good care of you. You'll never see this wretched island again, never. It's over now, all over."

There were two dark and motionless forms crouched close by, silent shadows among the rocks, and Vanaa said quietly, introducing them: "This is Maramaitera, the best sponge fisherman in all the islands, and a good man in a fight, too. And Teupootahiti, who builds canoes."

The shadows rose up out of the sand, like ghouls. Teupootahiti was squat and sturdy, a barrel-chested man in his early forties, with great splayed feet that seemed almost prehensile, close-cropped, curly black hair, and a face as dark as thunder. He wore denim shorts and nothing else, and the moonlight shone on his rippling chest muscles. He was gripping an adz, and I was astonished to see that its blade was made of stone, a great sharp wedge of granite fastened to its shining wooden shaft with a tight binding of plaited cord, a weapon out of the Polynesian past. He shook hands with me, a bone-crushing grip, and waved his adz and said: "Find me a head that I can break with this," and then he looked down at Tiare and corrected himself: "Find me ten heads..."

Maramaitera had taken a grip on my shoulder and was pointing out to sea. He said: "*Mea ha 'uti 'uti te miti*, you see? Something is stirring up the water. It is good." His voice was husky, and he was screwing up his eyes as he swung his arm around. "Over there, a storm gathering, and from there, the wind will soon come, a strong wind. For us, it is good. The water will boil, and on such a sea, only Hiro can live. The god Hiro, and the ketch *Pinaa*."

I could see the ketch out there, two miles or so offshore. It was rolling, pitching, tossing, though the surface of the water itself seemed calm. Vanaa growled: "Soon, nothing will live out there, he is right."

Maramaitera clapped him ferociously on the back, and whispered: "Of course I am right." He was gripping a cudgel of enormous size, intricately carved from what I thought might have been *'aito* wood, the *Casuarina equisetifolia*, though it was too dark to see well.

The Captain nodded. "Yes, the Pinaa will survive, if Auguste will let me take the wheel. By midday tomorrow, we'll make Papeete, and then..." He was peering up at me, squinting. He said softly: "But that's not what you want, is it?"

I said: "You and I, and the two Tahitians... Auguste and Teiho should man the ketch with the women in case they try and sneak up on her. That leaves four of us."

"There's one more man—Tera'i. He's over there, by the *marae*, keeping watch."

I looked, but could see nothing, and the Captain whistled softly through his teeth, a long, drawn-out sibilant. Part of a coral rock detached itself from its alma mater, and he was running lithely toward us, a slight, skinny man with a long spear clutched in his right hand. His movements were quick and jerky, his balance delicate, and Vanaa said: "Tera'i, another friend..."

He was in a permanent half-crouch, and he looked back and pointed to the dark line of the woods, and said of handedly: "One man out there, watching and seeing nothing."

I said: "You saw him?"

"I saw him. A big man who moves well in the dark. He was tossing a knife, like so, over and over in his hand."

"Ulricson, without a doubt; he's dangerous. Did he see you?"

Tera'i snorted. "He sees nothing, only shadows."

I said "Don't count on it, Tera'i," and Vanaz nodded. "Better get back, keep your eyes open."

I took the Captain's arm and led him a little away from the others, and we squatted in the lee of a jagged boulder and whispered together for a while.

I said: "The outcome of the battle at the house...can you make a reasonable guess? I was too busy with Tiare to see what happened."

He shrugged. "I saw two men die. Perhaps three. Do you know how many there were when it all started?"

"Who knows? Perhaps a dozen left. They have machine guns, rifles, revolvers... My God, they've even got missiles, and I wonder where the hell they're hidden away? And we have—what? One Bren, one Webley, a spear, an old stone axe, and a cudgel."

He grinned. "If the old weapons were good enough for our grandfathers, they should be good enough for us. And we are good men, and they are not. The gods will be on our side."

"Well, that's helpful. Ammunition?"

He grimaced. "Six rounds left in the Bren, two in the

revolver."

"Great. The five of us, practically unarmed, on their home ground, and two women to worry about..."

Yanaa said promptly: "We'll get the women out to the ketch, like you said. Under sail, with the motors on full power, Auguste can be a long way away by the time they rally their forces."

"That's what they're waiting for."

"Huh?"

I said: "Let's assume that they know we can't stay here, because sooner or later they're bound to find us. Let's also assume that they know we can get out to the ketch, and that once on board we can outrun anything they have here."

"Right."

"With a southerly wind, we'd have to use the motors, or we'd be tacking back and forth for hours on end just to get a reasonable distance from the island."

"Correct."

"I say again—that's what they're waiting for."

He ran a gnarled hand over his grizzled chin. "The missiles?"

"The missiles are heat-activated. Once we start the motors on the ketch, they need just one of their SAMs, and in a matter of seconds, we're dead, all of us. With nothing but debris to show we were ever here."

He was silent for a moment, thinking it out, looking for an alternative. He said at last: "Well, that's a cheerful thought, isn't it? *Mon Dieu*, if we run, we get blown out of the water. If we don't, we get picked off one by one as soon as daylight comes and they can start a thorough search."

"That's about the size of it."

"So?"

"We need help, Vanaa. What's the range of the radio on the *Pinaa*?"

He picked up a handful of black sand and dribbled it through his fingers; he looked a mite embarrassed. He said, awkwardly: "Well, it's a very good radio, an excellent radio, only..." He broke off and sighed. "Don't count on the radio."

I remembered the radio-telephone on board, a 50-wait Airmac, a very solid piece of equipment, and I said: "*Nothing* can go wrong with an Airmac."

He grunted. "The battery. When we left Tahiti, we found it was flat. I tried to recharge it, but the...what do you call it, the relay?"

"The overload relay?"

"Yes. It kept...popping, and shutting itself off."

"Did you isolate the motor's alternator?"

"What's that?"

"Oh my God. Did you disconnect the ground cable? Or even the positive?"

He shook his head. "I just switched on the charger, the same as I do on my own motorboat, it's easy enough. But it kept popping, and finally, I gave up."

"Auguste's equipment is a little more sophisticated than the stuff you're used to. He's got alternating current, not direct. And you burned out the diode rectifiers."

He snorted, "Newfangled rubbish."

"So now, we're on our own."

"Uh-huh." He didn't seem in the least concerned, "So we stay, and we fight them."

"With stone axes and spears."

"Well, I don't suppose it will be easy." He raised his hands in an expressive gesture. "All right, what do we do now?"

"Any more weapons on board the ketch?"

"No, of course not."

"Just a vague hope. Then Auguste will have to take the Bren. It's not likely they'll paddle out there in a pirogue, but they just *might*."

"They'd be seen..."

"But could they be *stopped?*"

He grunted again. "All right. Auguste looks after the women with the Bren gun. That leaves us with two bullets." He shrugged philosophically. "It will have to do, won't it?"

I said: "You're a good man, Vanaa."

"The best."

"But God save me from the hopeful optimists."

"I tell you again, my friend, our great ancestor Oro, who rules the whole world, will take care of us."

I hoped he was right. I said: "There's one small point in our favor."

He looked to question, and I said: "They will certainly assume that all our forces, whatever they may be—and they don't know how weak we are, remember—will be headed for the ketch. They'll have to give chase to get within good range for their missiles. That *means* they will be concentrated at the wharf. That's our epicenter of operations."

He said promptly: "So let's get the women to safety and go to work."

I found him a very refreshing man. We crawled carefully back to where the others were. There were three hours left until sunrise.

We found them still huddled around Tiare under a stark coral boulder that was gnarled and weather-beaten as Captain Vanaa's grizzled face, a silent, expectant little group, staring at us with eyes that seemed to shine in the darkness. Tiare was sitting up now, and as I squatted down beside her she reached out and laid a hand on my knee.

She said, a sound so slight could hardly hear her: "It's not really finished yet. Is it?"

"For you, yes it is."

"Not for you."

There was a terrible sadness in her voice. Maite was watching her obliquely, bleeding with her. I told Auguste what he had to do and, as I expected, he protested.

I said: "We need a good man on board the *Pinaa*, in case of a sneak attack. I don't really expect one, but... They know just what they can do with a few hostages in their hands again. So you, Teiho, and the two women, join Vaite on the *Pinaa* and wait for us. Take the Bren with you. Wait for the beginnings of daylight, and if we're not out there by then...get the hell out of there as fast as you can. Under sail only."

I told him about the heat-seeking missiles, and looked up at the sky and glowered. There were dark and heavy clouds coming in from the south.

He said: "If we get chased, do you know what they'll be using? Can you guess?"

"A Laguna. Eleven point five meters."

"Diesel?"

"Twin Ammarines, turbo-charged V8s."

"Oh Jesus! I'll never outrun that under sail, not unless I run due north on the wind."

"Then that's what you'll have to do."

"Run north? If I miss Hawaii, in about a month's time, there's nothing on this longitude I hit Alaska. And it's too damn cold up there."

"So stay on a course of a hundred and eighty-seven."

"Dead into the wind. Oh *mon Dieu!*"

"You're safe from everything except rifle fire as long as you don't use your motors."

He brightened suddenly. "It might be exciting at that. Maybe I can ram her. What's she made of, fiberglass?"

"Teak."

"What a pity. Well, I can try."

He really believed he could do that. I tried to imagine the fleet little Laguna running around him in circles while he tried, under sail, to bear down on her. How long before the launch would run out of fuel and be at his mercy? I thought it might be a very long time.

I said: "Give me exactly one hour from now. Then start your engines. Run them for thirty seconds precisely, and then cut them. And after that, for God's sake, don't start them again till you're back in Papeete."

"Thirty seconds...?"

"No more."

I put my arm around Maite and said: "You and Auguste, you'll both have to help Tiare. Shall we find you a log to help?"

She shook her head. "We'll manage."

But Tiare, pulling herself together with a strength I would never have imagined, got a little unsteadily to her feet and said: "I'll be all right. Once I get into the water...I can swim." She was still trembling, fighting the nausea. She laid a hand on my arm and said gravely: "I have a lot to thank you for, don't I?

"It was my fault in the first place. They thought you were my woman."

She looked at Maite and smiled, and then suddenly she was laughing again, that quiet, amused laugh she had when I had first met her up at the Belvedere. She said again: "I'm all right now, I promise you."

"Good. Then we'll see you on board the ketch in a little while."

Her eyes were grave one more, wide and solemn and very beautiful. "And what will you do now?"

I said: "I wish to God I knew."

And then, I was aware that Teupootahiti was staring toward the great purple slabs of rock that stood like a sentinel a hundred yards or so from the beach, the remnants of the old *marae*. He said, whispering: "*Tera'i...te aha ra oia?* What's Tera'i doing?"

There was alarm on his face, and when I swung round to see what had caught the attention of his night eyes, I could see the shadows over there moving; it seemed that *someone*—or was it only a shadow?—was sliding down one of the huge fallen stones, and it seemed, in the semi-obscurity, that his body was strangely twisted.

I said to Vanaa: "Get them into the water, quickly," and turned and raced up to the slope of the beach, and then Tera'i was on his feet and staggering toward me, and when I reached him he collapsed in my arms, and half-turned and pointed; and said thickly: "*E ta'ata...puai roa...ra...*a strong man...over there..." His head was rolling instantly from side to side, and he was clutching at his stomach, and then the hands, shining with blood, came up in front of my face, and he said, choking: "*Teie tipi...*this knife..."

He pulled it out of his stomach and held it out to me with a gesture that seemed almost reverent, as though the final symbol in his life were to be the means of its passing.

It was the ivory-handled knife that Ulricson had liked to play with; I saw it fall to the sand as Tera'i seemed to take a deep, shuddering breath. I felt the increase of his weight and felt the silence, and I knew that he was dead.

I laid him down gently, and ran fast toward the *marae* he had come from, not stopping to take any precautions at all, and leaped over one of the great stones, and there was Ulricson.

He had no need for silence now, and I heard his first and only bullet whistle past my head and shatter against the granite. He was in a crouch, ready to crawl up the slope of the rock, and my feet drove into his face as I leaped down, and I gave him no time at all even to fall to the ground, but caught him by the collar as he stumbled over, and swung him round, and drove his head into the *marae* wall, so hard that it burst like a crushed watermelon.

I threw myself flat on my belly in a patch of dark purple shadow, and stared at the somber edge of the forest, and listened; there was no sound at all.

In a little while, I rolled over quietly and looked at the dead body beside me. I took the gun from under it, a German Luger with the stock attached, and checked the rounds in the magazine and found that there were six. I found two more magazines in his pockets, a bunch of keys that I thought might come in handy, a second, smaller knife tucked into the top of his nine-inch boot, and a flashlight on a strap at his belt.

I took them all, and then, out of the dense dark vegetation some three hundred feet ahead of me, I heard the sound I had been half-expecting—the shattering clatter of a machine gun. I heard the bullets smashing into the sacred remnants of the old *marae* as I threw myself under the lee of one of the great gray slabs, heard the dismal whine of the ricochets speeding through the night.

There was a rapid rifle fire from my right now, three guns by the sound of it, and then a second machine gun opened up on my left, and soon the air was thick with sprayed bullets, a plethora of ammunition wasting itself as they put down a covering blanket of fire.

I lay flat on my belly and wormed my way back to where Vanaa and the others were waiting, one revolver, one axe, and one cudgel ready to do battle. Ignoring the fusillade entirely, Vanaa was on his feet with his head tilted back, staring into the darkness and watching the flashes of their guns. I said: "Get down, for Christ's sake, I'm going to need you."

He grunted. Teupootahiti and Maramaiters were peering out from behind a massive hunk of coral, and whispered: "The others?"

Teupootahiti turned and pointed. I could see the tiny pinpoints in the water that were the heads of Auguste, and Teiho, and Tiare, and Maite, already a hundred and fifty yards out now, little specks of black on the surface of the silver-gray water. Beyond them, the leaden overcast, dense as a shroud, was racing toward us; the ketch was already in its shadow, almost invisible now. Close inshore, the white caps of the surf were beginning to boil.

Vanaa said urgently: "Tera'i?"

"He's dead."

He swore softly. "In the name of God, how many are there out there?"

"Enough to give us a bad time if we don't get out of here, fast."

"In the water, then, the best thing, I think."

We ran fast, bent low, along the line of coral to where it entered the surf like a breakwater, and turned there to see what was happening behind us. I counted the violent red flashes of at least eleven, guns; one of them was firing tracer bullets, sweeping back and forth over the top of the *marae* walls. They were moving in on us now, and I knew that once they were over the top they could lower their trajectory. The Captain had the same idea, and he looked at the Luger in my hand and whispered: "A few rounds, to keep them back?"

I shook my head. "We don't want them to think we've only got one gun, do we? As far as they can guess, the ketch might have brought an army, let's not disillusion them."

As we slipped into the water, I could hear the sound of their bullets biting into the wet black sand; the first of them were already over the granite slabs and heading our way. We went down like seals and swam fast underwater, keeping close to the protective coral wall, hoping that sooner or later it might reach as far as the reef itself. It was hard to see in the black, black water, with the blacker sand below it, but I was conscious that the two Polynesians had taken to the sea like fish, swimming fast with quite effortless ease, with long, rhythmic motions that denoted long, long practice; I remembered Maite's similar expertise that time we had spent a difficult fifteen minutes together under the wreck of Hawking's plane.

I was worried about the Captain. He was tough, and he was angry, and that's a good combination; but he was also old. But he held his own down there with the rest of us, and when we finally found the reef and came up to fill our bursting lungs, he stared back at the beach and growled: "Now how do I get back there to bury Tera'i decently, can you tell me that?"

"Later."

"He was my friend."

We could see their silhouettes at the water's edge now, shadowy forms that seemed to blend with all the other shadows. They were spreading out, running fast, about ten of them. I heard one of them shout, and wondered if he had seen the signs in the sand of our entry into the water; I hoped he had.

I whispered to Vanaa: "They'll assume we're heading for the ketch. That means they'll go for their boats. Over there."

He nodded. Far over to the east, there was a brilliant gleam in the sky that was the reflection of the wharf bright lamps, and I thought: As soon as they get there, they ought to turn them out.

And, as we swam slowly along the reef toward them, that's just what they did. The sky was suddenly black again, and Vanaa said: "Ha! They make it easy for us, what we have to do."

"They are making it easy for themselves. A naval battle coming up."

"And they have all the weapons. Never mind. When I was in the Navy, many years ago..." He grinned suddenly. "One day, I tell you all about it. Now...we sink their boats, right?"

"If you'll tell me how to sink a hundred-and-sixty-five-foot oceangoing cruiser from underwater, with our bare hands."

"Oh. So?"

I said: "First, let's find out just what they're up to."

"They are getting ready to hit us, *sans doute*."

I was sure he was absolutely right. The water was body temperature, a strange and relaxing feeling to it, with the tiny currents swirling through the coral like the jets of a Jacuzzi.

I said: "Then let's hit them first, what do you say?"

He nodded; his eyes gleaming. The two Polynesians were waiting patiently, treading water. I looked at my Rolex; fifty minutes to go.

Then, the showdown would begin, with the sound of the *Pinaa's* motors.

CHAPTER 13

I could not believe the silence.

Again, there was that feeling of utter isolation, of being so remote from the rest of the world that *nothing* else existed. The only sound was the faint *lap-lap-lap* of the water eddying among the gaunt stark serrations of the black coral that was our bulwark. The reef seemed to have been frozen, by time, into a giant distortion of eroded black iron, cast into freeform by a demented sculptor.

But now, there was menace in the silence. Out there, *somewhere*, they were setting about our destruction. I could only guess what they were planning for us; but I knew that it would be horrible.

We were a hundred and thirty feet away from the little wharf, and the clouds had covered the moon entirely now, so that all we could see was the black silhouette of the boats ahead of us, set against the deeper black of the forested mountain behind them.

I wondered if it would be safe, if there would be time enough, to swim in closer, perhaps to the shelter of the looming cruiser, the big Feadship. There was scarcely any light aboard it, just a glimmer or two amidships. An ocean-going vessel of this size and quality would need a substantial crew, perhaps as many as twelve hands. But it occurred to me that it would probably not be in constant use—the kind of vessel a wealthy man uses perhaps once a year or so, for a round-the-world cruise, when he would hire a skipper and crew just for the voyage. A mere two or three people on board then, to keep her shipshape and all tidied up. Was I being too optimistic? I thought not; there was an air of emptiness about her, and I liked it.

And then, very faintly, I could hear the sound of hurrying feet padding along the jetty's timbers: four, five, perhaps six men. I whispered to Vanaa, urgently: "Now, before they turn the lights on again."

He nodded in the darkness, and we went down under the water again, and once more I was conscious of those two Polynesian experts beside me, watchdog porpoises, trailing along easily in the darkness. We reached the black hull of the cruiser in moments, and surfaced close by its stern. From here, I could make out more clearly the shadow that was the Laguna, chink of light showing through the drapes of its cabin windows. The double-ender was beyond it and the dugout canoes were scattered about like drifting logs in the darkness, low-lying and hardly visible, tossing lightly among the shallow crests. On the wharf itself, a half-dozen men were moving back and forth; it was too dark to see what they were doing; some were coming ashore, and some going on board. I touched Vanaa on the shoulder and whispered: "Wait, I'll be back."

I swam very quietly in the darkness, under four feet of water, and came up under the jetty, and from this point of view, against the gray of the sky, they were angulated puppets over my head.

Three of them were carrying long steel cylinders on their shoulders, and the others, coming off the launch, were empty-handed. It made me a very happy man indeed, because now all the problems but one were solved.

I swam back quickly to where the others were waiting, and whispered to Teupootahiti: "You and Maramaitera...I need a pirogue, the smallest one you can find."

They were staring across the water, squinting, Maramaitera nodded. "That one, there."

I followed his look. All I could see was darkness, but in a moment I could make out what looked like a free floating tree trunk on the surface. I whispered: "Are you sure?"

He was grinning. He touched his eyes and whispered back: "I see good in the dark. A pirogue, four meters long... Where do you want it?"

"Here, under the stern." I hoped they would not put the lights on again. If they did, it would still be in deep shadow.

Maramaitera jerked his head at Teupootahiti, and they both sank down and were gone, I signaled Vanaa, and we swam the few yards to the anchor chain. I grasped it, and looked a question at the Captain; he nodded, and stuck up his thumb in a gesture. I whispered: "Give me two minutes, then follow."

I pulled myself up the chain hand over hand, and clung there at the top for a moment or two, listening, and when I heard no indication of an alien presence, I slipped over the side and hid myself between the gunwale and the windlass, and peered back carefully over the stern.

Captain Vanaa was surprisingly visible down there; my eyes were fast becoming used to the sea darkness. So, too, from this elevation, were the men on the wharf, the enemy. The first load carriers had gone, and two others had taken their places and were hurrying aboard with their missiles, and I realized *exactly* what Aimata had to do. It was not a question of a single missile to destroy us all on board the ketch; he had other problems to worry about.

If he had not believed that his cover was still secure, and *if* someone back on the mainland knew that he really was Will Utter, then the game was up and he had to go, at once, as far away and as fast as he could. But if, on the other hand, there were merely the tale of some nasty business on Rangitefara circulating among the authorities, then all he had to do was make sure that he would not be caught with any compromising materials in his possession. If a search of the island should turn up his SAM Mark Sevens, he was in real trouble.

So? Obviously, he would get rid of them, fast. At the first indication of danger, they could be heaved overboard; there were four thousand meters of water under the surface here, I remembered.

His three nylon bags of the *Cressonus* as well? The starter sets with which he could begin all over, and blackmail half the world? Perhaps. I wondered about that. I assumed he'd keep them close by now, with him at all times. Unlike his load of stolen rocketry, they'd be relatively easy to move around.

Captain Vanaa was already scrambling up the anchor chain, using his feet as well as his arms but making an admirable job of it in spite of his age. When he had dropped down beside me, I whispered: "I'm going below, watch the deck for me."

His voice was almost inaudible: "Take care, they will never leave a ship like this unguarded. A skeleton crew somewhere..."

"Absolute silence, all the way..." He nodded, and I ran quickly from shadow to shadow, and went up the mahogany steps to the bridge; no one. I ran down again and waited a moment or two by the davits, listening.

And well I did. A door opened silently beside me, and a man came out, a tall, lanky, awkwardly-moving young man, about twenty-five years old. He was dressed in the same type of paramilitary clothing that I had seen on Faatua, and he carried a rifle. He let the door close behind him, and moved away, his back to me; I watched him move off toward the stern.

I waited.

In less than a minute, the sound care that I had been waiting for, a dull thud that might have been a fist coming down on someone's head, and a louder one as the body hit the floor; I knew he'd walked into Vanaa.

I went quietly down the companionway, and was glad to see that there were no lights in the long corridor. I moved in absolute silence, easing my way forward to the main cabin, empty, into a small passage on the other side of it, and beyond it into a large stateroom where one of the lights was glowing; the smell of cigar smoke was heavy here, and as I moved cautiously across to the door on the other side, I heard someone moving beyond it, I listened for a while to try and decipher what he might be doing, but quite uselessly.

And then, he solved the problem for me, by merely opening the door himself. I stepped back quickly, behind the door, and as he turned to close it I took hold of his wrist and threw the arm upward and down again in a wide, twisting sweep, and as he went flying over there was just time to see the look of acute surprise on his face and the reflection of the tiny lamp on his bald pate. It was Jason. As he hit the floor, head first, I stepped on his back and pushed the arm back, and heard the shoulder dislocate, then put one foot at the back of his knee, seized his foot, and bent his leg back over my instep. With the other hand, I took a firm grip on his neck and squeezed hard.

The trick is to hit the auricular nerve; the cervical becomes too dangerous. But his gasp of pain told me that I'd found it at once. If I'd kept up the pressure, he could have gone out like a light, so I released it a little, applied more weight to his foot to hold him steadily in position, and said quietly: "You have just one or two things to tell me."

He was sputtering, trying to fight the coma, a very determined man, so I applied a little more pressure, letting my middle finger slide around to the clavicular nerve for good measure. He said, gasping: "All right, you sonofabitch, all right."

"Where are the missiles, Jason?"

He was having trouble getting the words out. "They are... they're loading them on the...on the launch."

"What kind of launch?"

"It's a Laguna."

The truth; he was too desperately afraid to lie. I said: "Why?"

"He's going to...to jettison them...if he has to."

I said: "And the insects? He has three bags of them. Where are they?"

"Go to hell, Cain."

I dug my thumb into the hypoglossal, and there's no one alive who can stand much pressure there for long. He shuddered, and I released the pressure. "All right, all right, for God's sake," he said.

"Where are they?"

"They're on board...on board the Laguna, too."

"And where's he taking them?"

"I don't...don't know."

"Where to?"

"For God's sake...I don't know, Cain!"

He was trying to shout, and the words were hardly audible. I let go of his neck, grabbed him by the ear, twisted his head around, and struck him smartly on the base of the neck, just where the stems of the cervical plexus branch out. He went limp at once, of course, and I left him there, knowing that he wouldn't recover, if ever, for a couple of hours at the least; I knew that if he woke up at all, he'd be out of action with a dislocated shoulder, a thigh muscle pulled out, and a colossal headache that would stay with him for a week, together with constant dizziness and recurrent fainting spells. I went through to the other room.

As the smells that had come with the opening of the door had told me, it was a galley, and a very good one indeed, comfortably lit by four shaded lamps set around the walls, all decorated in blue and white, with heavy velour drapes over the portholes in the same strange cyanic blue I had seen in Aimata's paintings. It was modern and well-equipped, with a butane cooking stove and oven, a large freezer, two refrigerators, a dozen cupboards around the walls, a good-sized butcher's chopping block for a table, an impressive array of French carving knives from Dehilleran in Paris, all nicely set out on a magnetic plate, a very well designed dresser full of copper and cast iron cooking pots, and, against one wall, a line of six spare butane tanks, their key-wrench in the logical place on a hook just above them. They were all fifteen-gallon containers, in keeping with the extended range of this beautiful vessel.

I was glad to see that there was a very efficient fire-control system in evidence, well-concealed in the galley's molded ceiling: twelve spray-cocks in all, the excellent Graber Carbonic equipment.

I assumed that the burners on the gas range would be automatic, but I checked them one by one, eight of them in all, just to make sure. They all flared immediately, the pilot lights clean and well-kept. Good.

It seemed to me that I should not stay long under the galley's lamps, even though the beautiful drapes were well closed. If any other members of the skeleton crew were prowling around, I preferred to be in the kind of darkness where mischief is not only made but also best countered.

I took down the key-wrench and unscrewed the cocks on all of the butane tanks, and then got the hell out of there, fast, not being too sure how long it would take for the room to fill with gas, nor quite how much would be needed to set off the initial explosion. I went up the companionway three steps at a time, raced along to the afterdeck where Vanaa was, and whispered: "Quick, no time now..."

He was crouched beside the stern batch over the body of the man who had so carelessly walked into the fury of his clenched fists, leaning over him and waiting, as though not quite sure how much damage his blow had done; there was a very satisfied look on his face, the triumph of age over youth.

I said: "Quick, she's going to blow up any minute now."

He nodded, and whispered: "Three men in the crew's quarters, I saw them."

"Come on, for God's sake..."

We both went over the railings on the seaward side, and clung there for a moment, waiting.

And then the galley went up.

It was not much of an explosion after all. The first tank went off with a shuddering sort of *whoosh*, and the deck trembled very slightly. And then, three or four more tanks went off, and I saw the steam core pouring up out of the vents as the automatic fire-extinguishers took over, quenching the flames with a surfeit of bicarbonate of soda. I could smell the sour stench of the sulphuric acid which was turning it into carbonic acid gas under pressure and causing it to foam tremendously.

I heard a more welcome sound, too.

Coming from the wharf itself, there was the sudden surge of running feet, and I heard a voice, a roaring bellow, which I thought might be from Aimata. I gave them ten seconds, and then touched the Captain on the shoulder, and down we went, knifing into the water far below and diving deep. We swam forward under water and came up at the prow. From here, the little Laguna was only a matter of fifty yards away. I whispered: "Get the others; I want the pirogue close by the launch, on the other side of it. Hurry."

He was gone at once, and I swam fast to the lovely little speedboat and hauled myself on board.

It was one of those mistakes of urgency. Given a moment or two to think, I am sure they would have left a couple of men on board here, just in case. But I was counting on the unexpectedness of the attack on the cruiser, feeling quite sure that *everyone* would rush there at once, an instinctive reflex to find out what the hell was going on in this unexpected quarter; I wondered how long it would take them to realize that it was merely a diversion. Not long, I imagined; there wasn't much time.

There were small fifteen-watt lights in the cabin, but the drapes over its long windows were drawn, and the first thing I saw was a large wooden box of deep-red teak, bound in brass, on the small mahogany table on the port side. It was closed, but not locked, and I was sure I knew what was in it.

I lifted the lid. There were three green nylon mesh bags inside, and each of them contained twenty or thirty of the *Docciostaurus Cressonus*, the last, and perfect, specimens of the Professor's lifelong work, all that was needed for the less erudite, like Aimata, to carry on the breeding for purposes far removed from the original intent, and as sickening a process as a man could ever hate to see.

They were larger, or so it seemed, than I had remembered them. They were green in color, the green of verdigris, and they held their long wings tight to their little bodies. They had six fragile legs apiece, and quarter-inch antennae, and looked rather like the common *schistocerca*, except for that unusual color. And except for those startling mandibles—jawbones that seemed out of all proportion to the rest of the body, and were horrible to look at; they were *chomping* slowly, as though in expectation of delights to come. There was a picture flashing of the tired old drunk lying in Gerard's vineyard, a skeleton...

But it was their eyes that held me fascinated. They were almost hypnotic.

If an intellectual venom could so be described as apparent in the eyes of an insect...I found it hard not to shudder. The eyes were large, and round, and swiveled, with corneas of enormous size (an indication, perhaps, of remarkably large vitreous chambers), and drooping lids like those of frogs. But there was evil in them.

There were sixty, seventy, perhaps a hundred pairs of tiny, malevolent eyes fastened on me, staring at me, dissecting me, and calculating... I found myself looking around for something to destroy them with; I wanted to crush them with my bare hands, to send them into the oblivion of man's imaginings from which they had come, all uninvited.

But I knew that I could not; they had to wait their turn. With the insects gone, I would lose Aimata himself, and I wanted them both.

I closed the lid softly and went into the aft storage locker. And here was the solution to the whole problem, just as I had foreseen.

Neatly set out on the wide shelf there, I found a row of four-foot cylinders; shining brightly in the reflected light—the remaining SAM Mark Sevens. In a moment of panic, I wondered where the launching tubes were, and if perhaps there might be only one of them.

But there were nine of these, too, and it seemed to me, on reflection, that this made sense, since he had probably stationed them at strategic points all over his island, and each missile would therefore need its own individual tube.

I took one of each, and hurried back to the stern of the vessel. There, waiting at the side, was Maramaitera with his little pirogue; Teupootahiti was at its stern, and they were both looking up at me in the darkness with expressions of the purest delight on their faces.

I slipped the missile and its bazooka-like launcher down to them, slid into the water, pointed, and said: "Over there, on the reef, as fast as you can, *Te i hea o Vanad*, where's the Captain?"

Teupootahiti jerked his thumb downward, and at that moment the Captain surfaced close beside me, Neptune rising out of the dark sea. I signaled him, and we took hold of the little pirogue and shoved, and swam with it fast to the shelter of the reef, and not until we were close in its black, black recesses did we stop to listen for the sounds of agitation behind us. We manhandled the weapon up onto the coral, and I lay there close beside it, waiting.

Captain Vanaa touched it lightly with a calloused hand, stroking it like the flesh of a woman. He whispered: "Will they miss it?"

This was the crux of the matter: would they?

I said: "The insects are on board, and they'll be his prime concern. Once he sees they've not been touched, let's hope he won't check his missiles."

"He might."

"A risk we have to take. But he doesn't have much time now, and I'm counting on his haste."

"Ah, but does he know that?"

I looked at my Rolex. "If Auguste is on time...?"

"He will be."

"No worries, then. We keep him moving now, fast. Too fast to give him time to think."

Out there at sea, a deep rumble came to us across the vast expanse of water, the authoritative note of the *Pinaa's* engines; exactly on schedule, to the second.

188

And there was the sound of running feet again, hurrying down the cruiser's gangplank and racing along the wharf to the launch. There was no need for them to hide now, and in a moment the wharf's bright lights went on, and we could see them clearly, eight or nine of them, leaping on board the Laguna. I could see Aimata, and imagined I could even see the fury on his face.

And then they were gone from our sight, and I heard the massive roar as the twin Ammarine Diesels burst into life. She leaped almost out of the water like a dolphin and thundered toward us; we pressed ourselves into the black coral and waited. I whispered to Vanaa: "Where will the break in the reef be?"

He squinted up at the island's mountain, and looked over to the left, and pointed. "There. A dozen meters away, it will be very narrow."

"Too close for comfort. We must be very still now."

The launch raced for the opening and then throttled back, and we could see a man lying on the forward deck, peering into the dark water, signaling with his hand. She was moving at minimum speed now, and we heard him call out softly: "Starboard two points...steady as she goes."

Not easy, in the dark, to find the opening to the lagoon; the launch was rocking, moving forward with little bursts of power, then easing off again, searching.

And then, Aimata's voice was a sharp angry command: "Hold it! Cut the engines!"

The silence was broken only by the gentle lap of the water against the speedboat's hull. She was thirty feet away from us, bobbing in the swell. There were three men on the stern decks.

And on the flybridge, his head tilted back, his feet widely spaced and his hand on his hips, Aimata was standing. He was listening to the silence.

And the silence was intense. In a moment, he looked down at the others, and his voice was low and controlled; it came to me so clearly that he could have been close by my side:

"They've cut their motors. What happened?"

Someone answered him: "Engine trouble, maybe?"

"Maybe. Is he under sail?"

"I don't know, it's too dark."

"Give me the night glasses."

I saw a man climbing up to the flybridge, saw Aimata staring through the binoculars. The ketch was more than a mile away, deep in the dark of the thunderclouds.

Aimata said, growling: "Yeah, I can see her. Hell, these are good glasses."

The silence again, and then Aimata's voice once more: "Mainsail and mizzen, but she's luffed. Luffed, but good."

And the other man answered him: "Luffed? That's gotta mean they're ready to run on their canvas and engines, once they get them going."

"What's he got, do you know? Diesels?"

"Yeah, that's a good little ketch, I know it. And he's a good mechanic, not much he can't fix if he puts his mind to it."

Aimata said: "Yeah, working on his motors, no doubt about it, the only way he'll ever hope to get any speed in the wind that's coming up. Unless he heads straight for us."

He laughed and said: "All right, close in to a thousand yards. Bring her up on her weather side, nice and easy, we got all the time in the world now. Get me a SAM up here, just one. That's all I'm gonna need."

The other man called out: "All right, you heard, swing around to the south of her, a thousand yards, dead into the wind, about five knots."

The low, subdued rumble of the big Ammarines started up again, a powerful, ominous roll of drums. The launch had yawed considerably, and was behind us now on the swell of the water. She swung round and eased herself along the reef, and the man at the bow called out quietly, waving his arm: "Easy, take it easy, another point to starboard...another point...easy...steady as she goes..."

They passed by us not more than twelve feet away, and we kept motionless in the water, only our heads above the surface, tight into the black coral. A crab was gently waving its claws an inch from my eyes; we held our breaths.

And then she was heading through the gap in the reefs, where the river that ran down from the top of the mountain had cut, over the millennia, an exit and an entry for its turbulent presence. I gave them a minute and a half, and then climbed carefully up on the reef and lay there, and held out my hands for the weapon.

Vanaa steadied the dugout, and the two others handed me the SAM and its launcher, and I slipped the missile home and waited; I thought I'd give them another five hundred yards, just to be sure we wouldn't all be knocked out by the concussion.

And then, the voice, much fainter now but still brought with admirable clarity on the wind, the man who had gone below was raising a puzzled question. Quite clearly, I heard him say: "Hey, I thought we brought nine of them aboard. How come there are only eight?"

I swung the launcher round at once. I almost forgot that it was not in the least necessary to aim, just out of a distorted, contrary feeling that there was something unpleasant in the fact that the SAM finds its own target, whichever way it's pointed. I remembered how the first one had followed me out there, not far from this very point, twisting this way and that as I had tried to evade it, and finally blowing me and Teiho's Golden Eagle to near-oblivion.

I squeezed the trigger.

There was a long and sustained *Sssshhh* as the red flame of the tail swept past my ear, and in a moment of incongruity, I wondered how often people got their faces blown off through careless handling of these deadly rockets. And then the missile was streaking across the water at what seemed a phenomenal speed, its course illuminated by the bright red-yellow plume that followed it.

He had one more thing to say, Aimata.

I heard his frantic shriek, a yell of pure agony: "*Cut the motors! Cut the motors!*" It was the bellow of a wounded buffalo, the roar of a dying lion, the trumpet of an elephant brought to its knees by the hunter's magnum. It was a cannonade of sound exploding out of the night, filed with urgency, and hatred, and surprise, and terror. And it was still pounding into my ears as the missile hit home.

I dropped everything, and rolled into the water, and yelled: "Down!" and saw that the others were sinking like leaden weights under the comforting water.

Even beyond the reef, the shock of it was appalling.

First, there was the massive thudding sensation and a blinding light that lit up the surface above us; and then the reef itself seemed to split in two, and I thought of Hiro tearing Moorea apart in the dead of the night.

A great mass of coral tipped slowly off the reef and fell, rolling over and over almost lazily, past my body, and when I surfaced I saw that the Laguna—all that was left of it—was still high in the air, suspended in a great brilliant furnace of its own extinction. I could see the sharp point of its white-painted hull twisting over and over, and all around it, more explosions were erupting savagely into the clouds. There was a rumble of violent blasts, and great clouds of smoke were drifting, and a berserk fury took over the flames as the missiles went off one by one.

Beside me, Captain Vanaa had surfaced, and he was staring out to sea with a look of shock on his face. He said, awestruck: "*Mon Dieu*, I don't believe it..."

The debris was raining down into the water, and sheets of black smoke were blossoming into the night sky, and the flames were flickering over the oily sea, and then they went out suddenly, and everything was quiet again and there was nothing left to stare at.

Teupootahiti's mouth was hanging open in astonishment, and Maramaitera's face was a study in incomprehension. He said, stammering: "The first time...I ever really see...the *tupapaus* at work."

Vanaa said, pointing: "The *Pinaa*."

The leaden clouds behind her, as though they were trying to outrace her, the ketch was under way, her drawn canvas billowing, her motors thundering at full power, running before the wind with a speed I could only find remarkable.

She was a shadow on the dark sea, a ghost looming up out of the black waters, cutting through the swells with a white crest at her bow, heeling over as she crested the waves, I fancied I could see Auguste at the helm, like the warrior Pai with his bronzed, athletic body leaning into the wind, fancied I could see the three lovely graces he had with him, braced against the ratlines with the wind coursing through their hair, and Teiho fussing about on the deck, all my good friends together again, and safe now.

The storm was brewing, and in its vanguard, outracing it, the

Pinaa was plowing its own strong way through the water, headed for the reef and for us.

CHAPTER 14

Papeete had never seemed more relaxing, nor more colorful. It was as though the nights on Rangitefara had never existed, except in my imaginings.

The elderly women were still putt-putting along the broad, tree-lined esplanade on their motor scooters, long gray hair, flowered with hibiscus blossoms, flying in the wind or, in some cases, neatly tucked under their behinds.

The open-sided buses, *le truck*, were still honking their brightly painted, overcrowded ways around the tight corners past the Chinese stores, and people, as if in Gauguin pictures, were strolling by, plucking at their Paumoto guitars or fingering their leis. The leaden cloud still hung in the bright blue sky over the twin mountains as though trying to drag this loveliest island in the world up from the waters; I remember that the word *Tahiti* signifies, in the old language of the Polynesians, *"Raised to the skies from the bottom of the sea"*—a fantasy that seemed more than ever fitting. Out of the depths of the oceans, the ancient gods had dragged it, as though one single spot were needed for all the delights of a passing era to find refuge in; there was still the pleasing sense of detachment here, a feeling that the rest of the hectic, murky, oppressive world that lay beyond the confines of these calm and multicolored waters need never be faced again.

The languor was taking over again, inevitably, and I thought: Who needs the rat race?

We lay on the broad white sands below the Maeva Beach

Hotel, and the faint strains of the lunchtime music came to us. Up there, in the sun and under the palm frond shelters, the tourists were idly clinking the ice in their glasses as they watched the young girls dancing, a crowded *tamaaraa* going on. We heard the burst of applause as the music and the dancing came to an end.

A hundred yards offshore, beyond the gently breaking surf, the *Pinaa* was silent and still, its tall masts and furled blue sails reflected in the silver, shimmering sea; Auguste was on board with his Vaite, the bouncy Dropping Water, getting the little ship ready to take the Captain back to Huahine, where his Te Tua would be waiting for him. Teiho had bustled off to Faaa, to write up, happily, his claim for the second Golden Eagle, and the lovely Tiare had retired to her own secret hideaway to sleep off the effects of her tribulations. She had smiled and said: "Give me one day. Will you still be here?"

There were just the three of us here, the Captain, and Maite, and myself, and Vanaa was showing off his expertise with a sail-maker's needle. He had brought a large pitcher of ice down from the hotel and was using it as a local anesthetic as he stitched up the slit in my gut that Kanaka's machete had made; anesthetic or not, the iodine was burning great holes in my side, and I complained mildly and he grunted and said: "You're too soft, Cain."

My forearm was bound up with a white bandage, and there were others at my wrists; I felt a wreck. But Maite was beside me, kneeling in the soft sand with her long auburn hair picking up the sunlight, trailing down over her amber shoulders and looking lovelier than ever. She was watching the Captain's work with a certain fascination, wincing every time the needle went in, but turning away from time to time to sip, nonchalantly, from a coconut, a Naiad on the sand at the water's edge.

The Captain said cheerfully, easing the curved needle around: "No worse than a rent in a sail." He emptied the bottle of iodine all over me, and said, satisfied: "There. In a week, it will be as good as new." He sat back on his haunches and ran a gnarled hand over his face. "And now?"

I said: "Now...I must go home."

"Why? That's a ridiculous comment."

"I know."

I reached out and ran a hand through Maite's hair, and set it just so over the red-and-white *pareu* around her tiny breasts, and she put her fingers to my cheek, a touch to take a man to Paradise.

All the danger had gone, and it was forgotten forever, and she was smiling, all the pain and worry far away now. Four nights ago, we had been dining together up at the Belvedere, perched on the edge of space and of new, binding friendships. In the interim it was over now, and was no longer a matter for thought. No one even mentioned Aimata, or Rangitefara, or the deadly little *Cressonus*. Why should they? All these things were out of kilter here, and we wanted no more part of them.

I said to her: "Will you come back with me, Maite? To San Francisco?"

For a moment, her eyes held mine, and then she dropped them and looked at her fingertips, "Where is San Francisco? Where is America?"

"Oh...out there somewhere. Will you come back with me?"

She shook her head, very slowly. *"Non je n'ai pas envie*, I don't feel like it." Her eyes met mine again, and she was laughing, "Why do you have to go home? Home is where you are."

"I know that too, but..." I could not find a sensible reason to give her, and she waited, and then said: "Why don't you stay here with me? We'll make love every night, all night, for a hundred years. And then you'll be tired of me, and that will be the time for you to go home, Not before then."

"Please?"

"No. I will stay here now. Stay with me?"

"For how long, Maite?"

She said, laughing: "For eight days..."

There's a saying in the islands: *eight days in Tahiti is too long—and eight months is not long enough.*

There were two widely differing worlds confronting us now, hers and mine; and it was not easy to choose between them, San Francisco, and Paris, and Fenrek, and Gerard at his sad, burned-out vineyard, they all seemed so distant. Not only in time and space but also in the imagination, as though all that I had known, and felt, and loved, before these last few days, had really left no imprint on my mind.

The seduction: you fight it, or you give way to it; there can be no middle course.

Across the water, framed against the. distant purple mountains of Moorea, the sail of the *Pinaa's* mizzen was going up, and Vanaa got to his feet and stood there, staring at it, a tough, grizzled old man of the sea. He said: "He's ready, I must go now."

He turned back to me. "Will I see you again? Will you come to Huahine? My house there is yours."

I stood up and took his hand. "Perhaps I will. Thank you for the surgery. And for everything else."

He lifted Maite up and embraced her, and said gruffly: "Go to work on him, bring him over, you know what to do."

He put her down on the sand, and turned away, and kicked off his sandals, and slipped them into his pockets, and walked out into the surf. He turned back, and waved slowly, and called out: "*Parahi*, Cain. Goodbye. Come back to Tahiti." In a moment, he was swimming strongly toward the ketch, and we watched his bobbing head for a while, and then lay down side by side and looked up at the graceful sweep of the coconut palms above our heads, and the puffs of white clouds in the bright, bright sky, and felt the cool breeze wafting over our bodies, and I thought: Perhaps, if I am lucky, this day will never end.

THE END

ABOUT THE AUTHOR

Alan Lyle-Smythe was born in Surrey, England. Prior to World War II, he served with the Palestine Police from 1936 to 1939 and learned the Arabic language. He was awarded an MBE in June 1938. He married Aliza Sverdova in 1939, then studied acting from 1939 to 1941.

In January 1940, Lyle-Smythe was commissioned in the Royal Army Service Corps. Due to his linguistic skills, he transferred to the Intelligence Corps and served in the Western Desert, in which he used the surname "Caillou" (the French word for 'pebble') as an alias.

He was captured in North Africa, imprisoned and threatened with execution in Italy, then escaped to join the British forces at Salerno. He was then posted to serve with the partisans in Yugoslavia. He wrote about his experiences in the book *The World is Six Feet Square* (1954). He was promoted to captain and awarded the Military Cross in 1944.

Following the war, he returned to the Palestine Police from 1946 to 1947, then served as a Police Commissioner in British-occupied Italian Somaliland from 1947 to 1952, where he was recommissioned a captain.

After work as a District Officer in Somalia and professional hunter, Lyle-Smythe travelled to Canada, where he worked as a hunter and then became an actor on Canadian television.

He wrote his first novel, *Rogue's Gambit*, in 1955, first using the name Caillou, one of his aliases from the war. Moving from Vancouver to Hollywood, he made an appearance as a contestant on the January 23 1958 edition of *You Bet Your Life*.

He appeared as an actor and/or worked as a screenwriter in

such shows as *Daktari, The Man From U.N.C.L.E.* (including the screenwriting for "*The Bow-Wow Affair*" from 1965), *Thriller, Daniel Boone, Quark, Centennial*, and *How the West Was Won*. In 1966-67, he had a recurring role (as Jason Flood) in NBC's "*Tarzan*" TV series starring Ron Ely. Caillou appeared in such television movies as *Sole Survivor* (1970), *The Hound of the Baskervilles* (1972, as Inspector Lestrade), and *Goliath Awaits* (1981). His cinema film credits included roles in *Five Weeks in a Balloon* (1962), *Clarence, the Cross-Eyed Lion* (1965), *The Rare Breed* (1966), *The Devil's Brigade* (1968), *Hellfighters* (1968), *Everything You Always Wanted to Know About Sex* (*But Were Afraid to Ask)* (1972), *Herbie Goes to Monte Carlo* (1977), *Beyond Evil* (1980), *The Sword and the Sorcerer* (1982) and *The Ice Pirates* (1984).

Caillou wrote 52 paperback thrillers under his own name and the nom de plume of Alex Webb, with such heroes as Cabot Cain, Colonel Matthew Tobin, Mike Benasque, Ian Quayle and Josh Dekker, as well as writing many magazine stories.

Several of Caillou's novels were made into films, such as *Rampage* with Robert Mitchum in 1963, based on his big game hunting knowledge; *Assault on Agathon*, for which Caillou did the screenplay as well; and *The Cheetahs*, filmed in 1989.

He was married to Aliza Sverdova from 1939 until his death. Their daughter Nadia Caillou was the screenwriter for the film *Skeleton Coast*.

Alan Caillou died in Sedona, Arizona in 2006.

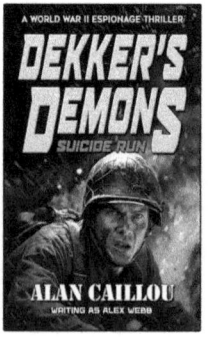

DON'T MISS ANY OF NEIL HUNTER'S NOVELS FROM CALIBER BOOKS

Reporter Les Mason is completing an expose on the Long Point Nuclear Plant. But before he can finish he dies an agonizing death. The doctors are baffled—and there are similar cases to follow...Chris Lane, his girlfriend, and organizer of the Long Point Protestors, discovers Mason's notes, and decides to find out for herself what the plant has to hide.

2 BOOK SERIES

In middle of the 21st century America – over-populated decaying cities are ruled by hi-tech gangs pushing every vice and wastelands are controlled by bands of mutants. Ordinary citizens are oppressed and face a hopeless future. But Marshal T.J. Cade is a new breed of law enforcer. Teamed with his cyborg partner, Janek, Cade takes on these criminals and works in the gray areas of the law to get the job done.

3 BOOK SERIES

The village of Shepthorne England wasn't being gripped, but strangled by a winter's blanket of heavy snow and Arctic temperatures. The trouble began innocently enough with a massive pile-up of autos on frozen roads leading to and from the village. Then, from the sky, a military transport plane with its top secret cargo of devastation crashed down towards the center of the village. Hell was just beginning to touch Shepthorne and its unsuspecting citizens...

FROM CALIBER BOOKS

CALIBER
B O O K S

www.calibercomics.com

CALIBER COMICS GOES TO WAR!

HISTORICAL AND MILITARY THEMED GRAPHIC NOVELS

**WORLD WAR ONE:
MO MAN'S LAND**

ISBN: 9781635298123

*A look at World War 1 from
the French trenches as they
faced the Imperial German
Army.*

**CORTEZ AND THE FALL
OF THE AZTECS**

ISBN: 9781635299779

*Cortez battles the Aztecs
while in search of Inca
gold.*

**TROY:
AN EMPIRE UNDER SIEGE**

ISBN: 9781635298635

*Homer's famous The Iliad and
the Trojan War is given a
unique human perspective
rather than from the God's.*

WITNESS TO WAR

ISBN: 9781635299700

*WW2's Battle of the Bulge
is seen up close by an
embedded female war
reporter.*

THE LINCOLN BRIGADE

ISBN: 9781635298222

*American volunteers head
to Spain in the 1930s to
fight in their civil war
against the fascist regime.*

**EL CID:
THE CONQUEROR**

ISBN: 9780982654996

*Europe's greatest warrior
attempts to unify Spain
against invading foreign
and domestic armies.*

WINTER WAR

ISBN: 9780985749392

*At the outbreak of WW2
Finland fights against an
invading Soviet army.*

**ZULUNATION:
END OF EMPIRE**

ISBN: 9780941613415

*The global British Empire
and far-reaching influence
is threatened by a Zulu
uprising in southern Africa.*

AIR WARRIORS: WORLD WAR ONE #V1 - V4 *Take to the skys of WW1 as various fighter aces tell their harrowing stories.*
ISBN: 9781635297973 (V1), 9781635297980 (V2), 9781635297997 (V3), 9781635298000 (V4)

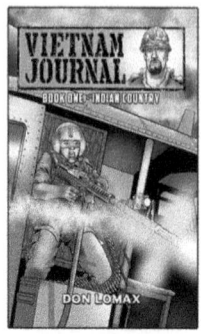   

CALIBER COMICS GOES TO THE EDGE!
Science Fiction and Horror themed graphic novels

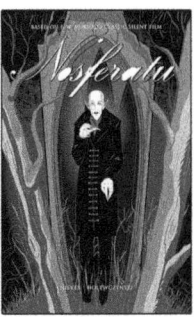